"May I remind you, Captain, that little is known of the Preservers and their technology. It is possible that a more rigorous examination may turn up subtle similarities between this probe and the obelisk, but they were apparently constructed of different materials, possibly at different points in the Preservers' history and development. Certainly, we lack the data to identify their relics easily."

"But these markings do look the same?" Kirk asked impatiently. He searched his memory, trying to remember exactly what the hieroglyphics on the obelisk had looked like. Spock had eventually deduced that they had corresponded to musical notes. "Don't they?"

"Yes, sir," Spock conceded. "They do."

Overcome with emotion, Kirk reached out to touch the symbols.

"Captain! Wait!"

STAR TREK®

THE RINGS OF TIME

Greg Cox

Based upon *Star Trek*
created by Gene Roddenberry

POCKET BOOKS
New York · London · Toronto · Sydney
New Delhi · Titan

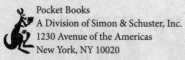
Pocket Books
A Division of Simon & Schuster, Inc.
1230 Avenue of the Americas
New York, NY 10020

This book is a work of fiction. Names, characters, places, and incidents either are products of the author's imagination or are used fictitiously. Any resemblance to actual events or locales or persons, living or dead, is entirely coincidental.

First Pocket Books paperback edition February 2012

POCKET and colophon are registered trademarks of Simon & Schuster, Inc.

For information about special discounts for bulk purchases, please contact Simon & Schuster Special Sales at 1-866-506-1949 or business@simonandschuster.com.

The Simon & Schuster Speakers Bureau can bring authors to your live event. For more information or to book an event, contact the Simon & Schuster Speakers Bureau at 1-866-248-3049 or visit our website at www.simonspeakers.com.

Manufactured in the United States of America

10 9 8 7 6 5 4 3 2 1

ISBN 978-1-4516-5547-6
ISBN 978-1-4516-5549-0 (ebook)

Dedicated (in advance)
to the future explorers of the solar system.

One

June 28, 2020

"Launch minus five minutes . . ."

The space shuttle *Renaissance* faced the early-morning sky at Cape Canaveral. Its enormous fuel tanks and boosters dwarfed the vessel as it towered over the launch pad. The launch tower pulled away, leaving the shuttle and its booster rockets clear for flight. It was a beautiful morning, the last Colonel Shaun Christopher would see for more than six months. It would be winter the next time he set foot on Earth.

Assuming all goes well, he thought.

Inside the cockpit, Shaun was strapped into his seat, staring up at the nose of the ship. A flight suit and helmet provided meager protection from the titanic forces about to be unleashed. The Atlantic Ocean could be glimpsed out the starboard window. A pair of old-fashioned military dog tags dangled above the lighted instrument panel in front of him. A good-luck charm, the tags had accompanied him into space before.

"Ready to go, Colonel?" the pilot sitting next to him said. Commander Shirin Ludden was among the first of a new breed of shuttle pilots. She seemed shockingly young to Shaun, who was in his early fifties.

"You tell me," he answered. "I'm just a passenger on this flight."

Despite their banter, the launch procedure continued on schedule. The sound-and-heat-suppression system fired up far below the cockpit, but Shaun could feel the vibration from all that water where he was sitting. He and Ludden closed the visors on their flight helmets. He took a deep breath of piped-in oxygen. The entire shuttle trembled as the launch engines gradually came online. Shaun felt a familiar excitement growing inside him.

The *Renaissance* had been intended to be the first in a new fleet of second-generation shuttles, but then the aerospace bubble had gone bust, cratering the economy again and creating entire districts of homeless people in many of the world's cities. The latest round of budget cuts had left the *Renaissance* as a one-of-a-kind prototype, kept alive primarily by private investors and international partners who couldn't afford to build ships on their own. She was an impressive vessel, state-of-the-art. A shame she had to fly alone.

Still, at least she would get him where he was going.

"Launch minus ten seconds . . ."

The engines ignited, and the shuttle strained to escape the eight-inch metal bolts holding it down. The spaceplane swayed violently before turning its nose back up toward the sky. Computerized systems went through their paces. Even though Ludden was nominally the pilot, the launch was out of her hands now. Rattling inside the cockpit, Shaun braced himself for what came next. A grin spread across his rugged face.

This never got old.

"Five . . . four . . . three . . . two . . . one . . ."

Liftoff!

Explosive charges blew away the hold-down bolts. The *Renaissance* blasted into the sky atop an inverted geyser of fire and smoke. Shaun was slammed back into his seat, then shaken back and forth like a rat in a dog's jaws. The shuttle rocketed up from the Cape, leaving Mother Earth far behind. The booster rockets fell away, having done the heavy lifting. Shaun felt a twinge of relief; like most astronauts, he felt safer rid of those enormous Roman candles. The bumpy ride quickly leveled off as the bright blue sky before him gave way to the blackness of the upper atmosphere.

The g-forces pressing down on him felt like an elephant standing on his chest. Shaun gritted his teeth; this part did get old after the first few minutes. He craned his neck to try to read the gauges on the instrument panel. So far, everything looked okay, although the elephant seemed to have gained weight since the last time he took this ride.

Or maybe that's just me.

Just when he thought he couldn't take it anymore, the elephant disappeared as though conjured away by

a Las Vegas magician. One last jerk shook the ship as
the empty fuel tank fell away. The pressure on Shaun
abruptly went from three g's to zero. His body lifted
away from the seat cushions, held in place only by his
safety straps. Glancing at the instrument panel, he saw
the lucky dog tags floating weightlessly.

We did it, Dad, he thought. *We're in space. Again.*

The tags had been worn by his father, Captain
John Christopher, during his Air Force jet-pilot days.
The senior Christopher had applied to the astronaut
program back in the 1960s but hadn't quite made
the cut. Shaun had taken his dad's tags up with him
on every mission, so that even though the real John
Christopher had only watched the liftoff from the
bleachers eight miles away, he was also flying beside
his son.

"So much for the fireworks," Ludden said, sounding
almost disappointed that the thrill-ride component of
the launch was over. "Smooth sailing from now on."

"Knock on wood," Shaun said.

She used the shuttle's smaller space engines to
guide the *Renaissance* into orbit approximately four
hundred kilometers above Earth. Circling the planet
at some twenty-nine thousand kilometers per hour,
she rotated the shuttle so that its belly faced outward
away from Earth. The engines cut off, and the cockpit
was suddenly so quiet that Shaun could hear the fans
and air filters whirring, along with his own breathing
inside the helmet. The payload bay doors opened,

exposing their cargo to the vacuum. This was standard procedure in space and essential to the next stage of their mission.

"Tell you the truth," Ludden said, "I wish I was going all the way with you."

"Now, Commander, you know NASA frowns on that kind of fraternization."

She punched him in the shoulder. "You know what I mean. This is just a taxi ride to the airport. You're making the real trip."

"Maybe next time," Shaun said to console her.

"Well, let's make sure you don't miss your flight."

The shuttle's launch was just the first leg of a much longer journey. Shaun waited impatiently, occupying himself with routine flight operations, while the shuttle caught up with his destination. Hours passed before Ludden nudged him.

"Heads up," she said. "There's your ride up ahead."

Peering through the cockpit window, he glimpsed a bright reflective object cruising above them. At first, it was only a shiny lure in the distance, but as they closed on the other vessel, a truly awe-inspiring spacecraft came into view. More than forty-five meters long, the ship was many times larger than the *Renaissance* and resembled several large tour buses linked together. Its modular components had been assembled in orbit over the course of the last five years. Shaun could count them off one by one: engine assembly, communications array, cargo bay, crew habitat, and command module.

The impulse thrusters fanned out from the tail of the ship, while a docking ring was attached to the nose of the command module. Antennae, EVA rails, and signal dishes sprouted from the ship's silvery titanium-polymer hull, although its delicate solar panels had been retracted in anticipation of breaking orbit. Additional insulation and padding protected the habitat. Lights shone in the windows. A NASA logo was emblazoned on the side of the cargo bay, along with the name of the vessel: *U.S.S. Lewis & Clark.*

Ludden whistled in appreciation. "Quite a ship."

Shaun had to agree. Even though he had trained on simulators, had familiarized himself with the individual modules on Earth, and already knew pretty much every inch of the ship by heart, he took a moment to admire it in its natural environment. *Savor the moment,* he thought. There had been times, during the economic roller coaster of the last few years, when he had wondered if the *Lewis & Clark* would ever get finished at all.

But here it was, waiting for him.

"*Renaissance* to *Lewis & Clark.*" Ludden hailed the other vessel. Like Shaun, she had shed her helmet and flight gear in favor of a comfy blue NASA jumpsuit. "Initiating docking procedure."

"*Roger that,* Renaissance," a husky female voice answered via ship-to-ship radio. "*We're ready on our end.*"

The shuttle approached the larger spaceship from

below. Onboard computers and laser-guidance systems steered the shuttle toward the docking ring. The *Renaissance*'s own docking mechanism was located in the forward payload bay, just aft of the crew compartment, so the shuttle presented its open back to the nose of the other ship. Multiple redundant systems ensured that the shuttle remained exactly on track. Ludden eyeballed it through the window, while Shaun watched the docking ring grow larger on a small television monitor. Even with the guidance systems constantly checking the shuttle's range, speed, and trajectory relative to the other ship, frequent small course corrections were required to stay on course. Ludden worked the brake and thruster control sticks like an expert, taking her time. By the time the ships were less than ten meters apart, the *Renaissance* was approaching the other vessel at roughly one-tenth of a foot per second. Pale yellow vapor jetted from the forward thrusters with each momentary burn.

Ludden's face was a portrait of concentration. "Almost there," she muttered under her breath. "Just a few meters more . . ."

Contact! The ships came together with a gentle bump, less jolting than a 747 touching down on the tarmac. Automatic latches grabbed onto the shuttle and pulled the two spacecraft together, creating an airtight seal, at least in theory. Shaun would have to double-check that carefully before they tried crossing over to the other ship, but he could not have asked for a more successful rendezvous with his new home away from home.

So much for the easy part, he thought.

"I believe this is your stop," Ludden quipped. "Don't forget to tip your driver."

He patted his jumpsuit. "I'm afraid I forgot my wallet. Guess I'm going to have to owe you."

"Okay, but you're looking at six-plus months of interest."

"Take it up with NASA."

"Are you kidding? They're more cash-strapped than I am."

Ain't it the truth, Shaun thought.

He unstrapped himself from his seat. He had never been subject to space-sickness, so he had quickly adjusted to the lack of gravity. Taking care to retrieve the dog tags, he floated to the back of the cockpit and opened the hatch to the mid-deck below. A convenient ladder helped him descend headfirst to the lower level, where the airlock to the docking ring waited. A red indicator light above the hatch warned that the airlock was not yet pressurized.

He rang the doorbell, so to speak. A video-com connected him with the spaceship's flight deck. "Permission to come aboard?"

"Just give us a second to roll out the welcome mat," the female voice replied. An attractive redhead appeared on a miniature video screen adjacent to the hatchway. *"Pressurizing now."*

Pumps rapidly filled the airlock with breathable air, so that the air pressure in the docking ring matched that of both the shuttle and the *Lewis & Clark*. The process took place with admirable speed; within minutes, he was able to unseal the hatch and rise through the vestibule connecting the two ships. The hatch at the other end opened onto the lower deck of the *Lewis & Clark*'s command module. The ship's onboard spacelab occupied most of the mid-deck. This was where he and the rest of the crew would be conducting many of their experiments over the next several months. Right now, everything was stowed away in preparation for their departure.

Two people floated just beyond the airlock.

"About time you got here," astronaut Alice Fontana teased him, her arms crossed over her chest. An athletic redhead of Amazonian physique, she was oriented in the same direction as Shaun. Her blue jumpsuit proudly bore a Canadian flag decal in addition to its NASA logo. Microgravity had given her a slightly fuller face than usual and added at least an inch to her height. Her naturally flame-colored hair had been cut practically short. In her mid-thirties, she was younger than Shaun but not so much that he thought of her as a kid. She was his copilot on this mission.

"Sorry to keep you waiting," he joked back. "Just be thankful you were safely up here, away from the dog-and-pony shows."

Prior to the usual prelaunch quarantine, Shaun

had spent the last few weeks doing publicity for the mission, in an attempt to drum up public and political support. Compared with the endless interviews, rubber chicken, and schmoozing, blasting off into space had been a breeze.

"Poor baby!" She gave him a hug that was slightly awkward, given their history, then disengaged quickly. "Better you than me."

"I have to agree," Dr. Marcus O'Herlihy said. Eschewing a hug, he shook Shaun's hand instead, while holding on to a handrail to anchor himself. "Welcome aboard, Colonel."

A distinguished-looking black man in his early fifties, about Shaun's age, O'Herlihy had a slightly professorial air befitting his status as one of the world's foremost astrophysicists. Combining disciplines, he was also the mission's resident physician. His neatly trimmed beard and mustache had gone gray, and, like Fontana, he was slightly taller and rounder of face while weightless. His deep voice had a slight Irish accent.

"Good to see you, Doc," Shaun greeted him. "You two been taking good care of my ship?"

"I think we've gotten everything battened down," O'Herlihy said. He and Fontana had been conducting system tests and checks while the *Lewis & Clark* was in orbit. Everything needed to be working perfectly before the ship set off for its ultimate destination; after all, it wasn't as if they could call for a tow if anything broke down later on. "We're merely awaiting your final inspection and that last load of supplies from the *Renaissance,* of course."

"Don't worry," Shaun said. "I remembered to get the groceries." He drifted further into the module. "So, which one of you ordered the pineapple pizza?"

"That would be me," Fontana confessed. "And don't even think of breaking into my private stock—unless you ask nice, that is."

"Duly noted," Shaun said. "I promise not to raid the fridge when you're not looking."

"I'm sure we'll all be on our best behavior," O'Herlihy said. "Or this could be a *very* long trip."

Shaun smiled. It was good to see them again. The three of them had been training together for months and had been judged psychologically compatible by the space shrinks back at Houston. *Good thing we get along,* he thought, *given that we're going to be stuck together for the next one-point-two billion kilometers.*

He made a mental note to give Ludden a tour of the *Lewis & Clark* before she headed back home.

"Prepare to engage engines," Shaun ordered.

Days had passed, and more than two thousand pounds of stores and equipment had been transferred from the *Renaissance* to the *Lewis & Clark.* The shuttle had returned to Earth, leaving the larger ship clear to depart. All final system checks had been completed. They were as ready as they were ever going to be.

Fontana and Shaun were strapped in at the helm, facing the front windows. O'Herlihy was off to the side at one of the auxiliary computer terminals. A steady stream of chatter flowed back and forth between the ship and Mission Control. The *Lewis & Clark* had orbited the Earth more than thirty times since Shaun had come aboard, once every ninety minutes. It was time to stop chasing their own tail and get on their way.

"*Mission Control to* Lewis & Clark," a voice spoke to them from Houston. "*You are cleared for departure. Bon voyage.*"

"Copy that," Shaun responded. "See you at New Year's."

He glanced over at Fontana. "You ready to get this show on the road?"

"Stop stalling and hit the gas," she shot back. "I don't know about you, but I'm not getting any younger."

"All right." He manually initiated the warm-up sequence. A chronometer on the instrument panel counted down to the precise moment they were scheduled to leave orbit. His father's dog tags dangled around his neck. "Here goes nothing."

The *Lewis & Clark*'s spanking-new "impulse" engines were state-of-the-art. To date, the technology had been tested on unmanned probes such as *Nomad*, but this was the first time it had been employed to carry human cargo out into the solar system. The system employed powerful fusion reactors to generate a propulsive stream of high-energy plasma. In theory, it would make interplanetary travel feasible at last.

In theory . . .

The reactors had been online for hours. The engines idled, ready to go to impulse. The chronometer clicked down to zero, and Shaun felt a sudden surge of acceleration, nowhere near as potent as what he had felt blasting off from the Cape, but the ship was obviously speeding up. He kept a close eye on the gauges and monitors before him, on the lookout for the slightest irregularity or sign of trouble, but everything seemed in order. He had run through this sequence in the simulator more than a dozen times before. It was almost hard to believe he was finally doing it for real.

"Breaking orbit," he said. "One-quarter power."

Not wanting to stress the engines right away or accidentally plow into any unexpected space junk at top speed, they planned to start off slowly and gradually accelerate to their maximum speed of 556,000 kilometers per hour. At that rate, they would reach their destination in a little more than ninety days.

"Goodbye, Earth," Fontana said. "Next stop: Saturn."

Just a few years ago, the prospect of reaching Saturn in only ninety days would have been nothing but science fiction, but the impulse drive promised to change everything. The stars were still out of reach, except for sleeper ships such as the late, lamented DY-100, but at least it wouldn't take years to reach the outer planets anymore.

Or so they intended to prove.

"Ninety days," Fontana mused. "Good thing I loaded plenty of crossword puzzles into my personal reader. Gotta keep my mind sharp."

Shaun kept his eyes on the gauges. "If your mind was any sharper, it would draw blood."

"Thanks," she answered. "I think."

In truth, they had plenty to keep them occupied on the way to Saturn: observations of Mars, Jupiter, and the asteroid belt, among other things. He had spent a lot of time over the last several weeks explaining why they were bypassing those nearer destinations in favor of Saturn, but they certainly had their reasons, only some of which he had been able to discuss publicly. Mars would have to wait, maybe for the *Ares* missions. Plans for future interplanetary jaunts were already being drawn up, contingent on the fluctuating economy and the success of this mission.

No pressure there, he thought wryly.

"What the devil?" O'Herlihy exclaimed.

His shocked tone immediately put Shaun on alert. He glanced back over his shoulder at the doctor, who was staring wide-eyed at the display panel before him.

"What is it, Doc?"

"Hold on," O'Herlihy muttered. "This isn't possible."

"What?" Shaun demanded. "Talk to me, Marcus."

"I picked up an odd transmission, a wireless signal, coming from the habitat module."

That didn't make any sense. There were no ship-to-Earth communication systems in the habitat, and nobody was there to operate them in the first place. "Must be a glitch."

"That's what I thought, but . . ." O'Herlihy hesitated, as though he could scarcely believe what he was saying. "There's activity in the hab. One of the computer terminals has been activated . . . and it appears that someone has just, er, used the facilities."

It took Shaun a second to realize what the doctor meant. "The head?"

There were two gravity-free toilets aboard the ship, one in the hab and one mid-deck below the cockpit. Shaun and his fellow astronauts had personally insisted on that particular redundancy. Nobody wanted to get stuck out beyond the asteroid belt without backup facilities.

But nobody was using them right now.

Were they?

"That's right," O'Herlihy confirmed. He called up a systems report on his screen. "Waste-disposal suction was activated for approximately five seconds about two minutes ago."

Shaun set the ship's controls on automatic, then unstrapped himself from the pilot's seat and floated over to see for himself. He peered over the doctor's shoulder at the monitor. "Could it have turned itself on and off?"

"I don't see how," O'Herlihy said. "Certainly, it hasn't been doing that while Alice and I have been testing things. Nor am I aware of any reports concerning such a malfunction."

"That's because there aren't any," Shaun said. He would have known about any problem with the ship's systems and hardware, no matter how trivial. The toilets were not supposed to switch on at random, and neither were the computer terminals. And then there was that unaccountable signal O'Herlihy had noticed.

"You don't think . . . ?" Fontana exchanged a baffled look with the two men. "A stowaway?"

"Get real," Shaun said. There had never been an actual stowaway in the entire history of human space exploration. That was the stuff of silly sci-fi movies and TV shows. Granted, the *Lewis & Clark* was bigger and roomier than an old-fashioned space capsule, with a lot more places to hide, but still . . . "It can't be."

"What's the alternative?" Fontana asked. "A ghost?"

There was only one way to find out. He activated the video-com and hit the speaker button. "Hello? Is anybody there?" He felt ridiculous even asking. "Please identify yourself."

Nobody answered, of course. The small video screen above the speaker remained blank. Shaun wondered what the hell he had expected. O'Herlihy chuckled and shook his head. "I must say, I didn't really expect us to go space-happy quite so soo—"

"Oh, hi!" a female voice interrupted him via the comm. A palm covered the video feed. *"Is that our skipper speaking?"* A playful tone made the moment even more surreal. *"I have to ask. Is it now safe for passengers to resume use of personal electronic devices?"*

The astronauts stared in shock at the comm. "Oh, no," O'Herlihy whispered in dismay. From the sound of his voice, only the lack of gravity kept the blood from draining from his face. "This can't be happening."

Fontana, on the other hand, acted more pissed-off than chagrined. Turning away from the comm, she glared at the hatch separating them from the habitat. "Did you hear that? Who the hell does she think she is?"

Shaun just wanted answers, pronto. "Who is this?" He pressed down on the speaker button with more force than necessary. "And what are you doing on my ship?"

"*Come and see*," the stowaway replied. "*I'm not going anywhere.*"

We'll see about that, Shaun thought.

He launched himself toward the hatch.

Two

Captain's log. Stardate 7103.4

The Enterprise *is nearing the end of its five-year mission. We have just finished surveying a previously uncharted star system. After nearly half a decade in deep space, seeking out new worlds and civilizations, one has to resist a tendency to take such accomplishments for granted. Exploring the cosmos has become almost routine . . .*

"Captain," Lieutenant Uhura said. "A priority message from Starfleet Command."

James T. Kirk sat up straight. His chair faced the viewscreen at the front of the bridge. "Put it on-screen," he said crisply.

"Yes, Captain."

Uhura patched the communication through. On the viewer, a starry vista was replaced by the head and shoulders of a dark-skinned older man with silver hair and a grave expression. Visual and aural static hinted at the vast distance between the *Enterprise* and Earth. A network of subspace relay beacons carried data back and forth across the quadrant. Uhura worked her communications console, and the transmission quickly cleared up. Kirk recognized Commodore Faris. The man was a Starfleet veteran who had once served under Robert April himself.

What's this about? Kirk wondered. *Are the Klingons acting up again? Or the Romulans?*

"*Kirk,*" Faris addressed him. "*Are you reading me?*"

"Loud and clear, sir." Kirk got right down to business. "What can I do for you?"

"*We've received a distress call from the Skagway colony. Are you familiar with it?*"

Kirk searched his memory. "It's a mining outpost. In the Klondike system?"

Faris nodded. "*Skagway is one of the moons of Klondike VI, a gas giant not unlike Saturn. For reasons unknown, the planet's rings appear to be destabilizing, possibly compromising the safety of the colony. Skagway's governor has requested Starfleet's immediate assistance, and I'm afraid the* Enterprise *is the only starship in the vicinity.*"

"Understood," Kirk replied. "We'll set course for the Klondike system at once."

"*Good.*" Care furrowed the commodore's brow. "*Skagway has proven to be a rich source of dilithium crystals. I don't have to tell you how important it is, to Starfleet and the Federation, that we keep that colony up and running, if at all possible. We need those crystals.*"

Dilithium was essential to warp-propulsion systems. And rare enough to make it one of the most precious substances in the galaxy.

"If I ever forget that, my chief engineer will be sure to remind me," Kirk assured Faris. He sought to anticipate the challenges ahead. "Sir, you said the planet's rings were 'destabilizing.' Do we know how quickly or what might be causing this?"

"*Details are sketchy,*" Faris admitted. "*You'll probably have a better idea of the situation once you get there. But I wouldn't recommend taking the scenic route. Governor Dawson sounded very concerned.*"

A mental image of a handsome, middle-aged woman surfaced from Kirk's memory banks. He vaguely recalled receiving a briefing on her appointment a few years back.

"Tell the governor she can expect us shortly." Kirk made this new mission his top priority. "You can count on us, Commodore."

"*Good luck, Jim.*" The other man reached to cut off the transmission. "*Faris out.*"

His image blinked away. An endless expanse of stars beckoned on the viewer. Kirk wondered which, if any, of those distant points of light was their new destination.

"Mr. Chekov." He addressed the navigator. The young ensign shared the conn with Lieutenant Sulu, who was at the helm. The ship's astrogator unit was positioned between them. "How far to the Klondike system?"

Chekov consulted his display panel. "Skagway is very remote," he observed. "At warp five, we're talking approximately nineteen days."

"Nineteen-point-four-eight, to be exact," Spock

amended. The Vulcan science officer was seated at his usual station at the rear of the bridge. Glancing back over his shoulder, Kirk noted that Spock had already called up a schematic of the Klondike system on his console's monitor. Streams of data regarding the system, its planets, and its moons scrolled along the edges of the screen.

"Increase speed to warp six," Kirk ordered. If the colony was truly in jeopardy, the sooner they got there, the better. Especially since it was unclear how rapidly the crisis might escalate.

"Aye, aye, sir." Sulu worked the helm. "Warp six."

Kirk tapped the intercom controls on his right armrest. "Kirk to Engineering. I'm going to need you to push the engines, Mr. Scott. We're in a bit of a hurry."

"*Captain!*" Chief Engineer Montgomery Scott protested via the speaker. A Scottish accent colored his inflections. "*Canna we take it a little slower? My bairns are no spring chickens, you know. They're overdue for a refit.*"

Kirk repressed a grin. Scotty's response was to be expected. He could be very protective of *his* engines.

"This is a rescue mission, Mr. Scott. Lives may be at stake."

Scotty couldn't argue with that. "*Ah, well. In that case, I'll see what I can do.*"

"Thank you, Mr. Scott." Kirk closed the line, then turned toward his science officer. "What do you make of this, Spock?"

"It is puzzling, Captain." Spock lifted his eyes from his data. "As the commodore reported, Klondike VI is a Class J gas giant. Long-range telescopes and unmanned probes have observed it for more than a century, beginning long before the mining colony on Skagway was established. During this time, the planet's rings have remained stable, within the standard parameters. A cursory examination of recent data from the colony suggests no obvious reason for the rings to alter their orbits. The primary gravitational factors have remained constant."

Kirk took his word for it. Spock's "cursory examination" was likely to put the most detailed computerized analysis to shame. "Then we have a mystery on our hands."

"So it appears," Spock agreed.

Kirk frowned. The prospect of studying such an inexplicable celestial phenomenon would be more appealing were innocent lives not in jeopardy. A troubling thought occurred to him. "What is the current population of Skagway?"

Spock looked it up in the ship's database. "Our records indicate that some one thousand seven hundred forty-six individuals currently inhabit the colony, give or take any recent births, deaths, or fissions. Including several families and small children."

Damn, Kirk thought. The *Enterprise* was not equipped to transport that many individuals at one time. They would be unable to evacuate the entire colony should it prove necessary. "And there are no other vessels nearby?"

"None, Captain." Spock confirmed the inconvenient truth. "Mr. Chekov was quite correct when he stated that the Skagway colony is notably distant from any other inhabited worlds. Aside from the *Enterprise*, the nearest Federation starship is the *Vancouver*, which is currently four-point-zero-three-three sectors away."

Kirk got the message. "Then it's up to us."

He just hoped that would be enough.

Three

2020

They found the stowaway waiting for them on the lower level of the habitat module. The crew's personal quarters were one deck above, while the mid-deck was a common area that served as gym, infirmary, galley, and general rec room. Sealed cupboards and pantries lined the walls. A treadmill was there for exercise. Circular windows offered a view of the endless void outside, but Shaun wasn't interested in sightseeing right then. He stared instead at someone who, to put it mildly, was not supposed to be there.

"Whoa," she said, tumbling in the air just below the ceiling. From the look of things, she was still trying to get the hang of navigating without gravity. She grabbed onto a hanging guide loop to arrest her uncontrolled flight. She groped in vain for a smart tablet floating nearby. "This is trickier than it looked on YouTube."

The stowaway was a petite Hispanic woman who appeared to be in her twenties. A neon-blue streak added flair to her dark brown hair and bangs. A floating ponytail wagged back and forth with every movement of her head. Her tank top and shorts set her apart from the astronauts in their standard-issue jumpsuits. As she rotated head over heels above them, Shaun glimpsed a tattoo at the nape of her neck. It was a series of concentric rings.

"Who are you?" he demanded. Grabbing her ankle to keep her from spinning away, he yanked her down until they were face-to-face. His own foot was tucked into a loop in the floor, holding him in place. "And how did you get aboard my ship?"

"Zoe Querez," she introduced herself. "Colonel Christopher, I presume? Pleased to meet you at last." She nodded at the other two astronauts floating behind him. "Captain Fontana. Dr. O'Herlihy." She held out her hand. "I've read so much about you, watched so many videos, that I feel like I already know you all."

"Are you freaking kidding me?" Fontana looked as if she wanted to throttle the stowaway. "You think this is some sort of goddamn meet-and-greet?"

Shaun ignored the woman's outstretched hand. He shared Fontana's outrage. How dare this glib intruder screw up their mission and treat the whole thing like a joke? He fought to keep his temper under control.

"You have a lot of explaining to do," he said sternly. "Start talking."

"All right," she replied, dropping some of the flippant attitude. "I can see where my being here must be a bit of a shock."

"To say the least," O'Herlihy said drily.

She tried to snag the tablet as it drifted by. "Short

version: I'm an investigative blogger. Maybe you've read my work?" She searched their faces hopefully, only to be disappointed. Shaun had never heard of her. She sighed before continuing. "And I crashed your party to get the scoop of the millennium and to find out the *real* story behind this trip."

"Real story?" O'Herlihy echoed. "What do you mean?"

"Never mind that right now," Shaun said. At the moment, he was less interested in her motives than in how exactly she had pulled this off in the first place. "How did you get aboard this ship?"

"Sorry," she said. "I can't divulge my sources. Journalistic ethics and all."

"Ethics?" Fontana said incredulously. "You've compromised a historic, multi-billion-dollar mission that's been years in the making, and you have the nerve to talk about ethics?" She confiscated the runaway tablet, which apparently belonged to the intruder. "I ought to cram your First Amendment rights up your—"

"Easy, Fontana," Shaun interrupted. "We'll get to the bottom of this."

He tried to figure it out. The stowaway could not have ridden up in a cargo bay, since those weren't pressurized or equipped for life support, so she must have been smuggled aboard via the *Renaissance* or one of the other ships servicing the *Lewis & Clark* while it was being prepped for departure. Maybe a Russian Soyuz capsule or one of the French construction crews? In any event, she could not have managed that without inside help, probably from one or more persons involved in the *Lewis & Clark*'s construction and assembly. Shaun shook his head at the very idea. Even with well-placed accomplices, the difficulties involved in slipping an extra person into space boggled his mind, but clearly this "Zoe Querez" had managed somehow. *There's going to be a hell of an investigation when this gets out,* he thought. *Heads will roll.*

Maybe even his.

"Are you nuts?" Fontana accused her. "We can't take on an extra passenger. Everything has been calculated for three people. The food, the weight, the oxygen, you name it." She threw up her hands in exasperation. "This is crazy."

"Please!" the stowaway shot back. "You think I didn't do my homework? I know that this mission was planned with wide safety margins, just in case something went wrong way out past Mars or wherever. You've got food, air, and water to spare. We're not talking a 'Cold Equations' scenario here."

Shaun caught the reference. She was citing a classic old science-fiction story in which an unlucky stowaway had to be jettisoned from a crucial space mission that had absolutely no margin for error. She was right about one thing: this Saturn mission was a lot less precarious than that fictional space flight. The ship's chemical fuel cells produced more than enough water for their purposes, weight was less of an issue since they hadn't needed to achieve escape velocity, and as for food, well, NASA didn't intend them to starve to death if one of the refrigerated pantries went on the fritz.

"Listen, you freeloader," Fontana said. "If you think you're eating any of my share, think again. I'm not doing without because some irresponsible gate crasher snuck in where she didn't belong."

"That's not going to be a problem," Querez said. "If you check your cargo bay, you'll find enough frozen dinners to sustain me for the trip and enough missing cargo to make up the weight difference."

"Missing cargo?" Shaun didn't like the sound of that. "What are you talking about? Every bit of that equipment was vitally important to this ship's mission."

"Yeah, right," she said sarcastically. "Like that time capsule from Ms. Hultquist's third-grade class at Thomas Jefferson Elementary School, the one with the large bronze plate with Senator Plummer's name on it?" She rolled her eyes. "C'mon, we all know that was a boondoggle to get one last vote on that funding bill. Somehow I think science will survive if you don't drop a crate of glorified souvenirs—including, as I recall, a school yearbook, a Bible, several personal letters and drawings, an autographed football, various stuffed animals and action figures, flash drives, CDs, baby teeth, and a complete set of *Harry Potter* novels—into orbit around Saturn for all eternity."

Touché, Shaun thought. He recalled posing for a photo op with the senator back in her hometown in

Kansas City. At the time, it had seemed a small price to pay for a crucial vote in the Senate. "I take it the time capsule didn't make it aboard?"

"Not exactly," she admitted, "although there's a package with all the right markings. And you know all those orchid bulbs that big perfume company sponsored?"

"I get the idea," Shaun said curtly. "You seem to have thought this all out, Ms. Querez."

"Please," she insisted. "Call me Zoe."

Fontana snorted. "That's not what I was planning to call you."

"You said something about the 'real story' behind our mission," O'Herlihy recalled. "What did you mean by that?"

"Like you don't know," she challenged him. "I mean, all of a sudden, we have to go to Saturn, even though Mars and Jupiter are much closer to Earth? Hell, Saturn is *twice* as far from the sun as Jupiter is, but we're going there first? You really expect people to buy that?"

"We've explained that before," Shaun said. "Dozens of times. Jupiter has a far more dangerous radioactive field, and Saturn just happens to be in alignment right now, or will be by the time we get there. We miss this chance, it's another thirty years before it comes around our way again. If ever we want to check out Saturn and its moons, now's the time."

"Plus, there's the comet," Fontana reminded him.

"That's right," Shaun said. He'd gone over this in

countless press conferences, so he knew the spiel by heart. "Hubble has spotted a previously unknown comet approaching Saturn. It should be passing by the planet about the time we arrive. How could we pass up an opportunity like that? It's a two-fer."

"Sure, sure, that's the official story," Zoe said skeptically, "and I'm certain it's true enough as far as the space science goes. Thirty-year solar revolution, dangerous Jovian radiation, incoming comet, yada, yada. But that's not the whole deal, is it?" She winked at them. "What about the trouble with the rings?"

O'Herlihy frowned. "What trouble? There is no trouble with the rings."

"That's not what I've heard," she said. "Word is, Saturn's famous rings are coming apart—'destabilizing' is the term my sources use—which could mess up the entire solar system."

"Nonsense," O'Herlihy said. "That's just a crackpot theory perpetuated by fringe elements. Contrary to what you might have read on the Internet, Saturn's rings are always full of irregularities and hardly uniform throughout. There are clumps and corrugations, froths and churns, some nearly three kilometers high." His voice took on a pedantic tone, as though he were addressing a classroom. "Think of them as raging rivers, complete with waves and rapids."

"Uh-huh," Zoe said, unconvinced. "But those rivers are getting wilder, aren't they, Professor?"

O'Herlihy sighed wearily. "Yes, conventional astronomers have recently detected some intriguing 'wobbles' in the rings, possibly caused by the approach of the comet, but that's just one more reason to visit Saturn and its moons at this particular juncture. There's no cause for alarm, despite the various doomsday scenarios on the Web."

"Really?" Zoe asked. "What if the rings break apart and the pieces come flying at the Earth?"

"A ridiculous fantasy," O'Herlihy insisted. "Even if the rings did disintegrate, Earth is much too far away to be significantly affected. Chances are, the loose debris would just add to the asteroid belt, if it didn't spiral into Saturn and burn up in its atmosphere."

Zoe almost looked disappointed. "Oh."

"Space is fascinating enough," Shaun said, "without having to sensationalize things. Trust me, we have plenty of good reasons to check out Saturn right here and now, but the end of the world isn't one of them."

Zoe shrugged. "Well, a girl can always dream, you know."

"Jesus!" Fontana said. "Why are we even wasting time talking to this flake?" She turned toward Shaun and O'Herlihy. "Now what are we going to do? Turn back?"

"Perhaps we should," O'Herlihy said. "Despite Ms. Querez's secret stores, her presence here completely upends our mission plans. We have no contingency plans for this." He shook his head dolefully. "Missions have been aborted for less."

He had a point, Shaun knew, but he hated the idea

of scrubbing the mission now that they were finally under way. "I don't know, Doc. A lot is depending on this mission. You know as well as I do that the space program is on life support as is, especially given the shaky state of the world economy. Plenty of people want to shut us down altogether."

He wasn't exaggerating. Back in the United States, thousands of homeless people were crammed into so-called sanctuary districts, with little hope of finding new jobs and lives anytime soon. The average citizen was more concerned with the economy, terrorism, global warming, wars, and the latest celebrity scandal than with humanity's future in space. Shaun's recent publicity tour had driven that home. Many today saw space exploration as a costly luxury that the world could no longer afford—or, worse yet, as the outmoded dream of an earlier generation. There weren't even any space shows on TV anymore. Hope was out of fashion.

"We need a successful mission, to get people excited about space and the future again. And NASA in particular could use a public-relations victory right now. The Eastern Coalition has already beaten us back to the moon. We can't come in second on Saturn, too." The more he thought about it, the more he realized what was at stake. "This is our last chance. We turn back now, that's it, not just for the Saturn mission but for the entire space program. We'll be grounded for good."

O'Herlihy scratched his beard. "It would be a shame to miss out on that comet," he admitted, "not to mention our chance to examine those intriguing ripples in the rings. As a scientist, I'll never have an opportunity like this again."

Shaun knew how much that meant to O'Herlihy. The doctor was a devout family man, very attached to his wife and daughter, yet he had agreed to leave them for 190 days and put hundreds of millions of kilometers between himself and his family, for the chance to take part in this mission. That was dedication.

"I won't be any trouble," Zoe insisted. "I'll just be along as an observer . . . to document your historic mission. And I'll help promote your success once we get back to Earth. Just think of me as an embedded journalist, like during a war."

"Shut up," Fontana said. "Nobody invited you along. You're an intruder, not a guest." She kept a wary eye on Zoe as she conferred with her colleagues. "And how do we know she is who she says she is, anyway? For all we know, she's a saboteur or a terrorist . . . like those HEL freaks back home."

The Human Extinction League was a radical environmental group that regarded humanity as a blight upon the planet and actually advocated its voluntary extinction, sooner rather than later. They had vowed to stop NASA from spreading the "plague" of humanity to other worlds and had even launched raids and attempted bombings against the space program. Just last week, the Johnson Space Center in Houston had received a threatening letter containing a suspicious white powder. Operations had been shut down for hours before Homeland Security determined that the powder was just an artificial sweetener.

"What if she's some sort of suicide bomber," Fontana asked, "out to sabotage the mission?"

"Then why haven't I done it already?" Zoe stretched out her arms. "Does it look like I'm wearing a suicide vest?" She scoffed at the notion. "Trust me, I've interviewed some HEL types, and they're a little extreme for my tastes."

"See?" Fontana said. "She admits she knows them."

"So? I've interviewed movie stars, too. That doesn't make me a Scientologist." She appealed to Shaun. "Look, Skipper, check out my credentials if you don't believe me."

"Oh, I will," Shaun promised. He wasn't looking forward to having that conversation with Houston. "And we're going to conduct a stem-to-stern search of this ship just to make sure there aren't any more hidden surprises."

"But that still leaves the burning question of what we're going to do with her," O'Herlihy said, "no matter which way we're going."

Fontana shrugged. "We could flush her out the airlock."

Shaun assumed she was joking . . . maybe. "We'll have to rig up a brig of some sort, perhaps in the airlock outside the cargo bay." Unfortunately, the *Lewis & Clark* had not been designed with prisoners in mind. "And keep a close eye on her regardless."

"Works for me," Zoe said. "At least until I can get you to trust me."

"Don't hold your breath for that," Fontana said. "What's the ruling, Commander? Are we seriously thinking about staying on course for Saturn?"

"That's for Mission Control to decide," he reminded them, "but if we present a unified front, our decision is likely to carry a lot of weight." He made up his mind. "I say we keep on going. We turn back now, we're never going to get another chance."

"All right, Shaun," O'Herlihy said. "You've convinced me. I'm game if you are."

"Thanks, Marcus." Shaun looked at Fontana. "What about you?"

As he knew from experience, his copilot wasn't fond of surprises, especially where a mission was concerned. She was all about advance planning and preparation. An X factor like their stowaway was bound to get under her skin.

She scowled, then let out an exasperated sigh. "What the hell. Far be it from me to be the spoilsport who kept mankind from going to Saturn. If you two are willing to put up with this juvenile idiot for more than two billion kilometers, you can count on me to back you up with Mission Control. But don't think I'm happy about it." She glared at Zoe. "If it was up to me, you'd be in a maximum-security prison cell as fast as we could turn this boat around."

"You may get your wish eventually," Zoe conceded. "If it's any consolation."

"Not really." Fontana gave Shaun a rueful look. "I really hope you know what you're doing, Shaun."

Me, too, he thought.

Four

"Klondike VI directly ahead, sir."

"Slow to impulse, Mr. Sulu," Kirk instructed, relieved to have reached their destination at last. The *Enterprise* had made good time getting there, but nineteen long days had passed since they had first received word of the crisis facing the mining colony. A yeoman offered him a cup of hot coffee, which he accepted gratefully. He leaned forward in his chair. "Let's see where we are."

The planet appeared on the viewscreen. Kirk was struck by its resemblance to Saturn. The stormy cloud belts striping its upper atmosphere were perhaps a touch more purple, and its glittering rings were configured slightly differently, but if you squinted, you could almost imagine that you were back in the Sol system. Although Klondike VI was still some distance away, the haloed orb filled the main viewer. It shone with reflected light.

"Beautiful," Uhura observed. "I've always liked ringed planets. There's something special about them."

"In what way, Lieutenant?" Spock asked. "Such rings are simply the result of predictable gravitational factors. Within a planet's Roche limit, tidal forces tear apart any large satellites and prevent new ones from being formed. Most rings are simply composed of random ice particles and other debris caught in a perpetual orbit."

"I know all that, Mr. Spock," Uhura replied. "But I still think they're gorgeous."

Spock did not argue the point. "I will concede that their symmetry has a certain aesthetic appeal."

"These particular rings are more than decorative," Kirk pointed out. He had been reading up on Klondike VI during the voyage. "Those aren't just ice crystals circling that planet. The inner rings are laced with significant amounts of dilithium, enough to make a mining operation both profitable and crucial to the future of space exploration."

The rings before them were like precious bracelets, sparkling with the rarest of gemstones. A shame they were destabilizing.

"Indeed," Spock said. "Prior to the present crisis, the Skagway colony was on its way to becoming the primary source of crystallized dilithium in this sector. It would be a significant loss should the operations there be curtailed."

"Not to mention the possible threat to the colony's population," Kirk reminded him. The captain squinted at the image of Klondike VI but could not make out the moon in question. "Are we within view of Skagway?"

According to their files, the moon occupied a gap between the inner and outer rings. Skagway's own gravity helped to keep the gap open—at least, until recently.

"Coming around now, Captain." Sulu brought the *Enterprise* into orbit above the planet's rings, then descended into the empty gap. Kirk spied a bright reflective object ahead of them. The moon grew larger as the starship quickly caught up with it. The *Enterprise* slowed to keep pace with the tiny moon. "There it is."

Skagway was a small moon, barely one hundred kilometers in diameter. An icy white glaze, pock-marked with craters, covered its surface. No atmosphere protected it from random meteor strikes. Only a fraction of the size of Earth's own moon, it was nonetheless home to nearly two thousand souls. Kirk hoped they weren't in too much trouble.

"Full magnification," he ordered.

A domed colony could be seen on the frozen surface of the moon. A crude spaceport surrounded the central dome. Automated harvesters and sifters, designed to extract dilithium from the nearby rings, were parked on landing pads composed of resurfaced ice. A small fleet of shuttles, tugs, and scout ships, ill equipped and insufficient to evacuate the entire colony, also occupied the spaceport. Crude hangars were presumably used to repair and service the various vehicles. Thermal collectors faced the planet, which, like Saturn, generated its own heat. Skagway rotated slowly on its axis, providing abbreviated days and nights for the people living beneath the translucent geodesic dome. The moon's dense core had made subterranean drilling both expensive and problematic.

Too bad, Kirk thought. The colonists might be safer beneath the ground, at least in the short term. *If only we had some Hortas at our disposal.*

Looking closer, the captain spied what appeared to be evidence of the emergency. Fresh craters pitted the frozen lunar landscape. Various shuttles and harvesters were visibly damaged, possibly beyond repair. And the colony's protective dome, while still intact, had been pitted by multiple high-speed collisions with falling objects. Even as Kirk watched the viewer, chunks of icy debris pelted the airless moon, throwing up clouds of crystalline powder. A slab of ice (or was it dilithium?) the size of a small shuttle barely missed the dome, hitting a landing pad outside the colony. A limited array of surface-to-air phasers had been deployed to defend the dome but were clearly inadequate to the crisis at hand; they had been intended to deal with only the occasional random object, not a constant barrage. Skagway was caught in a cosmic hailstorm that seemed to be growing in ferocity.

"Receiving hailing frequencies," Uhura reported. "It's Governor Dawson."

The *Enterprise*'s arrival had apparently not gone unnoticed.

"Put her through," Kirk said.

"Yes, Captain."

Skooka Dawson appeared on-screen. A handsome

woman in her late fifties who appeared to be of Aleutian descent, she was dressed simply in orange miner's overalls. Close-cropped white hair framed a drawn face that showed obvious signs of strain. Dark pouches beneath her eyes hinted that she had not been sleeping well. A framed photo of the aurora borealis could be glimpsed in the background. A chunk of unprocessed dilithium rested atop her desk.

"Hello, Captain. Thank you for responding so promptly to our distress signal."

"My pleasure, Governor." Kirk was eager to get the straight scoop from the ground. "What's your status?"

"Bad and getting worse," she replied, not mincing words. "My scientists tell me that the planet's rings are collapsing inward, which puts us right in the middle of an avalanche. We've had nonstop hailstorms for days now, and some of the bigger pieces are large enough to sink the Titanic, if you get the reference."

"I know my maritime history," he assured her. "How is your dome holding up?"

"We built this colony to last, but it was never meant to take this kind of punishment. The Yukon Gap is supposed to be clear of debris, or at least it always was before. Our deflectors are already being pushed to their limits, which is putting a severe strain on our resources. To be honest, I'm not sure how much longer we can hold out. We've already had to suspend all mining operations."

The lights flickered in her office. A heavy thud rattled the paperweights on her desk.

"I understand," Kirk said. "I'll have my engineering team see what they can do to reinforce your deflectors." He looked ahead to the bigger picture. "Do your scientists have any idea what might be causing these disturbances?"

"Not yet, but I'll see to it that all our data are transmitted to your ship." The lights sputtered again, then came back on. *"Perhaps you can spot something we missed."*

"Perhaps." Kirk could only hope that Spock could unravel the mystery. "I don't suppose there's any sign that this is just a temporary phenomenon?"

"I keep hoping as much," she said, *"but if anything, the storms seem to be worsening. There's also some concern that Skagway's own orbit could be affected. We could end up falling into the inner rings—or worse."*

Kirk imagined the moon descending into the gas giant's turbulent atmosphere. The planet's intense gravity and violent storms would make short work of the domed colony, even if it succeeded in passing through the inner rings in one piece. No amount of deflectors could save them.

Not for the first time, the captain wished there was a nearby starbase or M-class planet that the colonists could be transported to. But the distances involved made multiple trips impractical; if the situation was as bad as it appeared, there was not nearly enough time to get the entire population to safety.

"Let's hope it doesn't come to that," he said. "But we should be prepared to evacuate as many of your people as we can."

Dawson nodded. *"No offense, Kirk, but I wish that* Constitution-*class ship of yours was bigger. I'm not looking forward to deciding who lives and who dies . . . like Kodos the Executioner."*

Kirk winced inside. Governor Dawson probably didn't know it, but he had been on Tarsus IV when Kodos had condemned half the population to death during a planetwide famine. Kirk had only been thirteen years old at the time, but he still remembered the panic and heartbreak of those harrowing days, as Kodos had mercilessly culled the old, the infirm, and the "expendable." The nightmare had not ended until Starfleet arrived to halt the purge.

At least justice caught up with him, Kirk thought. *Eventually.*

"I met Kodos," he said, "and I'm certain you're nothing like him."

Dawson didn't ask for details. She clearly had other things on her mind. *"Let's be clear about one thing, Captain. If it comes down to it, I am not leaving this colony before any of my people. I'm going down with the ship if necessary. End of story."*

Kirk understood. The Skagway colony wasn't technically a ship, but the principle was the same. He could tell that her mind was made up. Photon torpedoes would not be enough to stop her from staying behind with the last of her people.

"That's not going to happen," he vowed. "We're going to find a way to save the entire colony."

Five

"Objection!" Zoe Querez gasped. "This is cruel and unusual punishment!"

Ignoring her protests, Colonel Christopher checked the timer instead. "Ten more minutes."

The stowaway was fifty minutes into her mandatory one-hour workout on the treadmill. Given the pernicious effects of zero gravity on the human body, it would have been grossly inhumane *not* to let her get some exercise at least twice a day. A harness kept her strapped down to the treadmill and gave her resistance to strain against; otherwise, she could have run in place for hours and not gotten much benefit at all. Attached to force plates on either side of the treadmill, the harness simulated gravity by pulling down on her shoulders and hips with more than a hundred pounds of pressure. Globules of perspiration clung to her face and skin. Her shorts and tank top were soaked with sweat. Shaun knew from experience just how hard she was working. Those straps got very uncomfortable, very fast.

"Sadist! It would have been kinder to chuck me out the airlock."

He chuckled. "Don't let Fontana hear you say that."

Thirty-plus days into the mission, Zoe had been a model prisoner so far. Talking Mission Control into continuing the mission, despite their unplanned passenger, had been a challenge, but Shaun and his fellow astronauts had ultimately prevailed. It had helped, of course, that the folks on the ground had been equally aware of the dire consequences of aborting the mission at the very moment public and political enthusiasm for the space program had reached record lows. Shaun knew that this decision was ultimately on him, though. He was still hoping that he hadn't made a monumental mistake.

NASA had also chosen to keep the stowaway's existence a secret for the time being, for fear of courting bad press. That was fine with Shaun. Let the PR flacks handle the spin control. He had a mission to complete.

A beep demanded his attention. He hit a button on his computer, and Fontana's face appeared on the monitor. "You called?"

"Hate to interrupt your babysitting session," she said drily, *"but I thought you'd want to know that as of sixty seconds ago, we officially entered the asteroid belt."* She smirked. *"No evasive action required yet."*

Shaun glanced out the nearest porthole. All he saw was the usual darkness and distant stars. No drifting boulders threatened the habitat module.

"We'll have to break out a bottle of the good stuff

for dinner tonight," he said. Officially, NASA frowned on alcohol in space, but their Russian partners were more inclined to look the other way where liquid refreshment was concerned. As it happened, some generous cosmonauts had smuggled a couple of bottles into one of the Soyuz capsules that had carried supplies up to the *Lewis & Clark* while it was in orbit. "I think this calls for a celebration, kind of like crossing the international date line back in the old days."

"Just as long as I don't have to be the designated driver," Fontana quipped. "I'm not sipping Tang while you hit the booze. Red wine is supposed to be good for combating weightlessness, you know."

"So I hear," he said. Studies had shown that a component of red wine, resveratrol, could help prevent bone-density loss and muscle atrophy, two common effects of life in space. NASA had prescribed resveratrol supplements for the whole crew, although the tablets lacked certain other benefits associated with a nice bottle of wine. "I suspect the doc will abstain. He's not much of a drinker." Shaun had never known O'Herlihy to indulge. "In the meantime, keep your eyes peeled for rolling rocks."

He was kidding, mostly. Although the asteroid belt contained thousands of microplanets, the matter was spread so thinly that the odds were a billion to one against the ship colliding with anything; over the last half-century, numerous unmanned probes had passed through the belt unscathed, and Shaun had every reason to assume that the *Lewis & Clark* would do the same. Still, the ship's LIDAR was on full alert for any potential hazards, and he and Fontana had agreed not to leave the cockpit unmanned until the ship was clear of the belt. They would be taking turns sleeping there for the next few weeks.

"*Roger that*," she said. "*You keep an eye on you-know-who.*"

"Hi, Fontana!" Zoe shouted from the treadmill. "How you doing, girlfriend?"

Grimacing, the other woman cut off the transmission.

"You know, you really shouldn't bait her like that," Shaun said.

"Everybody needs a hobby." She adjusted the straps digging into her shoulders in a vain attempt to relieve the pressure. Despite being short of breath, she kept on talking. "So, am I included in this crossing celebration? I gotta admit, I could use a drink, especially after fighting this torture device."

"Sure," he said with a shrug. "Why not? Provided you don't try to blow up the ship between now and dinnertime."

He wasn't really worried about that anymore. NASA had checked out her story, and she appeared to be just what she claimed to be: an unusually nervy journalist out to make a name for herself. Over the last few weeks, he had been gradually letting her out of their improvised brig more often, for the sake of her health and sanity. He wasn't about to grant her free run of the ship anytime soon, but as long as she behaved herself, there was probably no need to keep her locked up all the time. She actually wasn't bad company, although he suspected that his copilot felt otherwise.

"Fontana won't object?"

"Undoubtedly," Shaun predicted. Fontana had not yet warmed to Zoe; she still regarded the stowaway as an intruder. "But I'll see what I can do."

"Rank has its privileges, huh?"

"And seniority," Shaun said. "These gray hairs must count for something."

"Yeah, you've been at this game for some time now, haven't you? I did my homework on all of you before I boarded this cruise, as it were. You've got quite an interesting résumé, Colonel Christopher." She kept up a steady pace on the treadmill. Shaun could smell the rubber soles of her sneakers heating up from the friction. "Say, Skipper, at the risk of pushing my luck, do you mind if I ask you some questions about your illustrious career—including your stint at Area 51?"

Oh, boy, he thought, going on alert. *Here it comes.* He'd been expecting this; it was a wonder that she had waited so long to bring it up. *Probably wanted to ingratiate herself first.*

"That's classified, and you know it."

"Even after all these years? C'mon, Skipper. Throw me a bone. What else are we going to talk about the next umpteen million miles?"

"There's not much to tell," he lied. "If you must know, yes, I was assigned to the Groom Lake Facility, popularly known as Area 51, for a brief time back in the nineties, where I helped test experimental aircraft that I can't really talk about. Not exactly the stuff of tabloid headlines."

That wasn't the whole story, of course. In fact, he had been assigned to the development and construction of the DY-100, an experimental "sleeper ship" employing advanced technology reverse-engineered from a crashed "Ferengi" spacecraft recovered in Roswell back in 1947. If all had gone well, Shaun might have piloted the DY-100 on its maiden voyage, but the prototype had mysteriously vanished in 1996 under circumstances that puzzled him to this day. His friend and colleague, Shannon O'Donnell, had taken the fall for the loss of the DY-100, effectively ending her NASA career, but he'd always suspected that there was more to the story than she had ever let on. Last he'd heard, she had been involved with the Millennium Gate project in Indiana, and the DY-100 project had been tabled indefinitely. *Maybe they'll take those diagrams out of mothballs someday,* he thought, *if we pull this Saturn jaunt off without any more hitches.*

He liked to think so.

"Why am I not buying this?" Zoe asked aloud. "You must have some good dirt from those days."

"Sorry." He tried to wave it off as if it was no big deal. "Believe me, Area 51 was not nearly as interesting as the TV specials and conspiracy theorists make out."

"No alien autopsies or captured spaceships?"

"'Fraid not." He tried to change the subject. "Although my dad sighted a UFO once, back in the sixties."

"Really?" Zoe sounded intrigued. "How did I miss that?"

"Well, there's not much to the story." Shaun fingered the dog tags around his neck. "The Air Force picked up a UFO on radar and sent my dad up in a fighter jet to check it out. He thought he glimpsed something in the sky over Omaha, but then it was gone in a blink. To be honest, he's still not sure whether he really saw something or not."

"What do you think?" Zoe asked.

"Who knows? It *could* have been a visiting space-craft."

As a kid, he had asked his dad to tell him about that UFO sighting over and over again; hell, it had probably helped inspire his lifelong interest in space travel. And his tour of duty at Area 51, years later, had certainly left Shaun open to the prospect of intelligent life from other worlds. He wasn't about to dismiss what his dad had seen, however briefly, as just a trick of the light.

"Look at us," he said, gesturing around at the cramped interior of the *Lewis & Clark,* which had been named after two legendary explorers. "We're heading into space to see what—and who—might be out there. I have to imagine that other intelligent species are just as curious." He chuckled, just so she wouldn't think he was too much of a UFO nut. "Not that I'm expecting to run into any little green men on this mission."

"Or any sexy green girls?"

"Sadly, no," Shaun said. "But I like the way your mind works." He saw another way to divert the conversation away from Area 51. "I've been reading some of your blogs, by the way. NASA transmitted them to me—as part of their background check. It seems you have something of a cult following on the Internet."

Zoe beamed, clearly flattered. "So, what did you think?"

"To be honest, they were a little far-out for my tastes." He called up one of her online exposés on the computer terminal. "You really think Khan Noonien Singh is still alive?"

A notorious dictator, Khan had wielded consider-able power back in the nineties. At the height of his influence, he was said to have been the de facto ruler of large portions of India, South Asia, and the Middle East. He had been overthrown in '96—about the same time the DY-100 had disappeared, come to think of it. That had been a pretty tumultuous year.

"Maybe. They never found his body, you know—at least, not that it could be reliably determined. What's more, according to my research, some eighty of his closest advisers and followers remain unaccounted for."

Shaun hadn't heard that before. "Where do you

think they are? Tora Bora? A luxury estate in Kashmir?"

"Haven't figured that out yet," she admitted. "Who knows? Maybe we'll find them waiting for us out by Saturn."

"I wouldn't count on that," he said. "Although you certainly have a vivid imagination, I'll give you that."

She grinned. "I'll take that as a compliment."

The timer beeped.

"That's it," he announced. "You're done for the day."

"Thank God!" She switched off the treadmill and unhooked the harness. "My feet are killing me. They're not used to supporting all that weight, you know."

"Don't remind me." His feet always felt positively raw when he got on the treadmill. He traded places with Zoe and strapped himself in. Back in orbit around Earth, he had once jogged in place for a full ninety minutes, just so he could say that he had literally run around the entire planet. He flicked the treadmill on. It felt as if he was walking on a bed of nails.

And he still had an hour to go!

"Oh, my poor little piggies." She peeled off her socks and sneakers. Floating free, she massaged her aching feet. "Hey, Skipper, since we're finally opening up and all, mind if I ask you a personal question?"

"Not about Area 51, I hope."

"Nah, although don't think for a minute that I've given up on that angle." She wiped off her sweaty face and limbs with a towel. "This is just for my own curiosity. Off the record."

He started to pick up the pace. "Okay, shoot."

"What's the story with you and Fontana?"

Whoa! He missed a step but quickly recovered. "What do you mean? We're just colleagues, that's all."

Once again, that wasn't entirely the truth. He and Alice had conducted a discreet affair more than a year ago, shortly after his divorce, but had broken things off before it could get in the way of the mission. Ever since the Lisa Nowak scandal of 2007, NASA had frowned on excessive "fraternization" between astronauts. No way would they have both been assigned to this mission had the higher-ups known about their prior relationship.

"Uh-huh. Right." Zoe scrutinized the jogging astronaut. "I've been watching you two. There's a definite vibe there. I've seen the way you look at each other when you think nobody's looking and how awkward it is whenever you accidentally touch each other. 'Fess up, Skipper. You two practicing orbital maneuvers on the sly?"

Damn, Shaun thought. He had to give her points for observational skills, not that he intended to share his private life with a nosy reporter. Off the record or not, that was between him and Fontana. "Like I said before, you have a vivid imagination."

"But I also like to get my facts straight." She deposited the towel in a sealed hamper. "Seriously, what's the scoop? I mean, I know that the doc is happily married and all, but you really expect me to believe that you and Fontana aren't getting busy on this trip? It's a long way to Saturn and back."

Shaun hoped that zero g didn't make blushing easier. He quickened his pace on the treadmill, hoping the exertion would disguise any telltale flushes. "We have plenty to occupy us, thank you very much. This is a scientific mission, not a pleasure cruise." He tried to joke away the subject. "Besides, I'm holding out for one of those green girls you mentioned."

"You might want to clear that with Fontana first. I'm not sure she would approve."

Possibly not. "I'll keep that in mind." He adjusted the harness, which was already digging into his hips and shoulders. He had to be careful to avoid developing blisters and friction burns. "What about you? Hope you're not counting on an alien abduction."

"Nah. I'm not into ETs." She drifted over to the window and gazed out at the void. "But let me know if we run into Khan. Tyrant or not, he was a hottie."

"You'll be the first to know," he promised.

Six

"Impact in thirty-nine seconds, Captain."

All eyes were focused on the viewer as a slab of ice the size of an adult Horta came zooming at the dome protecting the Skagway colony. The frozen missile was accompanied by a rain of smaller particles from the outer rings. Flashes of blue Cherenkov energy flared whenever a sizable chunk struck the colony's fading shields. It looked like an old-fashioned fireworks display.

"Fire at will, Mr. Chekov."

A pair of brilliant sapphire beams, unleashed by the *Enterprise*'s forward phaser banks, converged on the speeding slab. The directed energy blasts disintegrated the massive object, which glowed brightly before dissolving into atoms. Vaporized water dispersed into the vacuum.

"Bingo." Sulu grinned at Chekov. "Right on target."

"Good shooting," Kirk agreed. "You're proving quite the sharp-eyed marksman, Mr. Chekov."

The young ensign shrugged modestly. "Sadly, I am getting rather too much practice."

Tell me about it, Kirk thought. The *Enterprise* had taken up a defensive position between Skagway and the crumbling rings of Klondike VI, where such exercises had become increasingly necessary. The colony's own defenses were no longer sufficient to keep its population safe. More than a day had passed since the ship had arrived at Skagway, and the storms were getting worse by the hour. Fresh cracks and craters marred the battered surface of the moon. Anti-meteor phaser arrays had been smashed to pieces by the very hazards they'd been designed to fend off. The Yukon Gap was supposed to be relatively clear of the debris. The colony had not been designed to cope with a barrage of this magnitude. Even as Kirk watched, another slab of ice hit the moon's uninhabited southern hemisphere. He guessed that the tremors could be felt from kilometers away.

The *Enterprise* was helping, but Kirk knew they were only buying time. As if the storms weren't bad enough, Spock had confirmed that Skagway's own orbit was deteriorating. The moon was doomed to spiral into the planet's atmosphere—unless some manner of solution could be found.

"Shuttle approaching the *Enterprise*," Uhura reported. "They're requesting permission to come aboard."

"Permission granted." Kirk had been expecting this. Governor Dawson had promised to send her best person to consult with his crew. He activated his intercom. "Kirk to landing bay, prepare for company."

On the viewer, the shuttle could be seen flying through the storm. Debris buffeted the small vessel, but its shields appeared to be holding. Kirk didn't envy the pilot.

"Keep an eye on that shuttle," he instructed, not wanting it to get nailed by an iceberg-sized missile before it reached the *Enterprise*. "Make sure it gets through intact."

"Aye, sir," Chekov said. "I will watch over it like a guardian angel."

"Just hang on to your halo, Ensign," Kirk quipped as he rose from his chair. He wanted to greet the delegation personally. "Would you please accompany me, Mr. Spock? I'm sure our guest would appreciate your scientific input."

"Of course, Captain." Spock stepped away from his station. "I am eager to 'compare notes,' as you might say, with the colony's own expert."

Kirk nodded at the helm. "Mr. Sulu, you have the conn."

"Aye, sir."

Sulu turned over the helm to Lieutenant Stoltzfus before taking the captain's chair. Kirk happened to notice how much at home Sulu looked in charge of the bridge. *Good*, Kirk thought. He knew that Sulu had ambitions of having his own command someday. *He'll make a fine captain, I'm guessing. After he gets a bit more seasoning.*

Spock joined Kirk in the turbolift. A short ride later, they arrived outside the shuttlecraft bay at the rear of the ship. "*Shuttle acquired,*" a voice announced over the intercom system. "*Repressurizing landing bay.*" Moments later, a green light flashed above the doorway, signaling that the deck was now safe to enter. Blue double doors slid open to admit them.

The shuttlecraft, which was smaller and of boxier design than the Starfleet models, rested at the center of the cavernous gray landing bay. Despite its shields, the shuttle's exterior was freshly dented in places. Its outer plating had been dinged and chipped. Kirk was impressed that the pilot had been willing to fly through the barrage to get here.

A single passenger exited the shuttle. Slight of figure, Qat Zaldana wore a neatly tailored emerald blazer and matching skirt. Dark hair was piled atop her head in a beehive. A metallic gold veil completely concealed her face, making her age hard to determine. The veil seemed to be composed of dozens of overlapping sequins that sparkled like a transporter effect. Kirk wondered how she could see through the shimmering fabric.

"Welcome to the *Enterprise,*" he greeted her. "I'm Captain Kirk, and this is my first officer, Mr. Spock."

"Pleased to meet you, gentlemen." She crossed the landing pad to join them. A shiny silver carry bag was slung over her shoulder. "I only wish the circumstances were less dire."

"As do I," he agreed. "But thank you for coming."

According to Governor Dawson, Qat Zaldana was Skagway's chief scientist and astronomer. Kirk was anxious to hear her views on the crisis threatening the colony. He offered her his arm. "If you'll allow me."

"You don't need to guide me, Captain," she said with a chuckle. "I can see perfectly well through my veil."

"It is composed of a sensor web, is it not?" Spock surmised.

"That's quite right, Mr. Spock. I belong to the Order of the Faceless, whose teachings require us to keep our visages to ourselves," she offered by way of explanation. "I assure you, I am not a Klingon in disguise."

"I never thought you were," Kirk said. He was not familiar with the sect she had mentioned but had no intention of asking her to compromise her beliefs. The Federation embraced all manner of creeds and philosophies, some more esoteric than others. "But I'm impressed by the craftsmanship of your veil."

Miranda Jones had worn a similar fabric, he recalled, but for a different reason. Apparently, the shimmering fabric was made of dozens of miniature sensors strung together in a complex lattice that probably allowed Qat Zaldana to perceive her surroundings better than either he or Spock could. For all he knew, she could see right through him—literally.

He couldn't help wondering what she looked like.

"This old thing?" she joked. "I've had it for years." She turned her shrouded face toward Spock. "I must say, Mr. Spock, I'm looking forward to working with you on this problem. Your reports to the Vulcan Science Council have made fascinating reading. I was particularly intrigued by your theories regarding temporal mechanics and mirror universes."

"Indeed?" Spock was too Vulcan to be visibly flattered by their guest's praise, but Kirk thought he detected a hint of pride in his friend's voice. Or perhaps Spock simply appreciated encountering an equally scientific mind. "I hope you found my work illuminating."

"Very much so," she insisted. "I have to ask, do you really think that the long-term relativistic side effects of the so-called slingshot maneuver can be calculated by means of a factored transdifferential equation?"

"That depends on the constancy of acceleration and the maximum fungibility of the space-time continuum. There are many other variables to consider as well."

"Such as the possibility of a quantum rift?"

"Precisely."

Kirk smirked in amusement. "I hate to break up this small talk, but perhaps we should get down to business?"

"Of course, Captain," she said apologetically. Her voice took on a more somber tone. "Is there somewhere we can talk? I have new data that may be of interest to you."

"We can speak in the briefing room," Kirk suggested. Before escorting her out of the landing bay, the captain cocked his head toward the parked shuttle. "What about your pilot? I imagine he might like to relax in one of our rec rooms, especially after that bumpy ride you just took." He shook his head. "You were both brave to go out in that storm."

Ordinarily, the *Enterprise* would have just beamed the scientist aboard, but that would have involved lowering the colony's shields. Under the circumstances, a shuttle flight from the spaceport outside the dome had seemed a safer bet—at least, for everybody back on the moon.

"That's very thoughtful of you, Captain," she said warmly, "but there is no 'both.' I piloted the shuttle myself."

"I see," Kirk said, impressed. Qat Zaldana was clearly a woman of many talents. "This way, then."

The doors slid shut behind them as they entered the corridor outside. Busy crew members, intent on their duties, hustled past them. An engineering team performed routine maintenance on an exposed power conduit. Kirk lowered his voice on the way to the turbolift.

"So, what's it like down on the colony?" he asked. "How are people bearing up?"

"No better than you might expect, Captain." Zaldana kept her voice subdued. "The governor is doing her best to try to keep everyone calm, but people are frightened. Who can blame them? Tremors are shaking the moon, the storms won't let up, and everyone's worried about what's coming next. Your timely arrival has reassured people a little, but nobody knows if that's going to be enough. Folks are on the verge of panicking, I'm afraid."

Kirk didn't like the sound of that. A rioting population could cost lives and make evacuation efforts even more difficult. He made a mental note to ask Governor Dawson if she needed any additional security forces.

"Panic is seldom logical," Spock observed, "but your fellow colonists have reason to fear for their safety. By my calculations, Skagway will soon fall out of its orbit unless we can determine the source of these anomalies and find a way to restore the status quo."

"I know," she said. "That's why you need to see my new data right away."

Kirk didn't have to see her face to know how urgent this was. He commandeered the nearest turbolift, which took them directly to a hallway outside the ship's main briefing room. The lights turned on automatically as they entered the chamber and sat down at the conference table. Kirk briefly wondered if he should summon McCoy or Scotty to this meeting but decided against it; he could get their advice later if necessary. Kirk activated the computer terminal.

"All right," Kirk said. "What do you have for us, Ms. Zaldana?"

"Please, call me Qat," she insisted.

"If you wish," he said. "Is that a name or a title?"

"Both," she answered. "But take a look at this."

She inserted a data card into the terminal. An image appeared on the triscreen viewer facing their seats. Churning clouds swirled around what appeared to be an enormous hexagon bordered by six dark purple jet streams. The vortex seemed to extend deep into the planet's turbulent atmosphere. Straight sides and sharp angles gave it an oddly artificial appearance, not at all like a natural weather pattern.

"What you're looking at," she explained, "is one of Klondike VI's most distinctive features: an enormous hexagonal vortex that permanently covers the planet's north pole. It's more than thirty thousand kilometers across, large enough to hold at least four Earth-sized planets, and it's been there for as long as anyone remembers."

Kirk examined the image, which looked familiar. "I've seen storm formations like this before. There's one just like it on Saturn."

"As well as on Myrddin V, Nova Limbo, Valhalla Prime, and various other gas giants throughout the quadrant," Spock added. "All ringed planets, as it happens."

"Just so," she confirmed. "The hexagon on Klondike VI is virtually identical to the one on Saturn, or at least it was." She advanced the file on the computer. "That image was taken months ago. Now look at time-lapse recordings taken over the last several weeks."

On the screens, the colossal hexagon began to

contract, gradually at first but with increasing speed.
Deep purple clouds lightened in color, looking pale
and washed-out. A time stamp at the bottom of the
recording charted the vortex's contraction. Weeks
clicked by rapidly.

"It's shrinking," Kirk said. "Growing smaller by the
day."

She nodded. "And at an accelerating rate."

"Fascinating," Spock observed. "Such formations
are known to be uniquely stable. To my knowledge,
a contraction of this nature has never been observed
elsewhere."

Kirk stared at the screen facing him. The hexagon
was only a fraction of its original size. "And you only
just noticed this?"

"We've been rather preoccupied with the outer
rings raining down on us," Zaldana pointed out.
"Besides, the process began so slowly that it was almost
imperceptible at first, like watching grass grow or a
glacier slowly melt over time. By the time you register
the change, it's already well under way."

Kirk could see that. The surface of Klondike VI was
vast and turbulent, after all. He could hardly expect
the colonists to monitor every square kilometer of the
planet at all times. Skagway was primarily a mining
operation, not a scientific outpost. The gas giant was
just background scenery to them.

"And the hexagon started shrinking around the
same time the rings began collapsing?" the captain
noted. "That can't be a coincidence."

"No," she agreed. "But is it a cause or an effect? Or is some other factor causing both phenomena?"

Kirk looked at Spock. "What do you think? Could what's happening to the hexagon be causing the rings to deteriorate?"

"That is impossible to determine without further data," Spock declared, clearly reluctant to speculate before all of the facts were in. "But this development certainly warrants closer study. I suggest we use the ship's scanners to examine the vortex."

"An excellent idea, Mr. Spock," Kirk said, "provided it doesn't get in the way of protecting the colony." He mentally charted the *Enterprise*'s position, trying to determine a location that would put them in the best place to observe the planet's north pole and defend the besieged moon at the same time. That was going to be tricky. "Don't forget. Hundreds of lives are at stake."

"I am quite aware of that, Captain," Spock stated, "but unless we can determine the source of the disturbances and find a means to reverse them, there will be no colony to defend."

Qat Zaldana inhaled sharply behind her veil.

"Forgive my bluntness," Spock apologized. "But the facts are what they are."

"You needn't apologize for stating the truth, Mr. Spock." Her voice was solemn but unshaken. "Skagway is doomed unless we can stop this. I know that."

Kirk was impressed by her bravery. He'd known Starfleet recruits to crack under less pressure. "Aside from the hexagon, is there anything else we should know? Another avenue of investigation?"

"Funny you should ask that, Captain." She placed a new card in the computer. "There is something else you should see."

The seething hexagon vanished from the screens, replaced by the image of a luminous white comet. A haze of dusty vapor surrounded its frozen nucleus. Its misty tail stretched out behind it, no doubt pointed away from the nearest sun.

"Our long-range scanners just detected this comet entering our solar system. And it appears to be coming straight toward us."

Seven

"Okay," Zoe said. "Now I understand why you all wanted to get here."

After more than ninety days in transit, Saturn loomed before them in all its majesty. Although still more than four million kilometers away, the ringed planet dominated the view from the cockpit windows. All three astronauts, plus one stowaway, had gathered on the flight deck to take in the breathtaking sight. The mustard-colored planet was immeasurably vast, second only to Jupiter in size. Horizontal bands of yellow and gold marked the passage of cyclonic winds zipping past one another in opposite directions. Saturn's winds were believed to be the most ferocious in the solar system, reaching speeds of more than eighteen thousand kilometers per hour, while its fabled rings, which could be subdivided into thousands of smaller ringlets, spread out in concentric circles from the planet's equator, not unlike the tattoo at the back of Zoe's neck. Shaun wondered if she'd had it done for the voyage.

"Almost there," Shaun said, proud of their accomplishment. They had passed through the asteroid belt unscathed, bypassed Jupiter and its deadly radiation field, and made it across the solar system to Saturn. They were farther from home than any explorer had ever ventured before—any human explorer, that was. "Well done, folks."

"Yes," O'Herlihy said hoarsely, choking up. "So much hard work, all our sacrifices . . . yet here we are. We made it."

Shaun patted him on his back. The doc was entitled to get emotional at a moment like this. "It's a great feeling, isn't it?"

"You bet." Fontana high-fived Shaun, wedging her foot into a rail to keep the motion from sending her flying across the deck. Her face was alight with jubilation; she didn't even seem to mind that Zoe was sharing this moment with them. "Just look at those rings. Earth's got nothing like that."

Zoe tapped away at her smart tablet, recording the moment for posterity. Shaun had returned the device to her after making sure its wireless capacity had been disabled and that it held no terrorist-friendly apps. He suspected that the authorities would confiscate the tablet once she returned to Earth, but in the meantime, it gave her something to do, especially since she wasn't allowed to touch any of the ship's computer terminals, not even for recreational purposes. Cabin fever could be dangerous in space, so it had seemed best to keep her occupied.

She looked up from the tablet and squinted at the windows. "So, that's the famous hexagon," she said. "Freaky."

As it happened, the planet was tilted toward them at about a twenty-six-degree angle, giving them a clear view of its north pole, where a distinctive honeycomb shape contained a colossal storm some forty thousand kilometers across. The hexagon had first been observed by *Voyager 1* more than forty years ago, Shaun recalled. Scientists had been arguing about it ever since.

"One of the solar system's odder natural wonders," O'Herlihy observed, somewhat less emotionally than before. His deep voice had regained its cool, professorial tone. "Quite remarkable."

"I don't know," Zoe said. "That doesn't look natural at all to me. More like evidence of some arcane alien intelligence."

O'Herlihy sighed; he had little patience for speculative pseudo-science. "Really, Zoe, you're worse than my students. You need to rely less on the Internet and crackpot theories and more on actual scientific research." He nodded at the view. "Although deceptively artificial in appearance, that vortex is nothing but an unusual storm formation created by rotational forces deep within the planet's turbulent atmosphere."

Zoe wasn't convinced. "But look at it. A perfect geometric figure with six sides of exactly equal length, unchanged for decades? You're telling me that just happened by accident?"

"The universe is a big place," Shaun reminded her. "There's time and space enough for all sorts of unlikely occurrences. Anything that can happen probably has."

"Like mysterious alien science projects?" Zoe said. "Who knows? Maybe there's some weird black monolith at the center of the hexagon."

"Not on this space odyssey," Shaun said. "I don't know about you, but I'm not planning to evolve into a higher form of life anytime soon."

Zoe winked at him. "Speak for yourself."

"Jesus," Fontana said, exasperated. "You really don't know when to give up, do you?"

"Would I be here if I did?"

"My point exactly."

Shaun intervened before Saturn witnessed its first zero-gravity catfight. "In any event, I hope we'll learn a lot more about that storm, and the rest of Saturn's weather patterns, while we're in the neighborhood."

The plan was to settle into a polar orbit threading the planet's rings and study Saturn and its moons for fourteen days before turning around and heading home. NASA expected them to accumulate enough data to keep scientists back on Earth occupied for years. With any luck, some of the data might actually explain the enigmatic hexagon once and for all.

"Indeed," O'Herlihy said. "I'm looking forward to checking out the magnetometer readings on that storm, not to mention getting a close-up look at that comet."

The comet was only a misty smudge in the distance

at this point. In theory, it would be joining them any day now.

"This is where your work really starts," Shaun said. O'Herlihy was the chief scientist on this mission; he would be taking center stage now. "I'm just glad we got you here in one piece."

"I appreciate the smooth ride, Colonel," O'Herlihy said. "My thanks to you and your esteemed copilot."

"You're welcome," Shaun said. "Recommend us to your friends."

"Hey, I've got an idea." Zoe waved her hand in the air to get their attention. "How about I take a snapshot of the three of you at this historic moment? Years from now, you can even pretend I wasn't here."

"Oh, I'm already doing that," Fontana said. "Trust me."

"Not a bad idea, though," Shaun said. NASA had issued them a couple of digital cameras so they could capture candid moments of life aboard the ship. The public-relations folks intended to get plenty of mileage out of the photos later; there was even talk of a coffee-table book and a calendar. "Let's do it."

He retrieved a camera from a supply locker and flew it over to Zoe. There was no need to lob it to her in an arc; momentum carried it across the cabin in a straight line. She snatched it out of the air and backed up to get the three astronauts in her sights.

"Okay, then," she said. "All together now, in front of the big pretty planet."

The crew posed in front of the cockpit windows, their feet not touching the floor. They were literally walking on air. Fontana took the center spot, flanked by the two men.

"Squeeze together closer," Zoe urged them. "C'mon, Skipper, put your arm around Fontana. Don't be shy."

Zoe gave Shaun a puckish smirk. He resisted the urge to glare back at her. That probably wouldn't look good in the photos.

Smiling, he hugged Fontana and felt her own arm slip around his waist. She gave his hand a furtive squeeze and beamed at the camera. O'Herlihy leaned in from the other side of her.

"Perfect!" Zoe decreed. "Everybody say 'hexagon.'"

"Hexagon!" they shouted in unison. A flash lit up the flight deck.

As Shaun recalled, they still had one bottle of champagne left.

"LIDAR still tracking the comet," O'Herlihy reported. "It's right on schedule."

Today was Comet Day. The *Lewis & Clark* had been in a polar orbit around Saturn, perpendicular to the rings, for more than seventy-two hours. That was more than a week by Saturn time, since the planet rotated completely every ten hours or so, giving them numerous chances to observe both its eastern and western hemispheres. They were orbiting the planet at a distance of twenty thousand kilometers, which conveniently allowed them to pass through the Cassini Division without colliding with the rings. The ship's hull was tough enough to withstand a few minor impacts, but nobody felt like tempting fate by plowing through the rings themselves.

Today, Saturn was just a backdrop, however. Their agenda was to observe the comet close-up and guide an unmanned probe to take samples of both its icy crust and its inner core. The probe, which had been christened *Sacagawea,* was already waiting outside the ship to intercept the comet. The goal was to land it on the comet's surface so that it could transmit its findings back to the *Lewis & Clark.* Christopher and Fontana had spent most of yesterday launching it from the ship's cargo bay.

Zoe drifted about the flight deck, staying more or less out of the way. "The comet's not going to hit the rings, is it?"

"Not a chance," Shaun said from the helm. "It's going to swing past Saturn at a distance of about two hundred twenty-five thousand kilometers, well clear of the rings."

"Too bad. That would have been quite a show." Zoe floated over to one of the auxiliary consoles, where O'Herlihy was directing *Sacagawea* by remote control. She tapped the scientist on the shoulder. "So, I've been meaning to ask you. Now that we're here, what's the story with the rings, anyway? Are they more or less wobbly than you expected?"

He looked up from his terminal with a slightly sheepish expression. "To be honest, my preliminary observations indicate that the rings do seem to be rather more . . . unstable than originally anticipated."

This was news to Shaun. He had been focused for the last few days on getting the probe launched in time to intercept the comet. He had left the pure scientific research to O'Herlihy, on the assumption that it was way too early to draw any definitive conclusions from the data they had just started accumulating. Chances were, scientists would be chewing over the data for years to come.

"How unstable, Doc?" he asked.

"Hard to say," O'Herlihy answered. "You have to remember, the rings have always been a dynamic system, full of troughs and waves and clumps. Some of the ringlets are even braided together, particularly out by the F Ring. The whole system is constantly in motion. Indeed, there's reason to believe that the rings are a relatively new and temporary phenomenon, that they did not even exist a few hundred million years ago, when the early dinosaurs were first roaming the Earth, and that they may be gone for good millions of years from now."

"And yet?" Shaun prompted him.

"Well, I'm hesitant to jump to any rash conclusions without further evidence . . ."

Shaun grew impatient. "Enough with the obligatory disclaimers, Doc. I don't want to wait for the peer-reviewed version. Cut to the chase."

"All right," the scientist said reluctantly, "but bear in mind that this is just off the cuff. I still need to collect more evidence and conduct a more detailed analysis."

"Understood. But . . . ?"

"The rings appear to be collapsing inward—at a steadily increasing rate. Debris from the outer rings is spiraling into the inner ones, whose orbits are gradually shrinking as well. The divisions between the rings are also narrowing, causing discrete rings to blur together much more than usual."

Shaun wondered what this meant for their mission. "Is there any danger to the ship?"

"I shouldn't think so. The ring matter is falling inward, toward the planet, not aiming at us, although I'm at a loss regarding what might be causing this or why it is happening now. Frankly, it's quite unexpected . . . and more than a little baffling."

"Told you." Zoe gloated. "I knew there was more to that rings angle than you wanted to admit earlier." She did a celebratory somersault in midair. "So, who is the crackpot conspiracy theorist now?"

"Watch your mouth, brat," Fontana snarled from the copilot's seat. "That's a future Nobel Prize winner you're talking to."

"It's all right, Alice," O'Herlihy said. "Our guest has reason to feel vindicated . . . to a degree. These findings are a humbling reminder that we are in unknown territory out here and that the universe can still surprise us."

Ordinarily, the scientist would have chided Zoe for letting her imagination run wild, but his response struck Shaun as uncharacteristically muted. He found that vaguely worrisome. When somebody like Marcus gave ground to Zoe, things were seriously out of whack.

"Still," O'Herlihy continued, "I'm sure it's just a temporary aberration, caused by the approach of the comet or some other factor. It's bound to correct itself in time."

"Oh, yeah." Zoe challenged him. "That's what they used to say about global warming. Tell that to the ice caps . . . or what's left of them."

Shaun scowled. Despite the scientist's provisos, this sounded like something he needed to stay on top of. "I want daily reports on those rings from now on. Let me know if you think there's even a chance that we might need to adjust our orbit to put more distance between ourselves and the rings."

Their mission had been plotted and predicated on the fact that Saturn would act like Saturn, and so would its rings. He recalled O'Herlihy's earlier description, months ago, of the rings as roiling rivers, complete with dangerous currents, eddies, and other hazards. Granted, the rings were only about half a kilometer thick on average, and the *Lewis & Clark* had been built to withstand random micrometeoroid strikes, but Shaun was in no hurry to ride the rapids.

"Will do," O'Herlihy assured him. "But I'm sure it's nothing to worry about."

"I like hearing you say that, Doc." Shaun turned his attention back to the day's agenda. "Let's just hope our cometary friend doesn't surprise us, too."

"Shh!" Zoe held a finger to her lips. "Don't jinx us."

"Says the jinx herself," Fontana muttered. She kept her eye on the view out the cockpit windows. "And they used to say comets were bad luck . . ."

The comet, designated C/2018-G2, had been visible for days as a faint white smudge in the distance, but it was growing clearer as it approached them. This far out from the sun, the comet had not melted enough to give it a truly impressive tail, yet it was already recognizable as a comet. A cloud of dusty vapor, known as the coma, formed an atmosphere around the comet's nucleus, while a misty white stream trailed behind it, pointing away from the sun, whose solar winds created the tail by blowing the ionized comet material away from it. C/2018 was extremely small by cometary standards, its nucleus barely more than a hundred meters across, yet its tail already stretched for thousands of kilometers. The comet's path was not expected to bring it anywhere near Earth, so this was their best chance to get a good look at it.

Like most comets, it was probably just a large, dirty snowball from the outer reaches of the solar system, but who knew where exactly C/2018 had been and what secrets it might hold? Past comets had been found to contain complex organic compounds, including amino acids. Nobody had discovered life on a comet yet, but the possibility was there. If nothing else, *Sacagawea* might provide clues to determine whether C/2018 was from the Kuiper Belt, the Oort Cloud, or someplace farther out in space. It might even prove to be that rare comet that was just passing through the solar system on its way out to interstellar space. If it was on a truly hyperbolic orbit, it might never pass this way again.

All the more reason to check it out when we can, Shaun thought. "You set, Doc?"

"*Sacagawea* is in position," O'Herlihy reported. "No orbital adjustments appear to be needed at this time. It should intercept C/2018 in approximately eighty-five minutes. We can initiate landing procedures then, assuming that—what the devil?"

Before their eyes, the comet suddenly veered to the left.

"Crap!" Fontana exclaimed. "Is it supposed to be able to do that?"

"No!" O'Herlihy frantically worked the LIDAR controls, trying to keep it locked on the detouring comet. "It was following a standard elliptical orbit, more or less. This should not be happening!"

Zoe flew toward the windows for a better look. She typed more notes into her tablet, then held it up to take a picture. "Holy cow. This trip is getting better and better."

Shaun was glad somebody felt that way. For himself, he was getting tired of the impossible biting them in the butt. "Talk to me, Doc. What the hell is that thing doing?"

"It's changing course, away from *Sacagawea,* and slowing down." The shocked scientist stared at his monitors. "It's heading in toward the planet, avoiding the rings." He shook his head, looking even more flabbergasted than when he had detected the stowaway aboard. Awe reduced his voice to a whisper. "It's not behaving like a proper comet at all, more like . . ."

"A UFO?" Zoe winked at Shaun. "What do you think, Skipper? Friends of your dad?"

Fontana look askance at Shaun. "You told her about that?" She knew what Zoe was referring to, of course. Shaun had shared that colorful bit of family history with Fontana back when they were dating. "Don't be ridiculous," the copilot snapped at Zoe. "There must be a sensible explanation for this."

"Like what?" Zoe asked.

Fontana groped for a response. "Maybe the same thing that's affecting the rings?"

Whatever that is, Shaun thought, scowling. He wanted answers, not more mysteries. "Where is it heading, Doc?"

"It seems to be heading for . . . the north pole of the planet."

"You mean the hexagon," Zoe said.

"Possibly," O'Herlihy admitted, with a distinctly pained expression. "At least, that general vicinity."

Zoe let go of her tablet, which remained floating within reach, and rubbed her hands together gleefully. "The plot thickens."

"Tell me about it," Shaun said. Their carefully planned operation, meticulously worked out by NASA and its international partners, had just gone out the proverbial window. *Sacagawea,* waiting in orbit for its celestial rendezvous, had been stood up. C/2018 had ditched them, almost as though it was on a mission of its own. *Careful,* he warned himself, *you're starting to think like Zoe.*

But maybe that wasn't entirely a bad idea. Their mission had just gotten a whole lot stranger and more exciting. Perhaps it was time to start thinking outside the box.

"Set a course for the north pole," he instructed. "We're going after that comet."

Fontana stared at him as if he had lost his mind. "But that's not part of the mission plan."

He couldn't blame her for being startled. NASA flights were not improvised. Every task and maneuver had been plotted out months, if not years, in advance, especially where dangerous new objectives were concerned. Hell, there had been *ten* trial runs before Apollo 11 had finally touched down on the moon. Space was no place to fly by the seat of your pants—except when something truly unpredictable happened.

"Screw the mission plan." He switched off the automatic pilot. "We're not robots, following a programmed script. What's the point of sending actual flesh-and-blood humans into space if we can't react to unexpected circumstances and take advantage of amazing new opportunities?"

"Woo-hoo!" Zoe cheered him on. "You tell 'em, Skipper."

"Hush!" Fontana said. "The grown-ups are talking." She gave him a worried look. "I don't know, Shaun. Maybe we should run this by Mission Control first."

"There's no time for that," Shaun said. Radio waves traveled at the speed of light through the vacuum of space, but there was still more than an hour's time lag when it came to communicating with Earth, and that wasn't even figuring in the bureaucracy factor. "That comet—or whatever it is—is going somewhere. I don't want it to get away while they're holding conferences back home." He looked her in the eyes, struck as always by their brilliant green depths. "I don't know about you, Alice, but I want to know what that so-called comet is."

"You think I don't?" She searched his face. "You really think this might be a UFO, Shaun?"

"To be honest, I don't know what to think." He toyed with the dog tags around his neck. "Like the doc said, we're in unknown territory here."

"Well, that's the job description, isn't it?" Fontana sighed and settled back into her seat. He recognized the determined set of her jaw. "All right. Let's go find out what's driving that puppy."

Shaun turned toward O'Herlihy. This decision could have an enormous, and possibly catastrophic, effect on their careers. They could even be risking their lives. He needed to make sure his whole crew was okay with it. "Marcus?"

"You're in charge of this mission, Colonel. It's

your call." The scientist's gaze remained glued to his monitors. "But personally, I would never forgive myself if we didn't at least try to solve this mystery."

Shaun felt the same way. "Okay, it's decided, then." He had never been more proud of his crew. "Keep the LIDAR locked on that comet. Track its every move."

"I wouldn't dream of doing anything else."

Zoe waved her hand in the air. "Hey, don't I get a vote?"

"No," Fontana said in no uncertain terms.

"Fair enough," Zoe said with a shrug. "Although, just for the record, I think you folks are acting like real starship heroes."

Fontana rolled her eyes. "Why don't I find that reassuring?"

It took several minutes to calculate an intercept course based on the comet's current trajectory. They would have to leave *Sacagawea* behind. The probe's thrusters had been intended for only minor course corrections; they lacked the power for this sort of chase. Shaun would have to be careful not to expend too much of the *Lewis & Clark*'s own engine power on this unplanned expedition. Mission Control would have a cow when they found out about it.

It will be worth it, Shaun thought, *if we can make contact with a genuine UFO.*

"Everybody strap yourself in," he advised the crew and the stowaway. Zoe took a seat at the computer station next to O'Herlihy. She tapped out a few last notes on her tablet before stowing it away for safekeeping. "We're hitting the gas."

"Tally-ho," Fontana said drily.

Shaun fired up the thrusters and initiated a controlled burn to accelerate the ship in the direction of the probe. The nose of the command module tilted as he altered the angle of their orbit to bring them into the same plane as their quarry. The *Lewis & Clark* climbed toward Saturn's north pole. The planet's axial tilt worked in their favor, as did the fact that Saturn was somewhat squashed in shape, being wider around the middle than from top to bottom, but because of the sheer size of the gas giant, it still took two-plus hours before they finally found themselves gazing down at the top of the planet.

"Whoa!" Zoe exclaimed. "What happened to the hexagon?"

Shaun was wondering the same thing. The celebrated six-sided vortex, which had been unchanged for decades, was visibly diminished. Its borders had contracted, so that it appeared to have shrunk in size by at least a third, and its color had faded, too, making it somewhat harder to make out against the planet's turbulent yellow atmosphere. It almost looked as though the vortex was gradually shrinking away.

But was that even possible?

"Marcus?"

"I see it," O'Herlihy replied tersely. "And no, our eyes are not deceiving us. The vortex has noticeably decreased in both size and intensity, almost thirty-two percent since the last time we analyzed it."

"Why didn't we notice this before?" Shaun asked.

O'Herlihy shrugged. "We weren't looking for it, and there's been a lot of Saturn, including its various rings and moons. Plus, it appears that the rate of the shrinkage has increased exponentially with the approach of the comet."

Shaun didn't like this. The hexagon, the rings, the comet—nothing was acting as it was supposed to. He supposed it could be seen as a lucky break that the *Lewis & Clark* had arrived in time to witness these astounding developments, but it didn't feel that way. He was starting to wish they had gone to Mars instead.

"What about the comet?" Fontana asked. "Where is it now?"

O'Herlihy consulted the LIDAR. "Oh, my God. You're not going to believe this."

At this point, Shaun was ready to accept just about anything short of a flock of winged unicorns. "Try me."

"It's come to a dead stop nine hundred kilometers above the planet's north pole." Zoe started to open her mouth, but O'Herlihy beat her to the punch. "Yes, directly above the hexagon."

"I don't understand," Fontana said. "How does a comet come to a stop?"

"You tell me," the scientist said, sounding somewhat overwhelmed by the unexplainable phenomena he had been confronted with recently. "But the comet is definitely parked in a stationary position above the pole. Not an easy feat to pull off, by the way, even for a satellite."

Shaun knew what he meant. Geosynchronous orbits were easier to maintain above a planet's equator, where the satellite's orbit could be matched to the planet's rotation. A satellite would have to be able to modify its orbit continuously to "hover" in place above the pole. Back on Earth, solar sails had been employed to attempt this, with mixed results. Shaun had no idea how a comet could do it—unless it wasn't really a comet.

"I'm bringing us in closer," he said. "I want to see that thing with my own eyes."

Operating the thrusters manually, he cruised a kilometer above the comet. Because the ship was in an inverted position, with its belly facing away from the planet, they were able to gaze up at the "comet" as it hovered hundreds of kilometers above the anemic hexagon.

C/2018 floated like a hot-air balloon beneath them. To Shaun's surprise, it was glowing much more brightly than before. Its misty coma expanded as jets of vapor steamed off the comet's frozen nucleus, which appeared to be dissolving before their eyes.

"Huh?" Zoe said. "Is it supposed to be doing that?"

"No," O'Herlihy said, sounding torn between dismay and wonder. "Not this far out from the sun. Granted, Saturn also radiates its own heat but not enough to melt a comet like that!"

Shaun stared at the comet, which was shrinking like an ice cube on a hot summer day. Its icy core seemed to be subliming directly from solid to gas, skipping the liquid state. Billowing clouds of vapor poured off the nucleus. Solar winds blew the gas back into the comet's tail, which was wrapping around the planet below before dissipating into the vacuum. He had never seen anything like it.

"What's happening, Doc?"

"Give me a second!" the harried scientist replied. He recalibrated their equipment, directing all of their sensory apparatus, including the trans-spectral imager, at the fuming comet. "I'm at my wit's end here. None of this makes any sense!"

Join the club, Shaun thought. He'd had more jolts on this voyage than in the rest of his NASA career combined, up to and including the disappearance of the DY-100. "Hold it together, Marcus. Just think of all the history we're making. We're discovering stuff that nobody ever dreamed of before."

"That's one way to look at it," Fontana said. She snuck her hand across the helm to squeeze his. "Count on you to see the upside."

He smiled back at her. "Astronauts have to be optimists. Who else would blast themselves into space?"

"As long as we keep one foot on the ground," she said. "Figuratively speaking."

"You do a pretty good job of that. That's why we make such a good team."

Was that a hint of a blush on her cheeks? "Nice of you to say so," she said, "but if we get abducted by aliens, it's all your fault."

She said it lightly, but Shaun knew she was right. If there was some extraterrestrial intelligence directing C/2018, there was no way of telling how it might react to their presence. There was no guarantee that first contacts had to be peaceful. *Just ask H. G. Wells*, he thought. *Or Montezuma.*

Steam continued to pour off the comet, which had already shed most of its mass, so that it was now smaller than the *Lewis & Clark*. A bright blue glow emanated from the nucleus, visible even through the thick clouds of vapor surrounding the core. The comet's tail extended beyond the curve of Saturn, almost like another ring.

"Curiouser and curiouser," Zoe murmured. She grinned like the Cheshire Cat.

Shaun watched as the comet dissolved into mist. What was causing it to sublime like that? Surely not the heat of the planet.

"Marcus?"

"It's heating up from within," the scientist reported, "as though there's some sort of internal heat source beneath the ice."

Zoe stared at him. "You mean, it's defrosting itself?"

"That would be one interpretation," O'Herlihy conceded. "Although I probably would have phrased it differently."

"That's why I'm a journalist and you're an academic." She peered at what remained of the comet. "What do you think is under all that ice and fog?"

"I don't know," Shaun said, "but it looks like we're about to find out."

The coma surrounding the nucleus was sucked into the comet's tail, exposing a shrinking chunk of ice that appeared to be no more than ten meters across. The glow seemed to be coming from beneath the icy crust, just as O'Herlihy had determined. Shaun wondered if the melting was taking place on purpose now that the "comet" had reached its destination. That seemed as plausible an explanation as any.

The last of the ice began to steam away. "Look!" Fontana said, pointing excitedly at the window. "You see that?"

Shaun saw. The icy crust had nearly misted away in spots, exposing patches of polished bronze plating. A glowing turquoise ring could be glimpsed beneath a frosty glaze.

A stunned hush fell over the flight deck. All present grasped the astonishing implications of what they were seeing. Even Zoe seemed rendered speechless.

"Okay," Fontana said finally. "That's no comet."

"No," Shaun realized. "That's a probe."

Eight

"A probe?"

"So it appears, Captain," Spock reported. "Of alien design and origin."

Kirk strode onto the bridge, having been alerted to a change in the comet's status. By ship's time, it was after two in the morning. The ship's corridor had been dimmed to simulate nighttime. The captain was gratified to see that his senior officers were already in place on the bridge. He dropped into his chair and peered at the viewer.

The probe, seen moving across the system under its own power, was shaped roughly like an hourglass, with wide concave dishes at both ends. Its dented bronze casing reflected the light from Klondike VI. A glowing turquoise ring orbited the neck of the hourglass. Kirk wondered if the spinning blue halo was the propulsion unit. Multicolored lights flickered along bands of instrumentation and sensors. The hourglass was oriented sideways on the screen. It was hard to judge its speed against the backdrop of the planet.

"Course and activity?" Kirk asked.

"The probe is approaching the northern tip of Klondike VI, its trajectory bypassing the rings and their hazards. It appears to be decelerating as it nears the pole." Spock manned his science station. The glow from his scanner cast azure shadows on the planes of his face. "In addition, the ice that formerly covered the probe has now melted away entirely, as a result of the activation of an internal heat source."

This can't be a coincidence, Kirk thought. A freak comet was unlikely enough, but an alien probe arriving at the same time that Klondike VI and its rings were undergoing massive distortions? There had to be a connection.

"Bring us closer," he ordered. "And dispatch a shuttlecraft to defend the colony." A shuttle's phasers were nowhere near the same class as the *Enterprise*'s, but they should be able to provide Skagway with a degree of protection while the starship was investigating the probe. "Have the shuttle equipped with auxiliary phasers as well."

"Aye, sir," Uhura said. "Relaying your orders to the hangar bay now."

Confident that the shuttle would watch over the colony, Kirk gave the probe his full attention. "What do you make of it, Mr. Spock? Any idea who might have sent it?"

"Negative, Captain." Spock looked up from his sensors. "The alloys and configuration do not match anything in our library banks. I am also detecting energy signatures of a highly unusual nature."

Kirk didn't recognize the design, either. It wasn't Romulan or Tholian or even Gorn.

"What about you?" he asked Qat Zaldana, who had apparently beaten him to the bridge. The veiled scientist stood between Kirk and Spock, leaning against the red safety rail surrounding the recessed command module. Kirk gestured at the probe on the screen. "Does that object ring any bells with you?"

"I'm afraid not, Captain. We've been studying this system for decades now, and there's no record of this comet—or probe—ever approaching Klondike VI before. I can't place its origins, either." She shrugged apologetically. "Then again, I'm an astronomer, not a xenologist."

"Careful," Kirk teased her. "Or our ship's doctor will sue you for trademark infringement."

Sulu and Uhura chuckled at their posts, but Qat Zaldana didn't get the joke. She tilted her head in a quizzical manner. "Excuse me?"

"I'll explain later," he promised.

The quip had been intended to lighten the mood on the bridge. So far, the mysterious probe did not seem to pose any immediate threat, but every member of his crew knew that such discoveries had proven dangerous in the past. Take the *Nomad* probe, for example, or Balok's radioactive warning buoy.

"Increase power to the deflectors," the captain ordered. Their screens were already in place to ward off stray debris from the rings, but the probe might have greater potential as a threat than random chunks of ice.

Kirk pressed a switch on his armrest. "Go to yellow alert."

"Aye, Captain," Chekov said.

Amber indicator lights flared around the bridge. The yellow alert signaled every crew member and department to go to an advanced stage of readiness. Emergency crews and systems were placed on standby.

"I'm attempting to hail the probe," Uhura reported. "No response."

Kirk was briefly tempted to ask if she had tried every frequency, but he knew that would be redundant. Uhura had hailed more alien vessels and planets than probably anyone else in this sector.

"Analysis, Mr. Spock?"

"Insufficient data, Captain. Although there are indications that the probe is many thousands of years old and perhaps running low on power. Meteoroid scoring has pitted its hull. Its energy signatures register as both erratic and fading."

Kirk nodded. "Is it emitting any harmful radiation? And what about weapons?"

"It appears to be unarmed, Captain."

"But why is it here? Why now?" Kirk frowned; he didn't need another mystery right now. "And what does this have to do with the anomalies affecting the rings? And the vortex on the planet's surface?"

"It is difficult to say," Spock stated, "without a closer examination of the artifact."

"I have to agree," Qat Zaldana added. "It might

be useful to inspect the probe itself. We could learn something that would help us save the colony."

Kirk had to smile. He suddenly felt as if he had *two* science officers at his disposal. That being the case, he would be foolish not to listen to them.

"Kirk to transporter room," he ordered via intercom. "Prepare to lock onto that object and beam it aboard. Employ standard safety and decontamination procedures."

"Aye, Captain," a female voice responded. A glance at the duty roster informed him that Lieutenant Mascali was manning the transporter this shift. *"Ready to proceed at your order."*

"Wait for me. I'm on my way. Kirk out."

He rose from his chair. "Mr. Spock? Qat? Care to join me?"

"After you, Captain," Qat Zaldana said. She tucked her data slate under her arm.

He headed for the turbolift. "The bridge is yours, Mr. Sulu. Notify me at once if that thing out there so much as burps."

"Aye, sir," Sulu promised. "You'll be the first to know.'"

The two scientists followed Kirk into the turbolift. Crimson doors *whoosh*ed shut. Kirk took hold of the handle. "Transporter room," he instructed the lift. "No stops."

They found Scotty waiting for them behind the transporter controls. "Thought I should do the honors myself, considering we don't know exactly what we're taking aboard here. Better safe than sorry." He glanced at Lieutenant Mascali, who stood by to assist him. Dark hair and olive skin hinted at Mediterranean roots, although Kirk believed she hailed from Alpha Centauri. "No offense, lassie."

"None taken, sir," she answered. "I'm glad you're here."

Kirk appreciated Scotty's initiative, too. Nobody aboard could operate the transporters as well as the ship's resident miracle worker.

"All right, then. Let's take a closer look at our surprise visitor."

Scotty nodded. "Locking onto the object." He pulled the levers down. "Energizing now."

The telltale whine of the transporter beam confirmed Scotty's report. A scintillating column of golden sparks manifested above a transporter pad, then coalesced into the shape of the probe. The radiance faded away, leaving only a hint of static in the air and a huge object resting on the platform. The image on the viewer had not quite prepared Kirk for the sheer size of the probe. At least twice as large as the conn stations on the bridge, the probe took up most of the transporter platform. Only sturdy Starfleet construction kept the platform from buckling under its weight. It lay sideways across the platform, resting on the rims of dishes at both ends, which crumpled slightly at the bottom. The glowing ring around its equator dimmed and slowed to a stop. Lights flashed intermittently here and there. Patches of melting ice clung to its hull. They dripped onto the transporter pads.

The probe had obviously seen better days. Its surface was badly scorched and corroded. Pitted metal testified to hundreds of microcollisions. The bronze plating was charred and melted in places. Kirk wondered what had inflicted the damage. Merely time and erosion, or had the probe had a run-in with an ion storm or something even more destructive? The probe's battered condition made it hard to guess how old it was. Hundreds of years? Thousands?

Millions?

"Remarkable," Qat Zaldana said. "Where do you think it came from?"

Kirk imagined her eyes widening behind her veil. He wondered how the probe appeared to her sensors. What else could she see?

"I'd like to know that, too," he said. "Mr. Spock?"

A tricorder was slung over the science officer's shoulder. He scanned the probe with the device. "Batteries low on power and fading. Unable to access its memory banks."

Kirk cautiously approached the probe. "Any reaction to our transporter beam?" He was concerned that the artifact might regard the act as hostile and respond in kind. "Has it activated any defenses?"

"Not that I can determine, Captain."

Kirk was glad to hear it. Perhaps the probe was merely an unmanned exploratory vessel from some distant civilization that had nothing to do with the crisis threatening Skagway. Or was that too much of a coincidence?

Qat Zaldana tilted her head to one side. "What are those markings on its casing?"

Markings? Kirk had not noticed anything of that nature, but evidently, her sensor veil was indeed more perceptive than his eyes. He stepped onto the transporter pad to get a closer look. Squinting, he saw what she was talking about. Beneath the scorch marks and corrosion was a string of alien hieroglyphics, partially eaten away by the damage to the hull. Kirk frowned. What was left of the symbols looked disturbingly familiar. He had seen markings like them before, but where?

Suddenly, it hit him.

"Spock," he said urgently. "Is it just me, or do those symbols look like the ones we found on that obelisk a few years ago?" His throat tightened at the memory. "You know the one I mean. The one the Preservers built."

Painful memories flooded Kirk. The obelisk in question had been constructed by an enigmatic alien race to protect a primitive world from an oncoming asteroid. While investigating the obelisk, he had been struck down by an unexpected energy discharge and separated from the rest of the landing party, who were eventually forced by circumstances to leave him behind. Suffering from amnesia, he had been taken in by the people of the planet, a tribe of transplanted Native Americans, and had eventually married a lovely young woman with whom he'd soon conceived a child. A deflector beam from the obelisk, of unimaginable power, had ultimately diverted the killer asteroid, but Kirk's bride had died at the hands of her own people when they turned against her and Kirk. Her tragic death, and the loss of their unborn child, still haunted him.

Miramanee . . .

If Spock was aware of just how agonizing this subject was, he was professional—and Vulcan—enough not to acknowledge it. Still, he seemed to choose his words even more carefully than usual.

"There is a resemblance, Captain, although the damage to the casing makes a detailed comparison difficult. It may be necessary to reconstruct the missing and obscured portions of the symbols before a definitive identification can be made."

The lack of certainty frustrated Kirk. "But I thought you said this probe did not match any in our computer banks?"

"May I remind you, Captain, that little is known of the Preservers and their technology. It is possible that a more rigorous examination may turn up subtle similarities between this probe and the obelisk, but they were apparently constructed of different materials, possibly at different points in the Preservers' history and development. Certainly, we lack the data to identify their relics easily."

Kirk knew that Spock was right. Nobody even knew

what the Preservers had looked like. They were known to have seeded the galaxy with various life-forms, sometimes transplanting specimens from one planet to another, as with Miramanee's people, but their origins and motives remained obscure. Some scholars had proposed that the Preservers were largely responsible for the proliferation of humanoid species and cultures throughout the universe, but that was just speculation. They were believed to have disappeared centuries ago, but whether they went extinct or simply departed the galaxy remained a mystery, much like this probe.

"But these markings do look the same?" Kirk asked impatiently. He searched his memory, trying to remember exactly what the hieroglyphics on the obelisk had looked like. Spock had eventually deduced that they had corresponded to musical notes. "Don't they?"

"Yes, sir," Spock conceded. "They do."

Overcome with emotion, Kirk reached out to touch the symbols.

"Captain! Wait!"

Spock's warning came too late. Kirk's fingers brushed against the ice-cold steel. An unexpected shock jolted his nervous system. A blinding flash consumed his vision.

The transporter room disappeared in a blaze of light.

Nine

"You sure you want to do this?" Fontana asked.

Inside the cramped airlock, she and O'Herlihy helped Shaun into his spacesuit. He began by climbing into the bottom half of the suit, which had not yet been pressurized. He had already donned his inner cooling garment, which looked like a cross between a skindiving suit and long underwear; cold water circulated through the plastic tubing laced throughout the elastic undergarment, giving him chills. The lower body assembly itself was composed of multiple layers of protective fibers and insulation. Its white outer shell was heat- and puncture-resistant. The legs ended in a pair of built-in boots.

"Not really," he admitted. "But I can't think of a better idea."

Their crazy notion was to capture the alien probe for transport back to Earth. Having already disposed of *Sacagawea*, a few other Earth probes, and nearly half of their provisions, they had room enough in the cargo bay for the mysterious extraterrestrial artifact now that its huge icy shell had sublimed away into the ether. Radio transmissions had been flying back and forth between the ship and Earth for hours, but Mission Control had ultimately approved the operation with laudable speed. Shaun guessed that the folks back home were already salivating at the thought of getting their hands on the probe.

"We could still try using the robot arm," O'Herlihy reminded him. The telescoping arm, which was installed in the cargo bay, could be quite handy when it came to loading and unloading heavy pieces of equipment, as well as for making repairs to the ship's outer hull. They could conceivably use it to try snagging the probe. "That might be less risky to you personally."

Shaun shook his head. "Too clumsy. We don't know how fragile that probe is." He checked to make sure the bottom of the spacesuit fit him securely. Multiple loops and clips were available to hook tools onto. "Every scientist in the world will have my hide if we break a genuine alien probe."

"I'm more worried about what might happen to you," Fontana said. "We don't know anything about that thing or how it might react. There could even be some sort of alien pilot inside. There are too many question marks."

"That's why we need to get a closer look," Shaun said. To be honest, he wanted to check out the probe himself, not via remote control. "Don't worry. I promise not to make any sudden movements that might alarm it. I wouldn't want to start an interplanetary war by mistake."

Fontana frowned, less than amused by his glib remarks. "I hope to God you're joking."

Me, too, he thought.

For several hours now, they had been maintaining a low polar orbit that brought them back over the probe on a regular basis, but the artifact had yet to react to their presence. Shaun chose to take that as a good sign. Braking thrusters had been deployed to keep them in the probe's vicinity long enough to carry out this operation. "We haven't been hiding from it," he pointed out. "If it's capable of spotting us, it doesn't seem to care."

"So far," she said.

"Hey, astronauts are optimists, remember?"

"Yes," Fontana countered, "but we're not supposed to be daredevils—or bomb-demolition experts."

Shaun hoped the probe wasn't wired to self-destruct. "Don't be silly. Who would bomb Saturn?"

"Pluto?" Zoe suggested. "Maybe it's still pissed off about not being a planet anymore."

The stowaway floated beyond the doorway, just outside the airlock. Fontana shot her a dirty look. "You know, it's not too late to lock you up again."

Fontana had proposed confining Zoe to the docking ring while they were using the airlock, but Shaun had vetoed that idea. For better or for worse, the intrepid blogger had been aboard the ship for months and had never given them any reason to suspect her of malignant intent. Furthermore, her story had checked out, so he figured it was safe to let her act as an observer.

"Nah," Shaun said. "This is possibly the biggest news story of all time. It would be a crime to exclude the only reporter in one-point-two billion kilometers."

More importantly, if things *did* get hairy, he didn't want anyone locked up with no escape route. What if they needed to evacuate part of the ship in a hurry?

"If you say so," Fontana said grudgingly. "Say, if there *is* an alien, maybe we can trade her for the probe." She thought better of the idea. "No, scratch that. I wouldn't wish that on any species."

"Love you, too," Zoe retorted.

Fontana ignored her. "Let me go with you," she volunteered. A second spacesuit hung in a niche on the wall. There was no suit for O'Herlihy; protocol dictated that one astronaut remain inside the vessel during every spacewalk. "I can help."

He shook his head. "I appreciate the offer, but I'm not risking both pilots. Somebody has to steer this ship if something happens to me." Glancing down at himself, he thought he looked like a clown with oversized pants. "Let's just finish getting me suited up. I've got an appointment with a probe."

The other two astronauts held up the hard upper torso assembly so he could wriggle into it. He was grateful for the lack of gravity; the bulky suit would have weighed more than a hundred pounds on Earth, and that wasn't counting the jet pack, which he had yet to put on. The life-support system on his back was loaded down with oxygen tanks, fans, pumps, and a water supply. Fontana and O'Herlihy locked the two halves of the suit together and made sure the connections were airtight. Shaun put on his "Snoopy cap" himself. The headphones pressed against his ears. He adjusted the miniature microphone in front of his lips.

"We'll be monitoring you every second," O'Herlihy said. He handed Shaun a pair of thick white gloves. Molded rubber fingertips were meant to provide a better grip. He slipped the gloves onto Shaun's hands and affixed them to metal rings at the end of the sleeves. "Take care . . . and good luck."

"Thanks, Marcus. Don't leave without me, okay?"

The doctor chuckled. "As if I know how to drive this thing."

Fontana approached with Shaun's helmet, which was made of a tough polycarbonate material. A gold-tinted visor provided protection from UV rays and any glare from the planet and its rings. Built-in cameras and lights were attached to the sides of the helmet.

"Don't forget your hat," she said. "I hear it's cold out."

O'Herlihy retreated to give them more room and perhaps a bit of privacy.

"I don't like this," she whispered. "Not one bit."

"I know." He retrieved his lucky dog tags from a hook on the wall, where he had hung them earlier. NASA frowned on accessorizing its high-tech spacesuits. He placed them around her neck. "Look after these until I get back."

"You know I will."

She leaned in and kissed him on the cheek. "For luck," she explained for the benefit of their audience. Zoe snickered in the doorway, while O'Herlihy refrained from comment. Shaun found a new appreciation for the cooling effects of his elastic undergarments. He was tempted to kiss her back, but the mike in front of his lips made that problematic.

"Thanks," he said inadequately. "For everything."

She lowered the helmet onto his head. "Be careful, Shaun. Come back to me."

He nodded at her through the gold-tinted visor. Her emerald eyes seemed to exert their own gravity, pulling him in. For a moment, he forgot about the probe.

Why exactly did we break up again?

Something to think about later.

Even after he was sealed into the suit, there was much to do before he was ready to exit the ship via the cargo bay. They had to pressurize the suit, frequently adjusting the pressure until it was just right, then test the life-support system and radio communications gear. Not until all of the gauges showed green did the other astronauts lift the jet pack onto his shoulders. The cumbersome device, officially known as the EVA

Maneuvering Unit, fit over the life-support backpack. He didn't want to think about how much the entire outfit would weigh on Earth or even Saturn.

"Very spiffy!" Zoe took a photo of him. "Now you look like a genuine spaceman."

Shaun hoped the probe would approve, too. He gave her a thumbs-up as his crewmates exited the airlock, dragging Zoe with them. The hatch closed behind them, and he waited impatiently for the airlock to depressurize so he could enter the cargo bay and get on his way. The probe had been there for hours. He was anxious to make its acquaintance.

Eventually, a green light signaled that he was cleared to proceed. He opened the far hatch and floated into the ship's cavernous cargo bay, which was large enough to hold more than six months' worth of provisions and equipment, plus, he hoped, a captured alien probe. As on the rest of the ship, handrails were mounted on the interior walls.

The space doors were already open, and Shaun could look down on the vast expanse of Saturn's pole. He was struck by how much smaller and more pallid its famous hexagonal vortex had become; it was now only a semblance of its former self, probably no more than fifteen thousand kilometers across. It was startling how much it had shrunk in the short time they had been there. At this rate, there might be nothing left of it by the time they got back home.

His visor shielded him from the glare of the planet.

The probe was silhouetted against the fading hexagon hundreds of kilometers below. Its metallic bronze casing reflected Saturn's amber light. No longer buried inside a huge ball of ice, the probe's true configuration had been revealed to resemble an hourglass with dishes mounted at both ends. A glowing turquoise ring orbited its midsection.

Okay, he thought. *That's as artificial as can be.*

Holding on to the handrails, he made his way out into the cargo bay until he was above the open space doors. A momentary sense of vertigo assailed him. Even though his mind knew that there was no gravity, all of his senses told him that he would fall to his death if he let go of the rail. He tightened his grip.

Shake it off, he told himself. He had experienced this sensation before; it was a fairly common reaction on spacewalks. He took a deep breath and loosened his grip. *You can do this.*

"Christopher to *Lewis & Clark,*" he said into the mike. By now, the others would be in place on the flight deck, monitoring his transmissions. "Preparing to exit vehicle."

"Copy that, Shaun," Marcus replied via the radio. *"Have a safe flight."*

"Just wait until you see the souvenir I bring back."

Letting go of the rail, he activated the jet pack. A burst of nitrogen gas propelled him out of the cargo bay and into the endless void outside the ship. Two dozen miniature jets, pointed at various angles, allowed him to direct his flight via the hand controls at his waist. Momentum carried him toward the probe.

Saturn's crown loomed before him, seeming even larger and more intimidating than before. As even the ship was nothing but an infinitesimal speck compared with the magnificent gas giant and its glittering rings, Shaun suddenly felt like the smallest of subatomic particles. "There is no zero," he whispered, quoting one of his favorite science-fiction movies. "I still exist."

Despite the crucial and risky task before him, he took a moment to marvel at the awe-inspiring vista, which boggled the mind. He wondered if people would ever get used to unearthly sights like that. Part of him still couldn't believe that he was really there, where no man had gone before . . .

That's enough sightseeing, he thought, snapping out of his reverie. His oxygen tanks held at least eight hours of air, but that was no reason to waste time gawking. He jetted toward the probe, letting Saturn's meager gravity, which, despite the gas giant's size, was roughly comparable to Earth's, add to his acceleration. Within minutes, the probe was directly ahead of him, approximately three hundred yards away.

The alien artifact looked like no Earthly spacecraft that Shaun was familiar with. At least three meters long, it had not budged from its stationary orbit high above the hexagon. He would have whistled in appreciation, but that wasn't an option; as generations of astronauts had discovered, pressurized space

helmets made whistling impossible. Inspecting the
probe with his own eyes, he noted how shiny and
undamaged it appeared, despite having traversed the
solar system inside a comet. He wondered how long
and how far it had traveled. All the way from another
solar system?

Probably, he thought. Millennia of observation of
Earth's brother and sister planets had never turned
up even a hint of a civilization capable of launching a
probe like this. The spacecraft had to have come from
an extrasolar planet light-years away. Unless, of course,
this was the world's most elaborate practical joke. *You
know, I wouldn't put that past Zoe.*

"Closing on target," he reported. "Will conduct
visual survey before attempting capture."

"Take your time, Shaun," Marcus said. *"No need to
rush this."*

"Copy that." Shaun used his braking jets to slow
his approach. He circled the probe cautiously, alert to
any unexpected developments, yet the onetime comet
continued to ignore him. That was fine with Shaun.

Where did you come from? he wondered. *And why
are you here?*

The next step was to determine whether it could
be easily moved. Its weight was no issue in space; as
an astronaut, he had routinely carted two-thousand-
pound satellites around. But it was still unclear what
means of propulsion the probe employed to hold itself
in place above the planet. It was very possible that it

might resist being relocated, in which case, they would have to rethink their plans.

Let's try just a little shove first, he decided. "Preparing to make contact with object. Stand by."

He moved in closer, a meter at a time. Ten meters, six meters, three meters—

Without warning, the probe's lower dish lit up. It fired pulses of incandescent cobalt energy at Saturn, straight into the heart of the faded polar vortex. The pulse crossed the distance between the planet and the probe at the speed of light. Shaun frantically hit the brakes to avoid flying into the path of the pulses.

"Crap!" he blurted. "What the hell?"

Despite the vacuum of space, a sort of drumbeat pounded in his head. He tapped the side of his helmet, but the staccato rhythm didn't go away, making it hard to think. He jetted away from the probe, which fired one last pulse at the planet below.

What was it doing?

He stared down at the probe's target. To his amazement, a bright blue glow flared up at the center of the vortex, then rapidly expanded outward. The image of a giant glowing hexagon, matching the storm's original dimensions, was briefly imprinted on his retinas before he was forced to look away despite his tinted visor. A blinding glare lit up the vacuum.

"*Shaun!*" Fontana shouted. "*Get out of there now!*"

Before he could respond, what felt like a shock wave hit him, sending him tumbling away from the probe.

He struggled to regain control of his flight but found himself tossed through space like a piece of cosmic flotsam. His jets failed to arrest his headlong flight.

Damn! he thought. *Maybe we should have used the robot arm after all . . .*

And then it was over. The light subsided, and the shock wave moved past him. Testing the controls, he managed to come to a halt thirty meters away from the probe. Gasping, he sucked down precious oxygen. His heart pounded in his chest.

Fontana yelled in his ears. *"Shaun! Talk to me! Are you all right?"*

"I think so." He conducted a quick visual inspection of his suit but didn't spot any burns or punctures. No vapor seemed to be escaping into the vacuum. All gauges read green. He patted himself just to be safe. "Just a little shaken up, that's all." He could still see the energy bursts pulsing in his memory. An afterimage of a shining hexagon lingered in his vision. "What just happened there?"

"Beats me," O'Herlihy confessed. *"I can't make head or tail of these readings. And I'm not sure I ever will. All I know is that the probe directed some sort of incredibly powerful electromagnetic discharge at the planet, and you were nearly caught in the line of fire."*

Shaun remembered the shock wave that had sent him hurtling through space. "What about the ship? Was there any damage?"

"Not that I can determine," O'Herlihy reported.

"There was some momentary turbulence but nothing we couldn't withstand. You don't need to worry about us, Shaun. We're fine."

"Glad to hear it."

"We can exchange status reports later," Fontana said impatiently. *"You need to get back to the ship, Shaun, pronto. This was a mistake. That thing, whatever it is, is too dangerous."*

The colonel knew she had to be kicking herself for agreeing to this operation in the first place, but how could they have anticipated the probe firing on the planet like that? Satisfied that he was still in one piece, he turned himself around to see what the probe was up to now.

The enigmatic device appeared to have gone dormant again. It had stopped blasting at Saturn and was just hovering above the north pole once more. His eyes widened behind his visor as he gazed at the planet. Was it just his imagination, or was the ailing hexagon looking more like its old self again? All six sides seemed to be spreading outward, as though heading back toward their original positions, while the swirling vortex within the hexagon appeared to be brighter and more energetic than before.

"How—?" he murmured. Had the probe done that?

"Please, Shaun," Fontana urged him. *"Turn around and come back. We don't know what that thing could do next."*

He knew he should listen to her, but he wasn't ready

to give up on the probe yet. If anything, what he had just witnessed made him even more eager to retrieve the probe if possible. Any technology that could affect storm patterns from space was too valuable to be left behind. He needed at least to get a closer look at it.

"I'm sorry, Fontana," he said. "I'm going in for another pass."

"Shaun, wait! Don't be crazy! It's not safe!"

The panic in her voice tugged at his heart, but he fired his jets anyway. He knew she might never forgive him, but he didn't have any choice. This was bigger than any of them. He needed to find out more.

"I'll be okay." He hoped that wasn't just wishful thinking. "I think maybe the worst is over."

O'Herlihy didn't try to talk him out of it. *"We don't know that, Shaun. Be careful."*

"Copy that."

Ignoring Fontana's heartfelt protests, Christopher warily returned to the probe. His fingers hovered over the jet controls, ready to execute a hasty retreat if the unpredictable artifact acted up again. Moving slowly, he came within arm's reach of the probe. The beam from his helmet light fell on the probe's metallic casing. This close, he was able to make out what appeared to be bizarre hieroglyphics embossed on the hull. The exotic symbols resembled no language, ancient or otherwise, that he was familiar with. Then again, he was no linguist.

"Are you seeing this?" he asked the others. In theory,

the camera in his helmet was transmitting the images back to the ship.

"Yes, Shaun," O'Herlihy responded, audibly awed. "*It's fantastic. This may be our first true glimpse of an alien language.*"

Not counting that classified Ferengi hardware back at Area 51, Shaun thought. He was suddenly very glad that he had not headed back to the ship right away. These images alone were worth the risk he was taking, not to mention their entire voyage. "What about you, Fontana? You getting this, too?"

"*It's amazing,*" she conceded. "*You're making history.*"

The unearthly hieroglyphics called out to him. He couldn't resist the urge to touch them. His fingers drummed impatiently. He reached out for the probe. A gloved hand made contact with the unknown.

A blinding white flash caught him by surprise.

"*Shaun!*" Fontana cried out.

Ten

One minute, James Kirk was standing in the transporter room aboard the *Enterprise.* The next, he found himself floating in space. An environmental suit, bulkier and more cumbersome than the Starfleet-issue suits he was accustomed to, protected him from the vacuum. Kirk blinked in surprise. His eyes watered from the brilliant white flash that had transported him there, and, without thinking, he reached to wipe them. A gloved hand bumped into the gold-tinted visor of a spacesuit helmet. His own breathing echoed in his ears.

What the devil?

He glanced around, trying to orient himself. The north pole of Klondike VI appeared to be thousands of kilometers below him, if below meant anything in zero g. Or was it Klondike VI? The color wasn't right, more mustard yellow than violet as before. And the furious hexagonal vortex at the pole looked much as it once had, not shrunken and pallid as in the most recent recordings. If Kirk didn't know better, he'd swear he was drifting above Saturn instead. But that was impossible, wasn't it? Saturn was months away, in a completely different sector.

The only familiar object in view was the probe, but even that seemed to have changed in an instant. The battered relic now looked much newer and less weathered than it had only seconds ago. He could see the alien hieroglyphics more clearly now; the gleaming bronze casing was no longer charred and pitted. The turquoise ring glowed more brightly than before. Additional lights flickered across its circuitry.

Kirk's fingers tingled beneath his gloves. He recalled touching the probe right before he found himself here, along with the mysterious relic, which was also not on the transporter pad where it belonged. Had the probe transported them both outside the *Enterprise* somehow? It seemed so, but Kirk was still confused. Why had the probe reacted this way? And where had this clumsy spacesuit come from?

He was anxious to get back to his ship and get some answers. *Come on, Scotty,* he thought impatiently. *Beam me back aboard.*

But as long moments passed and he remained adrift in the void, Kirk began to fear that something was amiss on his ship. Had the transporters been damaged by the alien energies unleashed by the probe? And what about the rest of the ship? And his crew?

Blast it, he thought. *Somebody open a frequency and talk to me!*

He glared at the probe, knowing that it was somehow

responsible for his predicament. He kept his distance, reluctant to touch it again. The glowing propulsion ring flared up brighter and started spinning faster than ever. Kirk could tell that something was happening.

The probe rotated in space, turning its dish arrays away from the planet. Kirk felt a surge of energy all the way through his spacesuit. All at once, the probe accelerated away from him at incredible speed. He watched in amazement as it left orbit and disappeared into space in a heartbeat. At the rate it was going, Kirk estimated that it would be out of the solar system in a matter of hours, if not minutes.

Heading home?

Kirk didn't know whether to be relieved or dismayed by the probe's abrupt departure. Even though the probe had brought nothing but trouble so far, he hoped it hadn't taken Skagway's last chance with it. They had never found out what it was doing there— besides transporting him into space.

"*Shaun!*" A frantic voice addressed him via the headphones inside his helmet. "*Oh, my God, Shaun! Are you okay?*"

Kirk didn't recognize the woman's voice. It didn't sound at all like Uhura, or Qat Zaldana, for that matter. And why was she calling him Shaun? Had she gotten the wrong frequency?

"Kirk here," he answered. "Who is this?"

"*What's that?*" the voice responded. Static garbled the transmission. "*I'm not reading you.*"

Where was the transmission coming from? The *Enterprise*? Skagway? A rescue shuttle? Kirk hoped for the shuttle.

"Who is this?" he repeated. "Identify yourself."

"Shaun? Can you hear me?"

Kirk tried to look for the *Enterprise,* only to discover that his helmet severely restricted his field of vision. Maneuvering in a vacuum, without anything solid to hold on to, made turning around problematic, but he bent backward at the knees until it looked as if he was competing in some kind of zero-g limbo competition and was able to gaze up and behind him. His jaw dropped.

The *Enterprise* was nowhere to be seen. In its place was an antique spacecraft only a fraction of its size, cruising in orbit several hundred meters away. The relic was composed of four large steel modules linked together in a chain. A pair of rectangular wings, extending from the rear propulsion unit, supported a series of solar panels designed to capture the distant sunlight while the ship was in orbit. Kirk immediately recognized the anachronistic vessel as an old, pre-warp ship of the sort used by human astronauts to explore Earth's own solar system back in the twenty-first century. A spaceship, not a starship.

He didn't understand. Ships like this were moth-balled centuries ago, at least on Earth. They were the stuff of history tapes and museum exhibits. But this ship looked brand-new and operational. What was it doing way out there in the Klondike system?

All at once, he thought of the *Ares IV*. That ship, one of the early Mars expeditions, had been lost in space more than two hundred years ago, when it had been swallowed up by an unexplained subspace anomaly. Was it possible that the ship had somehow ended up here, practically on the other side of the quadrant?

Maybe, he thought. Certainly, Khan's ship, the *Botany Bay*, had ended up far from home, and that had been an even earlier model of spacecraft, equipped with only crude, atomic-powered engines. The *Ares IV*, or some other twenty-first-century spacecraft, could have conceivably traveled just as far.

But that didn't explain what had happened to the *Enterprise*.

His own ship had vanished just as inexplicably as his spacesuit had appeared. A thought occurred to him, and he tilted his head forward to look down (up?) at himself. Upon closer inspection, his spacesuit was revealed to be as much a museum relic as the ship orbiting nearby. A hard white carapace protected his upper body. Cooling water seemed to course through tubes close to his skin. An old-fashioned microphone was mounted inside the helmet in front of his mouth. Fans and pumps churned within the breathing apparatus. The entire outfit was astonishingly stiff and bulky compared with a modern EVA suit. He would have been only slightly more surprised to find himself wearing a suit of chain mail.

Unwelcome questions pushed themselves into his brain.

Where am I? When am I?

"Shaun!" the voice shouted over the static. "*You're drifting away! Use your jets!*"

Jets? Kirk couldn't feel the weight of a thruster pack on his back, but he assumed it was there. He glanced down and spotted a pair of hand-operated controls jutting out on either side of his waist. Fortunately, the controls didn't appear all that different from those on the more advanced thruster suits he was used to. He guessed he could figure them out. There were really only three basic movements to master: yaw, pitch, and roll. He just needed to learn which toggle did which.

Maybe the one on the right was for basic propulsion?

"Message received." He hoped the woman could hear him. "Activating thrusters now."

He pressed the toggle forward slightly.

Nothing happened.

Kirk scowled inside the helmet and tried operating the other controls but with equally futile results. The thrusters refused to fire. Leaning back, he confirmed that he was indeed drifting away from the antique spaceship.

"*Shaun!*" the woman repeated. She clearly seemed to be hailing him from the old ship. "*Use your jets!*"

"I'm trying! They're not working!"

"*What's that?*" she shouted. "*You're breaking up!*"

Never mind, Kirk thought. In desperation, he smacked the controls with his hand, but they remained unresponsive. He recalled the blinding energy surge that had transported him there in the first place. Had the flash shorted out the thruster controls and perhaps the helmet's communications equipment, too? That might explain why the woman on the mystery ship couldn't seem to hear him.

The planet spun slowly beneath him. He seemed to be drifting toward it, although it was hard to tell. The sheer size of the gas giant, relative to himself, dwarfed any minor changes in his perspective. It would be a while before he could perceive it getting larger, but it already seemed intimidating enough. The fierce hexagonal vortex waited for him, even though he knew he would be long dead before he came within thousands of kilometers of it. He was doomed to burn up in its atmosphere, provided his oxygen supply lasted that long, which was doubtful. How much air could this primitive suit carry, anyway? Glancing around, he spotted a head-up display inside his helmet. Judging from an illuminated gauge, he still had about seven hours left.

It didn't seem like enough.

Why don't they just beam me aboard? he wondered briefly, then realized his mistake. If that old-school spaceship was actually what it appeared to be, it was unlikely to be equipped with a transporter. Earth-based vessels had not really started beaming people aboard until the historic voyages of Jonathan Archer, by which time ships like this one were already obsolete. Chances were, it probably didn't have any shuttles, either. *Where would they put them?*

"*Hang on, Shaun!*" the woman announced. "*We're coming for you!*"

Why did she keep calling him Shaun, whoever that was? Had she mistaken him for someone else? He looked around as much as he was able but did not spot any other astronauts drifting in the void. Where was this Shaun she was so worried about?

Old-fashioned RCS thrusters flared along the hull of the engine module, and the ship dipped toward him. Kirk wished there was some way to slow his progress to make it easier for the ship to catch up with him, but he was a victim of gravity and momentum, with no way to control his flight. He was just an object in motion, floating through space. Like one of the ice crystals in the planet's rings.

Slowly, steadily, the ship drew nearer, eating up the meters between them. Open space doors exposed an interior cargo bay. A mechanical arm, resembling a large metal crane, swung out of the bay toward Kirk. A clamp opened at the end of the arm.

The robotic arm reached for Kirk, but he was still too far away. He extended his own arm, stretching as far as the suit would allow. His gloved fingertips grazed the metal clamps, but, maddeningly, he couldn't get a grip on it. Or vice versa.

"Damn," he muttered.

It dawned on him that his legs were a good deal longer than his arms. He kicked upward, stretching out his right leg. The clamp closed tightly on his foot, which was protected by a rigid white boot. Kirk winced slightly. He prayed that whoever was operating the clamp knew just how much pressure to exert without tearing open the boot—or crushing his foot.

The arm drew him back toward the ship, feet first. It was hardly the most dignified way he had ever boarded a vessel, but he wasn't complaining. Seven hours of air would tick away far too quickly. Better to be taken aboard an unknown ship than to suffocate in a vacuum.

He wished he knew what was waiting for him, though. Lifting his head, he spied a name emblazoned on the hull of the spaceship. Large block letters spelled it out in English: *U.S.S. Lewis & Clark.*

For a second, he wondered if he was reading it right. This wasn't the *Ares IV,* he realized. It was Colonel Shaun Christopher's ship from the first Earth–Saturn mission. Well versed in the history of space exploration, Kirk was quite familiar with its celebrated voyage. He even had an odd bit of personal history with Colonel Christopher's family. He had read up on the Saturn mission only a few years ago.

Saturn . . .

He leaned back and saw the huge, mustard-colored planet filling the sky below him. Its crystalline rings sparkled in the reflected light of the gas giant, whose true identity Kirk could no longer deny.

That's not Klondike VI. That's really Saturn.

No wonder the woman kept hailing Shaun. Kirk suspected that the year wasn't 2270.

Somehow, he was two hundred fifty years in the past.

Eleven

Space went away.

Gravity seized Shaun Christopher for the first time in months, and he collapsed onto a hard red platform. His bare hands struck the platform, and he realized with a shock that he wasn't wearing his spacesuit anymore and was no longer floating above Saturn.

Instead, he found himself in a spacious, well-lit chamber that bore no resemblance to the familiar confines of the *Lewis & Clark.* Metallic disks the size of manhole covers were embedded in the elevated platform, which overlooked some sort of futuristic control room, complete with an instrument panel mounted on a pedestal facing the platform. Overhead spotlights or projectors were located above each of the metal disks. Shaun had no idea where he was or how he had gotten there.

But he wasn't alone.

Four unfamiliar figures faced him. A dark-haired man wearing a bright red tunic and a worried expression manned the instrument panel, assisted by an attractive young woman wearing a short red dress.

Another woman stood a meter away, her face hidden by a shimmering golden veil. An electronic tablet was tucked under her arm.

And then there was the other . . . man?

Pointed ears rose from both sides of a distinctly elfin countenance that reminded Shaun of the old *Sub-Mariner* comics he had read as a kid. The stranger wore a blue tunic bearing an unfamiliar gold insignia. He clutched what looked like a handheld Geiger counter. Cool brown eyes regarded Shaun with just a hint of dismay. He arched a sweeping eyebrow.

"Captain?" he inquired, getting Shaun's rank wrong. "Are you hurt?"

He lowered his gadget and came toward Shaun.

"Stay away from me!" Shaun blurted. He scrambled backward, frantic to get away. Gravity weighed him down; he wasn't used to it anymore. His limbs felt like lead. He banged into a solid metallic object resting behind him. Startled, he stared at the charred lump of machinery; it took him a second to recognize the probe, which looked much older and more damaged than it had only seconds ago. He didn't understand what was happening. "Where am I? How did I get here?"

"Captain?" the pointy-eared stranger repeated. He let go of his device, which hung from a strap over his shoulder. "You appear disoriented."

"What's happened, Mr. Spock?" the man at the control panel said. A pronounced brogue betrayed his Scottish roots. "What's wrong with the captain?"

"Page Dr. McCoy," the man named Spock ordered briskly, as though he was in command. "Tell him to report to the transporter room at once."

Transporter room? Shaun glanced around in confusion. *What the hell does that mean?*

"Where am I?" he demanded again. "What is this place?"

"You seem to have suffered a severe neurological shock," Spock attempted to explain. "You require medical assistance."

He reached out for Shaun.

"Don't touch me!"

Until he found out what this was all about, he wasn't going anywhere with anyone, let alone somebody who looked almost more devil than human. Back on Earth, he would have dismissed the man's tapered ears as just some sort of eccentric body modification, like tattoos or piercings, but out here in space, millions of miles from home, more alarming possibilities leaped to mind.

He reached instinctively for his father's dog tags, only to remember that Fontana had them now. He couldn't help recalling that UFO his dad had spotted and his own experiences at Area 51. Dr. Jeff Carlson, the head of the DY-100 project, had given Shaun a firsthand account of the notorious Roswell incident back in '47. Shaun stared at Spock with mixed fear and wonder.

Was this . . . a Ferengi?

Dr. Carlson had always said they had large ears, Shaun recalled, but what was a Ferengi doing out here by Saturn . . . with a Scotsman, of all people?

Oh my God, Shaun thought. *Have I been abducted?*

Nightmarish images of invasive biological probes and experiments flashed through his brain. He had always thought such stories were merely the stuff of cheesy sci-fi movies and supermarket tabloids, but now he wasn't so sure. How else to explain any of this?

"Please, Captain," Spock said. He gazed down at Shaun, while making no sudden moves. "Let me assist you."

Why did they keep calling him Captain? Did Earth ranks confuse them?

"I don't understand!" he protested. "This is insane!"

"It was the probe," the veiled woman stated. "There was an unexpected energy discharge. Please, let us help you."

She approached him from the left. Was she an alien, too, beneath the veil? Did she have three eyes or fangs? Was she even truly a woman?

"Keep back!" he shouted again. "All of you! You're not getting near me until you tell me where I am!"

He searched frantically for an escape route. Adrenaline gave him the strength to lurch to his feet, but the gravity still threw him off. He tottered unsteadily. Spock rushed forward to catch him, taking hold of Shaun under his shoulders. Shaun tried to break free, but his limbs were too heavy, and Spock was surprisingly strong. Despite the stranger's lean physique, his grip felt like iron. More proof that the man wasn't human?

"My apologies, Captain," Spock said. "But I fear you are not yourself."

His fingers pinched Shaun's neck . . . and everything went black.

The captain went limp in Spock's arms. He carefully lowered Kirk onto the transporter pad and scanned him with his tricorder. The device could not examine the captain as thoroughly as a specialized medical tricorder, but it reported that Kirk's vital signs were within acceptable ranges for a human. There was no obvious internal bleeding or burns, although Spock counted on Dr. McCoy to conduct a more comprehensive analysis. He hoped that Kirk had not suffered any lasting brain damage or memory loss.

That would be unfortunate, Spock thought. *For the mission and for Jim.*

"What's wrong with him?" Mr. Scott asked again. He abandoned the transporter controls to join Spock by the captain. "Is he going to be all right?"

"That remains to be determined," Spock said. "But it would be illogical to assume the worst."

Qat Zaldana crowded between them. "It was like he didn't even know who you were," she observed. "What did the probe do to him?"

An excellent question, Spock thought, but it

occurred to him that it might be best if she was not present at the moment. If the captain had been seriously incapacitated, that was information that perhaps should not be shared with civilians—or the colonists down on Skagway.

"Lieutenant Mascali, please escort our guest back to her quarters." He turned to Qat Zaldana before she could protest. "My apologies, but I'm afraid our examination of the probe will have to wait. The captain requires our full attention now."

"Of course." She backed away from the fallen captain. "I don't want to get in the way." She turned her veiled face toward Mascali. "There's no need to accompany me. I can find my own way. Stay with your captain."

"Thank you for your cooperation," Spock said. "And I must ask that you keep what you have just witnessed to yourself."

He did not want wild rumors undermining the crew's morale.

She nodded. "Understood. My thoughts are with your captain."

She exited the transporter room. Spock appreciated her swift departure. That was one fewer factor to complicate his computations.

"Maintain a safe distance from the probe," he warned Scott and Mascali. "We do not need any more casualties on our hands."

"Aye, that's for certain," the engineer agreed.

Stepping away from Kirk's supine form, Spock scanned the probe with the tricorder. He detected no energy readings; the device now appeared to be completely inert. The ring around its equator had slowed to a stop and was no longer glowing. The flickering lights on its surface had gone dark. Key circuits and components now read as burned-out. Had the discharge that had shocked the captain expended the last of its energy? It appeared so, but Spock was not inclined to take chances.

"Have the probe transported to a secure force-shielded location," he instructed Scott. "Take all necessary precautions."

"That I'll do," Scott assured him. "And a few unnecessary ones as well."

The doors *whoosh*ed open, and McCoy rushed into the chamber, clutching his medkit. His eyes widened at the sight of Kirk lying unconscious on the platform. "Good Lord! Is that Jim? What in God's name happened here?"

Spock succinctly described the incident, omitting any irrelevant details or speculation.

"Dammit," McCoy muttered. He glared angrily at the probe before kneeling beside Kirk. "We should have left that wretched thing alone."

That was not a viable option, Spock thought, although he allowed the doctor his emotional outburst, which did not seem unwarranted under the circumstances. Confident that Kirk was in good hands, he headed for the exit. "Attend to your patient, Doctor, and keep me informed of his condition."

McCoy looked up in surprise. "And where the hell do you think you're going?"

"I am needed on the bridge," Spock reminded him. "With the captain unwell, I must assume command and continue to carry out our mission. Skagway remains in jeopardy, and a solution has yet to be found." He paused to consider the probe. "And our most promising lead has proven to be more problematic than anticipated."

"You can say that again!" McCoy said.

"To do so would be redundant, Doctor, and time is running out. For Skagway and its imperiled population."

The Vulcan wondered how he was going to explain the captain's condition to Governor Dawson.

Twelve

The cargo bay of the *Lewis & Clark* was much smaller than the storage facilities back on the *Enterprise*. A primitive-looking probe waited to be launched from the historic spaceship. The crude devices were definitely of twenty-first-century origin; Kirk remembered seeing models of them at the Smithsonian and Starfleet museums. The equipment bore antiquated NASA logos.

They looked brand-new.

Kirk couldn't deny it any longer. Unless this was some sort of elaborate hoax, like the mock *Enterprise* that the rulers of Gideon had tried to trick him with a few years back, he was really aboard the very first Earth–Saturn probe, launched from Cape Canaveral way back in 2020, some two hundred fifty years ago.

Had the alien probe actually sent him back in time, not to mention space? But how and why?

The space doors sealed behind him, cutting him off from the vacuum outside. He floated across the cargo bay, struck by the lack of artificial gravity. He had taken part in zero-g emergency drills and exercises, of course, but it still felt odd to be aboard a spaceship that couldn't generate its own gravity. He couldn't remember the last time he'd had to navigate across a chamber like this, relying on his own momentum to carry him across open spaces. Grab rails along the walls, floor, and ceiling allowed him to control his flight. His spacesuit felt bulky and cumbersome.

An airlock sealed the bay from the rest of the ship. Its outer door slid open, and he drifted inside. Anxious faces stared at him through a small rectangular window in the sealed door at the opposite end of the airlock. The faces belonged to a handsome red-haired woman and an older man with a beard and a grave expression. He searched his memory for their names.

Fontana. O'Herlihy.

He would have to be careful what he said to them, Kirk realized, to avoid causing unwanted changes to history and the future. As he knew better than most, even a minor alteration to the past could send potentially catastrophic ripples down the timeline. He had learned that lesson the hard way. A lovely face surfaced from his memory, along with an aching sense of loss.

Edith . . .

He shoved the painful memory back. The door behind him closed. Moments later, a green indicator light indicated that the airlock had been fully pressurized. The door before him *whoosh*ed open.

"Shaun! Thank God!"

The woman, who had to be astronaut Alice

Fontana, launched herself into the airlock. She hugged him tightly as they collided in midair, her momentum carrying them backward to the rear of the airlock. He could feel her enthusiastic embrace even through his spacesuit. Her own figure was clothed in a much more flattering blue jumpsuit.

"Er, I think there might be a misunderstanding here," Kirk said, gently extricating himself from her arms. She had evidently mistaken him for Colonel Shaun Christopher, the leader of the expedition. He had no idea what had become of Christopher, but he suspected that the other two astronauts were in for a surprise. Unscrewing his helmet, he braced himself for their startled reactions. "I know this must be a shock, but—"

To his surprise, they didn't look startled at all. The other man—Marcus O'Herlihy—approached him. "The only error, Shaun, was letting you get up close and personal with that probe in the first place. We should have taken more precautions."

Kirk was confused. Why were they still addressing him as Shaun?

An alarming possibility occurred to him. He peeked at his helmet's reflective visor.

The face of a stranger stared back at him.

The face of Shaun Geoffrey Christopher?

The astounding truth hit him with the force of a photon torpedo. Never mind his own time or ship. He wasn't even in his own body anymore!

This is Janice Lester all over again, he thought, remembering the last time he'd found his mind inhabiting a body other than his own. He froze in shock. The helmet slipped from his numb fingers. It drifted away.

Fontana noted his stunned reaction. She gently took hold of his arm. "Shaun? What is it? What's wrong?"

Think fast, Kirk thought. *I can't let them know who I really am.*

History held no record of Colonel Shaun Christopher being possessed by the displaced consciousness of a starship captain from the twenty-third century. Kirk was pretty sure he would have remembered that part.

"It's nothing," he murmured. "I'm just a little shook up, I guess."

"Small wonder," O'Herlihy said. "After what you've been through. I think our first order of business is a thorough physical exam, once we get you out of that suit." He held up his hand to forestall any protests. "No arguments, Shaun. You just got zapped by a presumably extraterrestrial probe. A physical is the very least that's called for. Be thankful I don't want to dissect you."

"All right, Doctor," Kirk said. "Just give me a moment to catch my breath."

How long was he going to have to impersonate Shaun, he wondered, and how exactly did he expect to pull that off? Was there any way to get back to his own time and body?

"Are you sure you're all right?" Fontana asked. "You seem . . . different."

"Only a little fuzzy-headed, like I said." Kirk tried to figure out what the real Shaun Christopher would say next. *Probably the same thing I would.*

"What about the probe? Do we still have it on sensors?"

"Sensors?" O'Herlihy sounded puzzled by the term. "You mean LIDAR? We lost track of the probe right after you got zapped. We should try locating it again, after we get you checked out, but the way it was moving, I suspect it's long gone, possibly back to wherever it came from."

"Good riddance," Fontana said forcefully. She began to help Kirk out of his spacesuit. "I know, I know. That's not a very scientific attitude, but I don't like surprises, especially when they almost get one of us killed."

"You've got a point there." A new voice intruded on the discussion. "Who knew I was going to be the *second*-biggest wrinkle in your mission plans?"

The unexpected voice caught Kirk by surprise.

Who?

A petite, dark-haired woman stuck her head into the airlock. She was oriented at a one-hundred-eighty-degree angle to Kirk, so that she appeared to be hanging upside-down in the doorway. Unlike the other two astronauts, she was dressed like a civilian, wearing simply a T-shirt and shorts. A folded blue jumpsuit rested in her grip. She grinned at Kirk.

"Glad to have you back, Skipper. For a few moments there, I was afraid I was going to have to fill in for you on the rest of this cruise."

Fontana frowned. "Don't even joke about that."

Who the devil? Kirk tried not to stare at the newcomer. He had read up on this groundbreaking mission before, most recently after a certain time-warped encounter with a Captain John Christopher a few years back, and he was certain that there had not been a second woman aboard the *Lewis & Clark*. History recorded that the first Earth–Saturn mission had been conducted by a crew of three: O'Herlihy, Fontana, and Christopher.

So, who was this, and what was she doing there?

"I always joke," she replied, "especially after I'm nearly scared to death. You should know that by now." She turned herself right-side up and floated past Fontana to give Kirk a friendly hug. "No more of that, okay? I don't need a scoop that bad."

"All right," he said carefully. He didn't even know this woman's name, let alone what her relationship with Shaun was like. "Trust me, I wasn't planning on any of this, either."

At least he didn't have to feign confusion or fatigue. In the last forty-five minutes or so, he had been jolted by an alien probe, nearly lost in space, and found himself stuck in another man's body more than two centuries in the past. He had felt better.

With the others' help, he began to change out of the

heavy spacesuit into a fresh blue jumpsuit. Dressing in zero g was more challenging than he remembered, and he did so clumsily. Loose sleeves and pant legs floated about like underwater fronds. He thrust his leg into the jumpsuit too hard and accidentally launched his head into the ceiling. His scalp smacked against a bulkhead.

"Ow!"

Fontana shook her head. "Boy, you really are out of it, aren't you?" She grabbed his ankle and pulled him back down to the center of the airlock. "No uncontrolled takeoffs, remember?" She held him steady while he worked his arms into the sleeves. The texture was different from that of his Starfleet uniform, rougher and more loose-fitting, but he supposed it would have to do. She zipped him into the suit. "Okay, that's more like it."

"Thanks."

While it was mildly embarrassing to need help dressing himself, he appreciated her assistance and her obvious concern for his well-being. He couldn't help noticing that both she and the mystery woman were quite attractive, something Shaun's body noticed as well. He thought back again to that time he had switched bodies with Janice Lester.

At least I'm the right gender this time.

"Let's get you to the infirmary," O'Herlihy said. "Where I can conduct a proper exam."

Kirk had no idea where that was, so he let the others guide him out of the airlock into the habitat module beyond the cargo bay. Weightless, he didn't need to be supported, but both women took him by the arm regardless. Fontana watched him as if she half expected him to pass out at any minute. The other woman kept up a stream of friendly chatter. Kirk waited in vain for someone to address her by name.

"Oh, here's your lucky charm back." Fontana removed a pair of antique dog tags from her neck and placed them around Kirk's. "I kept them safe for you, as promised."

He didn't peek at the name on the tags. That might have been suspicious.

"Thanks."

With space at a premium, the infirmary seemed to serve as gym, mess, and rec area as well. Kirk looked about for a bed or examination table, then realized that there was no need for such furnishings in zero g. A padded mattress, with Velcro straps, was mounted on one wall, at a right angle to a nearby treadmill. There was no sign of a fully equipped biobed.

Not exactly sickbay, he thought.

"Over here, please," O'Herlihy said. "Make yourself comfortable, Shaun."

Kirk sat down on the pad, at a ninety-degree angle to the floor, and strapped a belt across his lap to stay in place, while the doctor retrieved what looked like a primitive medkit from a steel cabinet. The instruments inside the case were also strapped down to keep them from drifting away. Kirk winced at the sight of antique syringes, thermometers, and surgical supplies. He could just imagine what McCoy would have to say about such barbaric medical apparatus. There didn't even seem to be a standard medical scanner or hypospray.

"All right," O'Herlihy said. "If you ladies will leave me alone with my patient."

"Roger that," Fontana said. She took the other woman by the arm and guided her out of the infirmary. Kirk got the distinct impression that there was no love lost between them. "I'll be in the cockpit. Page me if you need me."

"Will do," the doctor said.

To Kirk's relief, the exam was both basic and relatively painless. He was a bit taken aback when O'Herlihy jabbed a needle in his arm to take a blood sample, but he acted as though such bloodletting was routine. Certainly, it stung less than a Klingon agonizer. He wasn't too worried that the doctor would figure out what had really happened. Mind transference was practically unheard of even in his own time. He couldn't imagine that twenty-first-century medicine was equipped to detect it. *Even McCoy had been unable to prove that Janice had taken over my body.*

"Well, you seem more or less undamaged," O'Herlihy pronounced at last. "I'm still recommending a couple of days' rest before you resume your full duties, but mostly just as a precaution. You had a fairly serious shock."

You have no idea, Kirk thought. Still, he was glad to hear that Shaun Christopher's body was apparently in working order. He flexed his arm experimentally. At least his new body seemed to be fit enough, although a bit stiffer and more wrinkled than he would have preferred.

How old was Shaun again?

He wondered what had become of Shaun's own consciousness. *If we've truly switched bodies, does that mean that Shaun is in my body and my time?*

He wished he knew what was happening—or, to be more precise, *would* happen—aboard the *Enterprise* more than two hundred years from now.

What will become of my ship?

Thirteen

2270

Captain's log. Stardate 7104.2. First Officer Spock reporting.

I have assumed temporary command of the Enterprise following Captain Kirk's traumatic encounter with the alien probe. Although our mission to render assistance to the endangered Skagway colony, and perhaps find a way to avert the disaster, remains paramount, I cannot help wondering what effect the probe has had on the captain's mental state.

Spock entered sickbay, where he found McCoy waiting for him just inside the doorway. The doctor's office preceded the examination rooms and recovery wards beyond. Spock didn't waste time with pleasantries. "You asked for me, Doctor?"

"That's right," McCoy grumbled. "About time you got here."

Spock felt a touch of impatience himself. He had been called away from other pressing duties, most notably the challenging task of saving the Skagway colony from total destruction. "If this is urgent, it might have been more efficient simply to transmit your report to the bridge."

McCoy snorted. "I think you need to see this for yourself."

That remains to be determined, Spock thought. He was uncertain why humans placed so much value on direct visual observations when eyewitness accounts were often notoriously inaccurate. Still, his curiosity had been piqued, and he remained concerned about Kirk's condition. More than one hour and sixteen minutes had passed since he had placed the captain in McCoy's care. By now, Kirk should have recovered from the nerve pinch. Spock could only wonder if he had recovered from his contact with the probe as well.

"How is your patient, Doctor?"

McCoy remained stubbornly uninformative. "Let me show you."

The doctor led Spock to a private examination room adjacent to the primary ward. The chamber was sometimes used to quarantine patients who needed to be kept isolated from the rest of sickbay. Spock found Kirk strapped to a bed, under restraint. A diagnostic screen above the bed monitored his vital signs, which appeared to be normal for an adult human male of Kirk's age and conditioning. Nurse Christine Chapel watched over the patient. A highly emotional woman, even by human standards, she could not conceal her anxiety, although Spock had no reason to expect this to affect her performance. She was the ship's senior nurse, after all, and had served aboard the *Enterprise* since the onset of its current voyages. Kirk lay silently on the bed, his eyes closed. His fingers drummed irritably against the sheets. Spock could not immediately determine if he was conscious or not.

"How is he, Nurse?" McCoy asked.

"A bit calmer," she reported, "but . . . the same."

An unnecessarily cryptic diagnosis, Spock mused. He trusted that more concrete data would be forthcoming soon. *Minus any more attempts at drama.*

Their voices roused Kirk, who opened his eyes and lifted his head from the pillow. His gaze zeroed in on Spock. His fists clenched at his sides. Only the restraints holding him down kept him from jumping off the bed and perhaps engaging Spock in a physical confrontation.

This was not an encouraging sign.

"You again," Kirk snarled. "What did you do to me before?"

Spock assumed that he was referring to the nerve pinch. "My apologies. You were resisting our efforts to assist you. It seemed necessary at the time."

"Necessary?" Kirk challenged. "Is that what you call it?"

"This is Mr. Spock," McCoy said, intervening. "Our first officer."

Spock frowned. That the doctor found it necessary to introduce him indicated that Kirk's memory was still impaired. *Don't you know me, Jim?*

Kirk regarded him warily. "And is he . . . human?"

"I am Vulcan," Spock stated. "As you should be aware."

"And why the hell should I know you're a Vulcan, whatever that is?"

"Because you are Captain James T. Kirk of the *U.S.S. Enterprise,* and we have served together for some time."

"Oh, God, not that again!" Kirk threw his head back, visibly agitated. "I already told the doc here. I'm not this Kirk person. I've never even heard the name before today." He tugged on his bonds. "I keep telling you. You've got the wrong guy!"

Chapel gave Spock a sympathetic look, as though she feared that Kirk's failure to recognize him might have hurt Spock's feelings. Despite her considerable skills and intelligence, she had always tended to underestimate his control over his emotions. If he was being completely honest with himself, though, he did find the captain's current behavior troubling.

He turned to McCoy for answers. "Amnesia, Doctor?"

"More than that, I'm afraid." McCoy addressed his patient. "Tell Mr. Spock who you think you are."

"I don't *think* anything!" Kirk insisted. "I am Colonel Shaun Christopher, commander of the *U.S.S. Lewis & Clark,* and I demand that you return me to my ship."

An arched eyebrow betrayed Spock's surprise. Of all of the eventualities he had considered regarding the probe's effect on the captain, this had not been among them.

"You see what I mean?" McCoy said.

For once, Spock was not certain what to think. He gestured to McCoy that he wished to converse in private. They moved to the other end of the cabin and lowered their voices.

"Interesting," he observed, even as Kirk glared at them as if they were strangers. Spock consulted the doctor. "A delusion?"

"You tell me," McCoy said. "I assume you recognize the name."

"*My* memory is unimpaired, Doctor." Spock easily retrieved the relevant data. "Shaun Geoffrey Christopher, son of Captain John Christopher of the United States Air Force, circa the late twentieth century."

He recalled the incident well. Exactly three years, ten months, and twenty-three days ago, the *Enterprise* and its crew had been accidentally transported back to Earth orbit in the year 1969. During that unplanned sojourn in the past, they had been forced to beam aboard an American jet pilot who had been in pursuit of what had then been termed an "unidentified flying object." Captain Christopher had been a reluctant guest aboard the ship for a time, until it was discovered that he needed to be returned to his life in order to father Shaun Christopher, the future commander of Earth's first manned mission to Saturn. Ultimately, a means was devised to beam John Christopher back to the precise moment he had been plucked from his aircraft, so that he would have no memory of his time aboard the *Enterprise,* which had returned to its own era shortly thereafter. Spock had given the incident little thought since.

"I don't get it," McCoy confessed. "Why Shaun Christopher, of all people? We never even met him. Just his father."

"A valid question," Spock said.

While the Earth–Saturn mission of 2020 was certainly an important milestone in the history of human space exploration, he was not aware that it held any special significance to Kirk, aside from their brief acquaintance with Colonel Christopher's father, and even that was now some years in the past. Kirk had been involved in any number of equally memorable encounters since. Why had he not fixated on, say, Zefram Cochrane, Commodore Matt Decker, or Apollo?

"I have not heard the captain speak of either Christopher recently," Spock noted. "Have you, Doctor?"

"Can't say that I have." McCoy scratched his head. "Heck, if Jim was going to go off his rocker and think he was some famous historical figure, you'd think he'd fixate on Abraham Lincoln . . . or maybe Casanova."

The object of their discussion grew restive. "You there!" Kirk fought in vain against his restraints. "Stop talking about me like I'm not even here. I've told you who I am. Now I want to know who exactly you people are and what I'm doing here!"

Spock returned to the foot of Kirk's bed. "My apologies." He started to call Kirk *Captain* but caught himself. It would not do to upset Kirk further. "I assure you, we find the present situation equally as puzzling as you do, perhaps even more so. May I ask what your last memory was before you found yourself in our transporter room?"

Kirk eyed him suspiciously. "Don't you know that?"

"Indulge my curiosity," Spock said calmly. "There is still much about your presence here that we do not entirely comprehend. Any data you can provide may ultimately benefit us all."

"Hmm." Kirk mulled it over for a few moments. "Okay. I'm not sure what your angle is, but I'll play along. I was conducting an EVA to retrieve what appeared to be an artificial space probe of unknown origin. I had just made contact with the object when there was a sudden flash . . . and I found myself with you and your buddies in your so-called transporter room." His brow furrowed. "What does that mean, anyway? Are you telling me you have some sort of teleportation device?"

"Affirmative," Spock stated. He found Kirk's unusual narrative intriguing, although it bore little resemblance to the actual circumstances of the captain's injury. "You encountered the probe in space? Where precisely?"

"In orbit around Saturn, naturally." His eyes

widened in alarm. "Wait! Aren't we there anymore?" He tried to sit up, only to be forcibly reminded of his restraints. "Where in the universe are we? Where is my ship?"

Spock chose not to answer those questions, uncertain how Kirk might react in his present state of mind. Instead, he continued his interrogation. "And you believe yourself to be in the year 2020 C.E., as reckoned by traditional Earth calendars?"

"Of course! Why shouldn't I?"

"Why, indeed."

Spock contemplated what he had just heard. The captain's delusion appeared to be remarkably consistent, aside from the fact that there was no record of the real Shaun Christopher ever encountering an alien probe on his mission to Saturn centuries ago. Humanity had not made conclusive contact with another sentient species until First Contact some forty-three years later. Had Kirk interpolated the probe into his fantasy of being Colonel Christopher? Spock was not certain why Kirk should do so, but the human unconscious, as he understood it, was even more irrational and unpredictable than their surface thoughts. It might require a specialist trained in abnormal human psychology to explain the nature of this obsession fully. Spock was more concerned with how to restore the captain to himself. He wondered what might be required to dispel the delusion.

"Doctor, a word."

He stepped away from the bed to confer with McCoy once more.

"Have you attempted to confront him with his true identity?" Spock asked. "Perhaps via the simple expedient of a mirror?"

"I considered that," McCoy said. "But I wasn't sure if that would make things better or worse. His mental state seems precarious enough as it is."

Spock swiftly weighed the pros and cons. Now was no time for a protracted course of psychological treatment. "Do it," he instructed. "The ship requires its captain."

"I don't know," McCoy said hesitantly. "Are you sure that's wise?"

"Your reservations are duly noted, Doctor. I will take full responsibility for any consequences."

"I don't care if my butt is covered," McCoy protested. "I want to do what's right for Jim!"

"As do I, Doctor. And the captain deserves a chance to recognize himself."

McCoy shook his head dolefully. "All right. If you say so." He resigned himself to the prospect. "God help me, I'm not sure what else to do."

Antique medical instruments were displayed on the walls of sickbay. McCoy retrieved a small hand mirror from one frame. "Physicians once used mirrors like this one to determine whether patients were still breathing," he explained, perhaps to take his mind off what they were about to attempt. He shrugged his shoulders.

"At least we don't have to worry about that, I suppose. Aside from his case of mistaken identity, he seems fit enough. Just confused and agitated."

"Wouldn't you be, Doctor, if you awoke thinking you were someone else? From a completely different time and place?"

"Good point."

Spock stood back, observing carefully, while McCoy returned to Kirk's bedside. The doctor held the mirror behind his back and conferred briefly with Nurse Chapel before speaking gently to his patient.

"Capt— I mean, Colonel, I'm going to show you something. There's no reason to be alarmed. I just want you to look in a mirror and tell me what you see."

"Fine," Kirk said sullenly. "Knock yourself out."

McCoy brought out the mirror and held it up to Kirk. Chapel stood by with a sedative, just in case.

This proved a wise precaution. A look of utter shock and horror came over Kirk's face as he spied his reflection in the glass. The blood drained from his features, so that he looked as white as a mugato. His jaw dropped.

"Nooo!" he wailed. "That's not me!" He tried to reach for his face, but his arms were still strapped down. "My face! What have you done to it?" He thrashed wildly against his bonds and stared down at his body, which was still clad in the uniform of a Starfleet captain. He didn't seem to recognize his own hands or clothing. "Oh, my God! What have you done to me!"

His face was contorted. His eyes bulged from their

sockets. Veins stood out against his neck. Spittle flew from his lips. He averted his eyes, unwilling to look at the mirror anymore.

"That's not me! I'm Shaun Christopher! Shaun Christopher, I tell you!"

"Nurse!" McCoy barked. "Sedative!"

"Yes, Doctor!"

She handed him the hypospray, and he placed it against Kirk's jugular. A hiss signaled the release of the drug. Kirk's eyelids drooped, and he sagged against the bed. His straining limbs fell still.

"Damn," McCoy muttered. "I was afraid of that."

"It was worth the attempt, Doctor," Spock stated. "If nothing else, we have demonstrated the considerable depth of the captain's delusion."

"He sounded so convinced," Chapel said. "So terrified. For a moment there, I almost believed him." A pensive look came over her face. "You don't think . . ." She paused, as though hesitant to complete her thought. "Is it possible he's telling the truth?"

McCoy scoffed. "That Jim Kirk is actually possessed by a dead American astronaut from more than two hundred years ago? That's ridiculous."

"Is it, Doctor?" Spock gave Chapel's query due consideration. "Upon reflection, have we not encountered similar phenomena in the past? Consider that incident involving Dr. Janice Lester or perhaps our experiences with the disembodied alien intelligences we made contact with on the planet Arret."

On that latter occasion, both he and Kirk and a

third crew member had allowed their bodies to be temporarily occupied by the bodiless survivors of an extinct civilization—with nearly irrevocable results. Spock was also acquainted with various ancient Vulcan legends that spoke of the transference of minds between two or more individuals. It was said that in ages past, even the very *katra*—or living spirit—of an individual could be imparted to another.

And, sometimes, back again.

"Well, I suppose it is possible," McCoy conceded. "Lord knows we've run into stranger things these past few years . . . maybe." He shook his head. "But still, Shaun Christopher? He's not some bizarre alien entity or superintelligence. He died hundreds of years ago on Earth. What would his mind be doing out here, centuries later?"

Spock considered the possibilities. "The captain, speaking as Colonel Christopher, told of encountering the probe during his celebrated mission to Saturn. If this event actually occurred and was omitted from the historical record, then it is conceivable that the real Shaun Christopher's consciousness was somehow stored or duplicated in the probe's memory banks until the captain came into contact with it earlier today."

"Maybe, possibly," McCoy groused. "But that's a heck of a leap, Spock. How can we know for sure this isn't just some wild theory?"

"There is a way to be certain, Doctor. One way or another."

Understanding dawned in McCoy's eyes. "A mind-meld?"

"Precisely. It may be our best means of determining the true nature of the captain's condition."

McCoy nodded. To Spock's surprise, the doctor did not automatically attempt to dissuade him. "Well, I suppose it has worked before," he said grudgingly. "But how can we be sure that you won't be affected by whatever has unhinged Jim's mind?" He indulged in a bit of mordant humor. "I don't want to end up with *two* confused twenty-first-century astronauts on my hands."

"I will endeavor to avoid being caught in the captain's delusion, if that is indeed what it is." McCoy's concerns were not without merit, but Spock felt confident that he could navigate Kirk's disturbed psyche safely. "As you just stated, Doctor, I *have* done this before."

"Don't remind me." McCoy stepped away from the bed. "You planning to do this now?"

"I see no need for delay," Spock said. "Although Lieutenant Sulu is an able officer, it is best that I return to the bridge as soon as possible. The Skagway colony remains in jeopardy, and an effective solution has yet to be found."

Chapel looked on worriedly. She prepared another hypospray. "Do you need us to revive him, Mr. Spock?"

"That will not be necessary, Nurse. I require only a few moments of mental preparation and perhaps a degree of privacy."

Despite his assurances to McCoy, a mind-meld was never to be entered into lightly. The lowering of one's psychic barriers to achieve telepathic communion with another was a profoundly intimate—and often shattering—experience. One he had no desire to share with an audience.

To his credit, McCoy seemed to grasp this. "That will be all, Christine," he said softly. "I can take it from here."

"All right, Doctor." She retreated from the ward, glancing back over her shoulder as she did so. Concern and compassion were evident in her voice. "Be careful, Mr. Spock. I hope you find the captain."

"That is my hope as well," Spock said.

McCoy remained behind. Spock did not object. It was only logical to have a physician overseeing the meld in the event that unexpected complications arose. They could not fully predict the effect the meld might have on their patient—or on Spock himself.

"Please do not interfere, Doctor," he instructed. "Unless you deem it absolutely imperative."

"Just get on with it." A shiver ran down McCoy's body. "This whole thing always gives me the creeps."

Spock recalled that McCoy had once been subjected to a forced mind-meld by an alternate-universe version of Spock himself. It was small wonder that McCoy regarded such invasions with distaste.

"If it is any consolation, Doctor, I would also avoid this if I could."

He took a moment to brace himself. Time-honored meditative techniques, passed down for generations, prepared his mind for the task at hand. He put aside any fears or misgivings; it would not do to sabotage the meld by clinging instinctively to his mental defenses. To carry out the meld, he had to make himself more vulnerable than any human could possibly imagine.

I have no choice, he reminded himself. *I must do this—for the ship and the mission.*

And for Jim.

He leaned over Kirk. Using both hands, he splayed his fingers against the sides of Kirk's face. It was a delicate touch, barely grazing the skin, but sufficient to anchor the neural connection. Kirk's flesh was cool to the touch compared with his own. Spock closed his eyes and concentrated on achieving the meld.

"My mind to your mind," he intoned. "My thoughts to your thoughts."

A minor tremor threatened his resolve as their individual minds began to blur together, but he took a deep breath and pushed past his natural impulse to protect his own identity. He had melded with Kirk before, on several occasions, so he reached out for the familiar signposts he had come to expect. Boyhood memories in Iowa. His proud parents, George and Winona. Older brother Sam. The massacre on Tarsus IV. Starfleet Academy. Carol Marcus. Ruth. The *U.S.S. Republic.* The attack on the *Farragut.* The launch of the *Enterprise* under his command. Gary Mitchell, his eyes glowing like pulsars. Sam Kirk's death on Deneva. Klingons. Romulans. Edith Keeler. Miramanee . . .

But instead, he found himself lost in an unfamiliar psychic landscape. Strange memories that had nothing to do with James Tiberius Kirk flooded his mind:

Earth, more than two centuries ago. Smoggy skies. Automobiles clogging endless highways. Television. Video games. High school. Making Eagle Scout. His first car. College. Marrying Debbie Lauderdale. Babies being born, then growing up right before his eyes. Kevin. Katie. Rory. Air Force training, just like Dad. Area 51. The DY-100. Shannon O'Donnell. NASA. The divorce. Docking with the Lewis & Clark. *Months in zero gravity. Fontana. O'Herlihy. A stowaway? Saturn looming in the distance, growing nearer by the day. The probe, floating in space. His hand reaching out to touch it—*

A blinding flash lit up Spock's synapses. The shock jolted him from the meld, and he staggered backward, reeling from the sudden dislocation. For a moment, he wasn't entirely sure who or where he was. Foreign memories and emotions fogged his mind.

"Fontana," he murmured. "Alice . . ."

"Spock!" McCoy rushed toward him. "What is it? Are you all right?"

"A moment, Doctor. Please."

Spock struggled to regain his composure and sense of self. He placed a hand against a wall to steady himself. The borrowed memories began to recede. Years of mental discipline and training restored order to his thoughts.

I am Spock, son of Sarek and Amanda. My mind is my own.

"Talk to me, Spock!" McCoy pleaded. He took hold of Spock's arm. "What happened?"

"Forgive me, Doctor." He straightened and stepped away from the wall. He politely but firmly removed his arm from McCoy's grip. "The meld was broken abruptly, and the transition back to myself was rather more jarring than I would have preferred."

McCoy examined Spock with a palm-sized medical scanner. "Well, you seem to be more or less normal. Your blood pressure, heart rate, and neural activity are a bit elevated, even for a Vulcan, but they seem to be dropping back to their usual freakish levels." He lowered the scanner. "So, what did you find in there? What's wrong with Jim?"

The anachronistic memories lingered at the back of Spock's mind. The evidence was irrefutable; there could be only one conclusion. He turned toward their unconscious patient, who twitched and murmured in his sleep. The man's fingers drummed restlessly.

"That, Doctor, is *not* James T. Kirk."

McCoy gaped in astonishment, but the truth had to be faced.

"Despite all outward appearances, that is Colonel Shaun Geoffrey Christopher."

"I can't believe it," McCoy murmured. He sank into the chair in his office, still trying to process the astounding diagnosis Spock had just delivered. He had no reason to doubt Spock; the Vulcan usually had his precious facts in order. It was just a lot to take in. "This is insane."

Spock remained standing, seemingly unshaken by his discovery. "At least we now know that the captain is *not* insane," he pointed out. "Merely . . . dispossessed."

That was small comfort.

"Dammit, Spock," McCoy cursed. "I'm a doctor, not an exorcist. What are we supposed to do now?" An urgent question came to mind. "What about Jim? Is he still in there somewhere? Beneath Shaun Christopher's memories?"

"Negative," Spock said. "I regret to say that I found no traces of the captain's consciousness still remaining within his body. His mind appears to be entirely absent."

"Good God," McCoy said. "You don't think it's been . . . erased?"

The thought that all of Jim Kirk's personality and life experiences—everything that had made him who he was—might have been wiped away forever filled McCoy with despair. It would be the same as if their friend had been vaporized by a Klingon disruptor. He would be gone for good.

"Or perhaps merely displaced," Spock suggested. "It could be that Colonel Christopher's memories were not simply copied into the captain's brain. There might have been a two-way transference instead."

"Across time?" McCoy's mind boggled at the notion. "Is that even possible?"

"There are always possibilities, Doctor. Some are simply more probable than others."

McCoy wanted to believe him but had his doubts. "But isn't it more likely that the probe simply replaced Jim's mind with a copy of Shaun Christopher's? I mean, I hate to be the one citing logic here, but what about Occam's Razor? Isn't that a simpler and more plausible explanation than assuming that Jim and Shaun somehow switched minds over a span of centuries—and umpteen light-years to boot? What makes you think Jim's mind is still around . . . somewhere?"

"A feeling, Doctor." Spock grimaced, as though the admission pained him. "I cannot put it into words precisely, but what I sensed just now did not feel like a *copy* of Shaun Christopher's memories but rather his actual living consciousness, somehow displaced in time and space. Which suggests that the same might have occurred to the captain's mind."

"A 'feeling,' you say." McCoy couldn't help being amused. "Look at us. I'm the one talking logic, and you're relying on some vague impression you can't really explain." He snickered at the sheer irony of the moment. "Somebody check on Tartarus Prime. I think it may have frozen over."

"Mind-melds do not lend themselves to spoken vocabulary," Spock replied, perhaps a tad defensively, "let alone your own unsophisticated human languages.

I believe my reasoning is perfectly sound, given my observations during the course of the meld."

"Uh-huh." McCoy didn't buy it. "Sounds more like wishful thinking to me. Not that I blame you. Anything's better than thinking that Jim's mind is lost for good." He settled back into his chair and crossed his arms. "All right, then. Let's run with that theory. What now? Where do you think Jim is?"

"If my hypothesis is correct," Spock said, "then the captain's mind may now occupy Shaun Christopher's body, during the Saturn mission approximately two hundred fifty years ago."

"Then let's go find him!" McCoy urged. He seized on Spock's theory as their last, best hope of getting Jim Kirk back. Hope flared inside him for the first time since Spock had revealed that Jim's mind was truly absent. If there was even a chance that they could save Jim, they had to take it. "Saturn is a ways from here, but if we hurry at maximum warp, we can be there in a matter of weeks. And we've traveled back to that era before. More than once, actually. Jim's probably wondering what's keeping us!"

Of course, even if they did somehow miraculously locate Kirk's mind in the past, they would still have to put it back into his body where it belonged, but McCoy was inclined to cross that bridge when they came to it. Another mind-mind, perhaps, or that alien machine Janice Lester had discovered. There had to be a way to put Jim back together.

We just have to find him first.

"Easier said than done, Doctor," Spock observed. "While I appreciate your sense of urgency, the situation here in the Klondike system must take priority. We cannot abandon the Skagway colony to go searching the past for our lost captain."

McCoy refused to accept that. "But what about Jim? He could be trapped in the past, waiting for us to rescue him!"

"If he is in the past, Doctor, then there is no hurry. Whatever might have become of the captain occurred centuries ago. Our present duty remains before us. Perhaps later, if and when the crisis here is resolved, we can follow up on my hypothesis."

McCoy seethed in frustration. He knew from personal experience what it was like to be marooned in the past with little hope of rescue. How could Spock be so cool and analytical about the situation? "This is Jim we're talking about!"

"I am fully aware of that, Doctor." Spock's voice held a hint of regret, although one probably had to know him well to hear it. "But I also know that the captain would want us to carry out our duties in his absence and not sacrifice the Skagway colony on the basis of a . . . supposition."

"I know." The hell of it was, Spock was absolutely right. McCoy's shoulders slumped in defeat. He felt as though his hopes had been raised, only to be crushed beneath the combined weight of logic and duty. "That's what Jim would want, but that doesn't mean I have to like it."

"Nor do I," Spock admitted.

Sighing, McCoy nodded at the private exam room beyond. "In the meantime, what am I supposed to do with our misplaced friend there? It looks like he's not going anywhere."

"For the time being," Spock advised, "it is probably best that we share the particulars of the captain's condition with only select members of the crew. I suggest we keep Colonel Christopher confined to quarantine and limit any contact with him. As far as the rest of the crew and any civilians are concerned, the captain is simply recovering from his injuries—under doctor's orders."

McCoy didn't have a better idea. "And what exactly do I tell my patient?"

"As little as possible," Spock stated gravely. "If we do hope someday to return him to his own place in history, we must limit his exposure to the future—as we did with his father."

McCoy nodded. "And just how long do you think we can keep him in the dark?"

"Long enough, Doctor. I hope, long enough."

Fourteen

Kirk examined his new face in a mirror. Only a couple of days had passed since he had found himself in Shaun Christopher's body, and he was still getting used to it. He wondered if he ever would.

Oddly familiar blue eyes stared back at him. Shaun resembled his father, whom Kirk had met just a few years ago, although, paradoxically, Shaun was noticeably older than Captain John Christopher. Gray hair infiltrated his temples, and decades of experience had added both creases and character to his features. Kirk calculated that Shaun was probably in his early fifties, although it was hard to tell. People in the past tended to age faster than the humans of his era, where the life expectancy was considerably longer. Although he was in excellent shape for a man his age, Shaun's body was still older than Kirk would have preferred. He felt as if he had aged thirty years overnight.

Not quite as bad as that time on Gamma Hydra IV but disturbing nonetheless.

The crew's personal quarters were on the upper deck of the habitat module, above the gym and the infirmary. He had been relieved to discover that NASA had been thoughtful enough to provide each of the astronauts with his or her own private compartment, probably not a bad idea on a flight of this duration. The small, rather monastic cell was only a fraction of the size of his stateroom back on the *Enterprise,* but that was made up for in part by making use of the walls and ceiling as well. A personal grooming area, complete with mirror, occupied one corner. A sleeping bag was tethered to a wall. A narrow corridor connected the compartments. Kirk kept his door open. He didn't want to appear to be hiding.

Stubble dotted his cheek as he attempted to shave in zero gravity, which was trickier than he had anticipated. He carefully applied a dollop of water, procured from a wall dispenser, to his face, then squeezed a little NASA-approved shaving cream from a small tin-foil packet. In theory, the mixture would cling to his whiskers without floating away and would also stick to the razor blade. He would have to keep wiping the blade clean and roll up the hand towel to keep the shorn whiskers from getting loose. He started work on his chin but accidentally dislodged a tiny blob of shaving cream.

"Damn." He chased after the blob with the towel. Starfleet zero-g drills had seldom focused on matters of personal grooming and hygiene.

"Having trouble?"

Zoe Querez floated into his quarters without

waiting for an invitation. She executed a midair flip so that they were oriented in the same direction. Her slender fingers snagged the elusive blob, then wiped it on her shorts. She had no quarters of her own, he had learned, but was spending more and more time outside the brig. Nobody really had time to babysit her anymore.

"A little." He handed her the towel so she could wipe off her suit. "Thanks for the assist, Ms. Querez."

Even though he had since learned who she was, he remained dumbfounded by her presence on the ship. So far, the *Lewis & Clark*'s mission was playing out very differently from what he recalled from the history tapes. A stowaway? A briefly glimpsed alien probe? None of that was in the official accounts of the mission, let alone history as he knew it. Which just made his current predicament all the more challenging. How was he supposed to avoid changing the past when that past wasn't what he thought it was?

All he could do was try to get through this mission without blowing his cover, then find some way to send a message to the future. Perhaps a letter in a safe-deposit box, to be delivered to McCoy at an appropriate date hundreds of years from now? Or a time capsule built to survive World War III? Or, better yet, an old-fashioned radio message directed to where a starbase would be two hundred fifty years from now? In theory, his SOS would arrive at just about the right time for Starfleet to receive it.

Granted, the brass increasingly frowned on unnecessary trips to the past, for fear of wreaking havoc with the timeline, but surely they would grant the *Enterprise* some leeway in this case. He hoped that Spock and the others would come looking for him. Then maybe they could deal with the little matter of putting his mind back into his own body!

In the meantime, he had to keep pretending to be Shaun.

"What's with this 'Ms. Querez' stuff?" Zoe asked. "We're not on a first-name basis anymore?"

Oops, Kirk thought. "Sorry. Just a little distracted."

"Yeah, I can see that." She hooked her foot into a wall loop to keep from drifting around the chamber. Her striking brown eyes inspected his unshaven face. "Maybe you should just let it grow out. A little stubble looks good on you."

"Thanks," Kirk said. "But given the length of this cruise, I need to shave sometimes or end up looking like Rip Van Winkle." *Except that Rip woke up in the future,* he thought, *and I'm stuck two centuries in the past.*

"Good point," she agreed. "Probably not a great look for you. Why hide that rugged, *Right Stuff* mug of yours?"

Kirk raised an eyebrow. Was she flirting with him?

Despite his unusual circumstances, he couldn't help being intrigued. Zoe was an attractive woman. And he *was* going to be stuck on this slow-moving spacecraft for weeks to come . . .

But how would Shaun react to her overtures? Was he married, engaged, or otherwise attached? Not for the first time, he wished he had access to the *Enterprise*'s computer banks. Back on his own ship, he could have called up all of the particulars on Shaun in a moment. By contrast, the *Lewis & Clark* was too far away from Earth even to have access to—what did they call it these days? The Interweb?

"I tried growing a beard one summer," he divulged, assuming that revelation was harmless enough. What human male hadn't stopped shaving at some point? "It was not a universal success."

"I'll take your word for it." She reached for the razor. "Here, let me help."

Taking the razor from his hand, she leaned in closer, and he caught a whiff of a delicate fragrance. She deftly shaved his cheeks and chin with a gentle touch. His two-day-old shadow was quickly transferred to the razor blade and from there to the towel. Not a single stray whisker escaped into the closed environment of the ship. When she was finished, she paused to admire her work. "Yeah, that's more like it."

Kirk checked himself out in the mirror. He liked what he saw.

"I have to agree. Thanks." He rubbed his chin, which was now as smooth as a Deltan's cranium. She hadn't nicked him once. "Where did an intrepid journalist-slash-stowaway learn to use a razor like that?"

"Hello?" She smirked at him. "Have you seen my

legs?" She wiped the razor clean and handed it back to him. She gave him a sly look. "Maybe you can return the favor someday."

Kirk grinned. "I think I'd like that."

"Ahem." Fontana appeared in the doorway. "Am I interrupting something?"

"Not at all," Zoe replied, completely unruffled. "How can we help you, astronaut?"

Fontana ignored her and spoke directly to Kirk instead. "Daily mission briefing in five minutes, remember?" She scowled at Zoe. "If you're not too busy."

"Right," Kirk said. "The briefing." He was still learning the ship's routine. "Thanks for the reminder. Guess I'm still a bit foggy from that zap the other day."

He wondered how much longer he could milk that excuse. Certainly, it was plausible enough. Powerful electric shocks were known to cause memory loss. Should he take advantage of that angle more, or would that risk affecting the mission in a significant way? He wouldn't want to get Shaun relieved of command on grounds of partial amnesia or suspected brain damage. That might have a serious impact on history.

"No problem," Fontana said, her tone softening. She eyed him with obvious concern before finally acknowledging Zoe's presence. "If you could give us a few minutes."

It was not a request.

"Sure. Whatever." Zoe shrugged. "I need to brainstorm my next blog, anyway, not that I'm going to be able to post it anytime soon." She rolled her eyes. "You'd think a spaceship this high-tech would have free Wi-Fi, at least." She winked at Kirk as she glided out the door. "Don't forget. You owe me."

Fontana watched to make sure the other woman left. Her feet claimed the loop Zoe had been using before. She crossed her arms over her chest.

"What was that all about?"

"Nothing," Kirk said, unclear if he was fibbing or not. "She was just helping me shave."

"Since when do you need help with something like that?"

Careful, Kirk thought. He wasn't sure what Fontana's problem was. Did she simply disapprove of him socializing with the stowaway, or was it more than that? Once again, he wished he knew more about Shaun's personal life. How was he going to fake this for the rest of the voyage? He didn't know enough about who he was supposed to be.

"I was just being polite," he assured her. "After all, the four of us are going to be in close quarters for a long time. We might as well try to get along."

"I suppose," she said doubtfully. She peered the way Zoe had gone. "But I still don't trust her. She doesn't belong here."

Kirk couldn't disagree. "You can say that again."

That seemed to mollify her. "I'm sorry. I know I must sound like a stereotypical jealous ex, but . . ." Her eyes moistened, and she drew nearer. "Oh, Shaun. I thought I was never going to see you again."

Her face was only inches away from his. Her lips parted expectantly.

Kirk didn't know how Shaun would respond. "Fontana . . . Alice . . ."

"I know, I know." She seemed to take his hesitation in stride. "We both agreed that it was a bad idea, that our careers—and the mission—took priority, but that was before I watched you drifting off into space. I almost lost you, Shaun."

Kirk stalled. "I'm sorry to put you through that."

"It just got me thinking, you know." Her eyes entreated him. "Did we make a mistake, Shaun? Are we wasting precious time?"

Time is definitely an issue here, Kirk thought. The oddity of his situation was not lost on him. Had he really traveled two centuries into the past to find himself in the middle of a complicated love triangle? And the devil of it was, he had no idea which, if either, woman he—or, rather, Shaun—was supposed to end up with.

Good thing McCoy isn't around to see this. He'd never let me hear the end of it.

The video-com buzzed.

"Paging Christopher and Fontana." O'Herlihy's voice interrupted the awkward moment. His face skyped onto the miniature video screen. *"What's keeping you two?"*

Kirk tried to conceal his relief. "We should probably get going." Fontana looked disappointed and maybe even a little hurt. He gave her a smile to ease the sting. "We can . . . talk more later."

If Zoe didn't get to him first.

"Roger that." She gave him a funny look, as if something wasn't quite right, before hitting the speaker button on the comm. "Hold on to your horses, Marcus. We'll be right there."

Kirk hoped that she would chalk up his reticence to ordinary human misunderstandings and relationship issues. That would certainly be the most likely explanation as far as she was concerned. How could she possibly guess the truth?

He could barely believe it himself!

"Don't forget your lucky dog tags," she reminded him.

"What? Oh, right." The metal tags, which had apparently once belonged to Shaun's father, were tethered to a hook. Kirk wondered if they were the same tags John Christopher had worn when he was beamed aboard the *Enterprise.* He placed them around his neck. "Can't forget these."

"You never did before," she said.

The briefing took place on the ship's flight deck, since the *Lewis & Clark* lacked the space for a separate conference room. Kirk couldn't help comparing it with the bridge of the *Enterprise.* Like the rest of the ship, it seemed remarkably cramped and primitive by comparison. There wasn't even a yeoman to serve coffee.

"There you are," O'Herlihy said as Kirk and Fontana arrived. He had the copilot's seat turned toward the back of the module. "Dare I ask what was keeping you?"

Kirk sighed inside. Did everyone on this ship know more about Shaun's private life than he did?

Probably.

"Nothing that you need to know about." Fontana adopted a light tone that was probably at odds with her true feelings about what had just happened. She took a place on the ceiling, where she could keep an eye on the two men. "Don't be a dirty old man."

"Occupational hazard," O'Herlihy quipped, not unlike McCoy. "Just ask my wife."

"Sorry for the delay, Doctor." Kirk settled into the pilot's seat. He guessed that was Shaun Christopher's usual spot. "My fault. I guess I'm not exactly at the top of my game."

"Don't apologize," O'Herlihy said. "If we were back on Earth, you'd already be on medical leave, if not under observation twenty-four/seven."

Yes, Kirk decided. *He definitely reminds me of Bones.*

"We have a job to do, Doctor. I intend to do it."

He had already started covertly studying the ship's operations manuals. The technology was remarkably simple by twenty-third-century standards. Scotty would have been appalled by the unsophisticated systems and engineering. Why, they were still getting by on a first-generation impulse drive. Zefram Cochrane hadn't even been born yet.

If nothing else, Kirk reflected, he had been given a front-row seat to space history in the making. The *Lewis & Clark* was a covered wagon compared with the *Enterprise,* which just made its crew's dedication and courage all the more impressive. Fontana and O'Herlihy, not to mention Christopher, were true pioneers, venturing out into the unforgiving void with nothing but a crude titanium hull to protect them. They had no deflectors, no phasers, no photon torpedoes, no transporters. Not even artificial gravity or universal translators.

I need to appreciate this opportunity, he thought. *Not take it for granted.*

"All right, then," O'Herlihy said. "Let's get down to business." He leafed through a stack of printouts. "We've received the latest updates from Mission Control. Seems they're keeping a tight lid on any info about that probe, and they expect us to do the same."

"So, they're keeping the whole thing quiet," Fontana said. "Just like they did about our unwanted guest earlier."

Kirk observed that Zoe had not been invited to the briefing. No surprise there. He wondered what the enticing stowaway was up to at that moment. Just working on her "blog," whatever that was?

"Exactly. They don't want to stir up any more controversy about this mission, especially since we didn't manage to retrieve the probe." O'Herlihy clucked in regret. "A pity it zipped away like that. Just think of all we could have learned from it!"

Don't worry, Kirk thought. *We'll run into it again—two hundred and fifty years from now.*

"It's completely gone?" Fontana asked. "There's no sign of it?"

O'Herlihy shook his head. "LIDAR tracked it to the edge of the solar system before losing it. Hubble has lost sight of it, too. It's long gone."

Kirk frowned. He hoped that they hadn't also lost their best chance of putting him back where he belonged, both physically and temporally. He remembered how battered and decrepit the probe had appeared in his time. What if the future version of the probe was too damaged to reverse whatever it had done the first time?

Is it already en route to Klondike VI, he wondered, *or does it have other errands to attend to first? Maybe some other gas giants to observe?*

"I wonder where it came from," Fontana said. "And what it was doing here."

"We may never know," O'Herlihy said sadly. "In the meantime, however, NASA wants us to continue with our mission and complete our observations of Saturn and its moons. And, Lord, is there plenty to observe."

"Such as?" Kirk asked.

"Take a look at this." O'Herlihy relocated to one of the auxiliary terminals and called up an image on a monitor. Kirk and Fontana looked over his shoulder. "These are our latest photos of Saturn's north pole, taken during our last pass."

The famous hexagonal vortex looked just the way Kirk remembered it from the future, spread vibrantly for thousands of kilometers atop the planet. It looked just like the travel photos and calendar shots he had seen his entire life, not to mention his own personal memories.

"It's back to normal," he realized. "Just like before."

"That's right," the scientist confirmed. "What's more, I've been running an analysis of the rings. They've also stabilized. The vast majority of the ring matter has already fallen back into its usual formations."

"Just in the last day or so?" Fontana stared at the monitor. She voiced the thought they were probably all thinking. "Was it the probe? Did it do something?"

"Possibly. Probably." O'Herlihy scratched his beard. "There *were* those energy pulses right before you ran into difficulty, Shaun. As nearly as I can tell, the pulses were directed at the planet's north pole, right into the heart of the vortex."

Kirk pondered the scientist's report. "What kind of energy, Doctor?"

"I'm not sure," O'Herlihy admitted. "Possibly a stream of charged particles or directed plasma waves. Like a laser, almost."

Or a phaser? Kirk wondered. Actual phasers would not be developed by Earth science for at least two centuries. Had the probe fired some variety of phaser at Saturn? Spock had not detected any defensive systems aboard the probe, but perhaps its phaser banks operated on different principles and were not recognized by the *Enterprise*'s sensors. Or maybe the beams were simply a previously unknown type of directed energy. In either case, they would be beyond O'Herlihy's experience.

"So, the beams rebooted the hexagon somehow?" Fontana speculated, apparently more interested in their function than their nature. "Which stabilized the rings? That's fantastic!"

But not unheard of, Kirk thought. He recalled the alien hieroglyphics on the probe and that obelisk back on Miramanee's world. Once activated, the obelisk had projected a powerful deflector beam that had kept the planet from being struck by an oncoming asteroid. Was it possible that the probe had been designed to serve a similar purpose, fixing Saturn's deteriorating rings? Or, more likely, resetting some other mechanism hidden somewhere deep within the mysterious hexagon?

"You may be on to something," he told Fontana. "Perhaps the probe *was* here to repair Saturn's rings."

"And it left once it completed its mission?" Marcus seized on the idea, visibly fascinated. "But who sent the probe? And what interest would they have in maintaining Saturn's rings?"

Good questions, Kirk thought. He wished he could tell O'Herlihy and Fontana more about the Preservers, not that there was much to tell. The ancient aliens were a mystery even in his own time. Had they anticipated humanity colonizing this solar system in the future and wanted to keep Saturn and its moons stabilized for Earth's benefit? Or did they have another motive for fixing the ringed giant? Perhaps they simply wanted to preserve one of the sector's natural wonders for conservation or aesthetic reasons. *It would be funny,* he mused, *if the Preservers ultimately turned out to be some sort of cosmic park service.*

"Shaun," O'Herlihy asked him, "you were out there when those pulses fired. What did you see before the probe shocked you?"

You mean, what did Christopher see, Kirk thought, *before I set up shop in his body.* In truth, his last memory before finding himself in orbit was of touching the probe in the *Enterprise*'s transporter room. He hadn't seen the pulses O'Herlihy was talking about.

"To be honest, it's all kind of a blur," he said. "Sorry."

Marcus sighed. He sounded disappointed but not too surprised. "I was afraid of that. A little traumatic short-term-memory loss was to be expected, I suppose."

"Is that serious?" Fontana asked, sounding worried.

"I doubt it," the doctor said. "Patients who have been in accidents often have little recollection of the actual events. It's probably nothing to be concerned

about, provided the rest of Shaun's memory is intact."
He looked Kirk over. "You do remember who I am,
right?"

He made it sound like a joke, but Kirk thought he
heard something more serious underneath.

"A nervous mother hen?" Kirk said with a grin.
"Seriously, I admit I was a little shook up, but I'm
feeling better every day. Stop treating me like a basket
case, both of you. That's an order."

"Fair enough," O'Herlihy said. "But you'll tell me if
you're having problems, right?"

"You'll be the first to know," Kirk lied. He felt bad
about deceiving the two astronauts. They deserved
better. But he couldn't risk changing history by
revealing that he was actually a time traveler from the
future. "But really, I just want to get back to work."

Fontana looked relieved. "Okay, that's the Shaun
Christopher I'm used to."

Kirk was glad to hear it. It occurred to him that
if he had to impersonate a human of the twenty-first
century, the commander of an exploratory space vessel
was not a bad fit. He and Shaun probably had much
in common, including similar instincts and training.
Could be worse, he thought. *I could be stuck in the body
of an opera singer or a brain surgeon.*

When in doubt, maybe he just needed to act like
himself.

"On a lighter note," O'Herlihy continued, "Mission
Control also forwarded a new batch of personal e-mails

from home. Not quite as good as a care package of homemade brownies, but they will have to do. There appear to be plenty of photos and videos to review at our so-called leisure."

Interesting, Kirk thought. He looked forward to studying Christopher's correspondence in private. He hoped they would tell him more about Shaun as a person.

Fontana flew down to the nearest computer terminal. "Duty be damned. I think we can take a few minutes out of our busy schedules to check out those e-mails right away." She grinned at Kirk. "If that's all right with you, Colonel."

"Indulge yourself, Commander." He figured that Christopher would say the same. "After what we've been through the past few days, I think we can all use a little taste of home."

Too bad he wasn't likely to have any messages from his real home.

Or century.

The crew members floated off to various terminals to enjoy their personal correspondence in relative privacy. Kirk was grateful that the other two astronauts were preoccupied with their own messages. That gave him a chance to skim Christopher's messages without being watched too closely. He felt a twinge of guilt at reading Christopher's e-mail but assumed that any assumption of privacy vanished when he took over the other man's body. Besides, for all he knew, Shaun's consciousness was residing at the back of his brain somewhere—if it hadn't been erased or transferred elsewhere.

Was Shaun about to read these letters, too? Kirk hoped not. He knew from experience how hellish it could be to remain aware but helpless while another mind controlled your body.

I had enough of that on Platonius.

Shoving the unpleasant memory aside, he checked out the first missive.

"Hi, Dad!" the message began.

Kirk blinked in surprise. Shaun had children? Not too surprising, considering the astronaut's age, he realized, but the filial salutation still hit him like a phaser on stun. He scanned the e-mails quickly, trying to get his bearings. Shaun seemed to have three kids, two in college and one much younger.

Color photos, attached to the letter, showed a Fourth of July picnic on a beach. The youngest boy, Rory, looked about eight years old.

The same age as David, Kirk thought.

Kirk had never met his own son. Carol preferred it that way. It dawned on Kirk that David—and his mother—would not be born for centuries. He found himself envying Shaun.

"Mom is taking us to Colonial Williamsburg," Rory wrote. *"She says hi."*

From the sound of things, Christopher's kids were staying with their mom while he was in space. Kirk read the passage again. Just "hi" from the mom? He wondered what the story was with her and Shaun. Were they married, divorced, separated, or had they never lived together at all? Scrolling quickly through the e-mail, he didn't find a separate note from the unnamed mother. The other letter appeared to be from Christopher's sister—and his father.

Kirk chuckled to himself. He couldn't help being amused to receive a personal message from Shaun's dad, retired Air Force Captain John Christopher. Only four years had passed, by Kirk's reckoning, since he had bid farewell to Captain Christopher on the bridge of the *Enterprise,* but of course, decades had passed for Shaun's father, who had not even conceived his son the last time Kirk saw him. And now Kirk was occupying Shaun's body!

Talk about a small universe, he thought. *Or should that be a small space-time continuum?*

What were the odds that they would cross paths like this again, despite a gap of centuries? Kirk had to wonder if some cosmic intelligence was playing games with him, or was it just that time-travel conundrums were like some kind of persistent infection? Maybe once you caught one, you were always susceptible to a relapse? Spock would surely have a theory on the subject, possibly involving temporal linkages or chroniton entanglement. McCoy would probably just chalk it up to a bizarre twist of fate.

Maybe the truth was somewhere in between.

Over at an adjacent terminal, Fontana looked up

from her own correspondence. "How are the kids? They having a good time with Debbie this summer?"

"Sounds like it." Kirk wished he could pump Fontana for more details on Christopher's family but changed the subject instead. "How about you? Any exciting news from home?"

"Not unless you count my idiot brother breaking his ankle snowboarding. And my mom has a new gallery opening next weekend." She snickered. "I told her I probably couldn't make it."

"I suspect she understood," Kirk said, relieved to be talking about anything other than Shaun Christopher's mysterious loved ones. He resolved to scour the e-mail more thoroughly later for whatever personal info he could glean from it. "You'll have to catch her next show."

He wondered if Fontana's mom was a painter, a sculptor, or what.

Watch out, he warned himself. *Don't let on that you don't know.*

"I just hope she's taking good care of Gus," Fontana said. "God, I miss the little guy."

Wait. Fontana had a child, too?

"Any message from him?" he asked.

She looked puzzled by the question. "Last time I checked, bulldogs weren't much on letter writing."

Damn, Kirk thought. *I got it wrong again.*

"Well, you never know," he said, trying to recover. "You can do wonders with dog training these days."

"Ha, ha, ha," she said. "Very funny—not."

O'Herlihy sniffled over at the far terminal. His back was turned to the other astronauts. Kirk thought he heard the man choke back a sob.

He seized on the distraction. "You all right, Doctor?"

"I'm fine," O'Herlihy insisted. He rotated to face them. "Just a little choked up, that's all." He wiped a tear from his eye and licked his finger to make sure it didn't get away. "What can I say? I miss my family."

Kirk had already picked up on the fact that the doctor was a devoted family man. He had previously caught O'Herlihy mooning over home-video footage of a wife and a college-age daughter. They had looked like lovely women. He couldn't blame O'Herlihy for missing them.

"Nothing wrong with that," Fontana said. "Everything okay with Jocelyn and Tera?"

"They're well," he reported, although his hoarse voice betrayed how powerfully the letters from home had affected him. He made an effort to regain his composure. "My apologies. I shouldn't get so emotional."

"Don't be too hard on yourself," Kirk said. "After all, you're human, not Vul—" He started to say "Vulcan" but caught himself. "I mean, you're only human."

"We all are," Fontana added.

"I know," O'Herlihy said. He stared plaintively at the screen before him. "They just seem so far away sometimes. Like I'm never going to see them again."

Kirk tried to remember O'Herlihy's biography but couldn't bring up the details. He just remembered the name from the mission logs.

"You will," Fontana promised. "They'll be there waiting for you when we get back."

And so will Christopher's family, Kirk realized. They were millions of kilometers away now, but what about when he got to Earth? How in the world could he face Shaun's own flesh and blood?

He couldn't even tell them what had become of the real Shaun.

If he even still existed at all.

Fifteen

"Here comes another one!" Sulu blurted.

A boulder-sized chunk of ice hurled toward the domed colony on the viewer. Between its size and its velocity, it had a good chance of breaching Skagway's fading deflectors and maybe even the lunar habitat itself. A breach in the dome was a worst-case scenario that seemed to be growing more likely by the moment.

"Got it," Chekov said.

Without waiting for a command to fire, Chekov unleashed a salvo of phaser beams that shattered the frozen meteoroid into hundreds of smaller fragments only moments before it would have slammed into Skagway. Vaporizing the object would have been cleaner, but they needed to conserve the phaser banks' power. Pulverized ice crystals rained down on the besieged colony.

Chekov let out a held breath. "That was a close one."

"Just like the last two," Sulu commented. "Is it just me, or are these giant hailstones getting more and more frequent?"

"Your perceptions are quite accurate, Lieutenant,"

Spock stated from the captain's chair. "The frequency of such near-collisions has increased by a factor of six-point-seven over the last twenty-four hours. As the rings continue to destabilize, ever more debris is being drawn toward Klondike VI, placing Skagway in jeopardy, even as the moon's own orbit brings it steadily closer to the inner rings—where it will face additional hazards."

They were fighting a losing battle, Spock knew. Once Skagway entered the inner rings, the challenge of defending the colony would increase exponentially. And the *Enterprise*'s tractor beams, while state-of-the-art, were hardly sufficient to hold even a small moon in place.

He called up the latest tracking data on Skagway's orbit. The figures scrolled across the display panel on his right armrest. He performed the necessary calculations in his head. The analysis took only seconds.

"Mr. Sulu." He addressed the helmsman. "Skagway's orbit has contracted by a factor of nine-point-two. Please adjust our own orbit to compensate."

"Already on it, sir," Sulu said. "Matching course and speed." He kept his gaze fixed on the wayward moon. "Don't worry, Mr. Spock, I'm not letting those people out of sight."

Chekov sighed. "Too bad those drifting icebergs aren't letting them alone, either."

Spock detected a note of fatigue in the ensign's

voice. By his calculations, Chekov had now been on duty for fourteen hours, twelve minutes, and forty-four seconds. A swift review of Chekov's defensive phaser fire indicated a slight but significant loss in reaction time. Spock made a decision.

"Lieutenant Ita," he instructed, "please relieve Ensign Chekov at the nav station. Mr. Chekov, you are relieved."

"Sir?" Chekov looked back at him in dismay.

"No criticism is intended, Ensign," Spock assured him. Five years of working alongside humans had taught him the importance of taking their egos and emotions into account in command situations. Maintaining crew morale was not his forte, but he had learned that it was not a factor that could be safely overlooked, particularly where humans were concerned. "Your performance has been exemplary, but you, like all living organisms, are subject to fatigue. It is only logical to rotate key personnel as required. You may resume your duties after a suitable interval of rest."

"Well, when you put it that way." Chekov grudgingly surrendered his seat to Maggie Ita. He yawned and stretched. "I suppose I could use a *little* break."

"Get some sleep," Sulu urged his comrade. "You deserve it."

Sulu sounded faintly envious. Spock resolved to relieve the helmsman, too, once Ita settled into phaser duty. It would be inadvisable to replace both Sulu and Chekov at the same time, but Spock calculated that approximately thirty-six-point-five minutes would allow for a smooth turnover at the conn. Any sooner might compromise their defense of Skagway, while any longer might decrease Sulu's efficiency beyond an acceptable margin.

"*Da.*" Chekov trudged toward the turbolift. "I will be in my quarters if you need me."

"Thank you, Ensign," Spock stated. "That will be all."

The turbolift doors closed on Chekov.

"What about you, Mr. Spock?" Uhura asked from her station. "You've barely rested since the captain . . . was taken ill."

Spock appreciated her discretion. As planned, the reality of what had befallen Captain Kirk had not been shared with the entire crew. This, too, was a matter of maintaining morale. Only key officers had been made privy to the truth. As far as the rest of the crew was concerned, the captain had been temporarily incapacitated by his encounter with the alien probe and was now recuperating in sickbay. That seemed preferable to letting them know that James Kirk's body was now occupied by a confused astronaut from twenty-first-century Earth and that the captain's own mind was missing and presumed lost in the past.

"Your concern is duly noted, Lieutenant," he replied to Uhura, "but, with all due respect to Ensign Chekov, I am afraid that I'm not so easily replaced. Fortunately, my Vulcan heritage also grants me greater endurance and ability to concentrate in such circumstances."

Uhura did not sound convinced. "Are you sure that's not just Vulcan pride speaking, Mr. Spock?"

"Merely an objective statement of fact, Lieutenant." He did not object to Uhura questioning him. He knew that she was only thinking of the best interests of himself and the ship and that she had never been afraid to speak her mind. "False modesty is not logical."

While accurate, his assertions did leave out certain qualifications. He had been in command of the *Enterprise* for precisely fifteen-point-six hours now, and fatigue *was* becoming an issue, even for him. Certain meditative techniques, along with the occasional bowl of *plomeek* soup, had helped to conserve his strength so far, but he could not maintain his focus indefinitely. Although he was reluctant to hand the bridge over to Lieutenant Commander Scott before the current crisis was resolved, especially since Mr. Scott was more usefully employed in Engineering, logic dictated that he eventually seek rest, too. He was half-human after all, even if he was loath to admit it.

"Incoming!" Sulu warned.

A trio of icy missiles threatened the colony. "I have them," Ita reported. The slim Asian woman had recently transferred over from the *U.S.S. Darrow.* "Firing now."

Sapphire beams targeted the first two meteoroids, which blew apart into—relatively—harmless hail. She hastily attempted to blast the remaining missile, too, but it was accelerating too fast. The massive hailstone cratered into the spaceport outside the dome. A cloud of shattered ice erupted from the shattered landing pad.

"Damn," Ita muttered under her breath. She turned to look at Spock. "I'm sorry, sir. That last one got by me."

Spock had observed her reactions carefully. "Why did you target the other two meteoroids first?"

"They seemed to be heading straight for the dome itself," Ita replied. "I thought they posed the greater threat to colonists, sir."

"Precisely so," Spock agreed. "By my calculations, the meteoroids you destroyed were on course for more vulnerable targets. Do not fault yourself, Lieutenant. You made the correct choice."

"Thank you, sir."

Spock suspected that such decisions would become more difficult—and common—as time went by. Wide-dispersal blasts could be employed to target multiple hazards but only at the cost of reducing the overall intensity of the phasers. They would have to weigh the effectiveness of such a strategy against the need to ensure that no single large ice boulder breached the dome. None of which would matter if the entire moon ultimately spiraled into the crushing immensity of Klondike VI. The ship's phasers and photon torpedoes were no match for the ringed giant's gravity.

"Mr. Spock," Uhura said. "Governor Dawson is hailing us. She wants an update on the situation."

Spock understood her desire for fresh information. The destruction of the landing pad must have been a dramatic reminder of the danger her colony was in. He only wished he had a concrete solution to present to her.

"Please inform her that we are continuing our efforts to the best of our abilities."

"I've tried, sir. She wants to talk to you."

"Very well." Spock accepted the interruption as unavoidable but decided that such a discussion was best conducted away from the bridge. "Please patch the frequency to the briefing room." He thought ahead to the meeting. "And have Qat Zaldana report to the briefing room as well."

The colony's chief scientist was continuing to study the data from the shrinking hexagonal vortex on Klondike VI. No doubt Governor Dawson would want to hear from her, too.

"Aye, sir."

He turned the captain's chair over to Sulu, whose rest period was apparently going to have to wait. Ensign Brubaker assumed Sulu's place at the helm.

"Notify me at once if there are any significant new developments," Spock stated. "And divert additional power to the phasers."

He did not want Skagway to be struck by an ice ball while he was conferring with the governor.

"Where is Captain Kirk?" Governor Dawson demanded. *"I need to speak to him."*

She scowled in triplicate on the triscreen viewer in the briefing room. Spock and Qat Zaldana sat opposite each other. A sealed doorway ensured their privacy.

"My apologies, Governor," he replied. "But, as I explained earlier, the captain is recovering from an accidental energy discharge. Our ship's doctor has instructed that he not be disturbed."

"That's all very well and good," Dawson objected, *"but we're fighting for our lives and home here, or have you forgotten that? I think that warrants 'disturbing' your captain."*

"The timing of the captain's injury is unfortunate," Spock said. "But the situation cannot be helped. I assure you that Captain Kirk would speak with you were he able."

His answer was apparently not good enough for Dawson. Bypassing Spock, she directed her queries to Qat Zaldana instead. *"What's going on there, Qat? Have you seen the captain? What's wrong with him? How bad is it?"*

The veiled scientist paused before answering. "I have no reason to doubt Dr. McCoy's assessment," she said diplomatically. "Given the current emergency, he would not restrict the captain to bed rest unless it was absolutely necessary." She spoke calmly, without excess emotion or dramatics. "In the meantime, Mr. Spock and the rest of the crew are working around the clock on our behalf. I believe we are in good hands."

Spock was grateful for her measured words. She

had, after all, seen "Kirk" behaving erratically after his contact with the probe. A vivid description of those events, including the captain's apparent amnesia, would have done little to assure Governor Dawson that the situation aboard the *Enterprise* was under control. It seemed that Qat Zaldana also understood that.

"*If you say so,*" Dawson grumbled. "*A hell of a time for Kirk to get himself banged up, though, I have to say.*" She let out an exasperated sigh. "*I don't mean to sound uncaring, Mr. Spock, but right now I've got an entire colony on the verge of panicking, so you'll forgive me if I can't afford to worry about how your captain is feeling.*"

"Understood," Spock said. "The preservation of Skagway must remain your top priority . . . and mine. The *Enterprise* is devoting every resource to this crisis, as the captain would have us do."

If he were truly here, he amended silently.

Spock remained troubled by the uncertainty regarding Kirk's fate. Although he had no doubt where his duty lay at the moment, he could not help wondering what had become of his captain—and his friend.

Where are you, Jim? Do you still exist?

Governor Dawson called him back to the present emergency. "*And have you made any progress?*" she asked. "*Don't get me wrong. I appreciate all of that fine skeet shooting you've been doing, but we're still getting pummeled down here, and our shields are about shot. And they tell me this entire moon is circling the drain.*"

An apt metaphor, Spock thought. "That is correct. Your orbit is contracting steadily, and you can expect to enter the inner rings in forty-nine-point-eight standard hours."

"Fantastic," Dawson said sarcastically. *"As if we didn't have enough to worry about."* She gazed at Spock hopefully. *"I don't suppose that high-powered starship of yours can nudge us back where we belong?"*

"Regretfully, no," Spock said. "Our tractor beams are insufficient to the task."

"I was afraid of that." She didn't sound too surprised. *"So, what else have you got?"*

Qat Zaldana spoke up. With Spock now occupied commanding the *Enterprise,* the bulk of the scientific analysis had fallen on her. "We're still studying the situation, but we've determined that the trouble with the rings—and our moon—may have something to do with an unusual phenomenon we've detected down on the planet."

"What phenomenon?"

Qat Zaldana explained about the apparently simul-taneous contraction of the hexagonal vortex at the planet's pole. The governor was familiar with the land-mark, naturally, but was clearly uncertain about the significance of this development.

"I don't understand," the governor said. *"What does that damn hexagon have to do with us?"*

Spock wished he knew. "I have given the matter some thought," he informed her. "We lack the data to reach a definitive conclusion, but let us theorize that the hexagon—or whatever lies within it—was somehow instrumental in maintaining the gravitational integrity of the planet's rings. If that is so, then perhaps that ancient mechanism is now malfunctioning, with the results that we are currently witnessing."

"Maybe it's finally just broken down after all these years," Qat Zaldana speculated. "I've been reviewing the data on both Klondike VI and other ringed planets such as Saturn, and I've determined that the hexagons might well be an artificial phenomenon, possibly along with the rings themselves. We think we understand the gravitational forces creating the rings, but what if the mass of the planet's core is actually much less stable than we've always believed? I mean, it's not like anyone has ever actually visited the core of a gas giant; that's beyond our technology, even today. What if Klondike VI and planets like it are actually much denser than we suspect, and the hexagons somehow act as counteragents creating the conditions that allow the rings to exist?"

Governor Dawson shook her head. *"Is that even possible?"*

"Conceivably," Spock stated. "The mass and density of a planet are not always fixed constants. I have personally witnessed the disintegration of a dying planet, whose gravity fluctuated dramatically in its final days." The planet in question, Psi 2000, no longer existed at all, and the *Enterprise* had nearly been caught in its gravitational death throes. "It may be that Klondike VI is similarly variable—without the stabilizing influence of the hexagon."

Dawson nodded. *"All right. So, how do we get the hexagon working again?"*

"That has yet to be determined," Spock confessed.

"Why did I know you were going to say that?" She groaned aloud. *"Look, this is all very interesting scientifically, but what about my people and this colony? What's our time frame here?"*

"As I said, we have more than two days before Skagway enters the inner rings, which will increase the danger by several orders of magnitude, and perhaps another twenty-seven hours before the moon enters the planet's atmosphere." Spock considered whether the time to find a solution that would save the colony, and all of its inhabitants, was running out. "We should accelerate our plans to evacuate the colony."

By his calculations, it would take sixteen-point-thirty-three hours to bring aboard as many evacuees as the *Enterprise* could safely transport. Even allowing for an adequate margin of error, they still had time to spare, but they needed to prepare for the worst.

"I've already begun drawing up lists of who gets to leave and who has to stay," she admitted ruefully. *"Children first, of course, but after that, the choices will break your heart. I know they have mine."* The strain of her position showed on her face. *"I knew I should have retired years ago. I*

could be on New Pangea now, playing with my grandchildren, not deciding who lives and who dies."

Spock was Vulcan, but he still grieved with her.

"Perhaps it still won't come to that," Qat Zaldana said, but her words rang hollow. Unknowable cosmic forces were in play, and they were running out of time.

A warning siren sounded in the governor's office. She looked up in alarm as the room shuddered on the screen. Dust fell from the ceiling. A paperweight rolled off her desk. *"Helfrost,"* she muttered. *"Not ag—"*

The transmission was cut off abruptly.

"Governor!" Qat Zaldana exclaimed. "Skooka!"

The intercom whistled. Spock hit the speaker button on the viewer. "Spock here."

"Sorry to interrupt, sir," Sulu reported from the bridge. *"But another barrage of meteoroids just hit the moon, about twenty kilometers west of the colony. Probably shook things up a bit."*

Spock overlooked Sulu's typically human lack of precision. He had already deduced as much from the tremor that had cut off the transmission.

"And the colony itself?" he asked.

"No direct hits on the dome," Sulu reported. *"It's still in one piece."*

For now, Spock thought.

But for how much longer?

Sixteen

The specs for the *Lewis & Clark*'s first-generation impulse engines were enough to give Scotty conniptions. Kirk couldn't believe how primitive they were. Poring over the technical data on an old-fashioned "laptop" computer, he saw all sorts of ways to make the antique engines safer and more efficient. Perhaps by reconfiguring the drive coils to increase the plasma output . . .

Too bad he couldn't share those innovations with the crew. He could spare generations of future spaceship engineers decades of trial and error. But humanity would have to discover those advances in its own good time, as he knew it would.

Provided he kept his mouth shut.

He floated in the middle of his quarters, stretched out facedown in the air, with the portable computer tethered to his wrists. A foot loop secured him to the wall. Scrolling through the files by means of a keyboard struck him as just as quaint and inefficient as those so-called engines. He missed the helpful female voice of the *Enterprise*'s computer. He hadn't realized how much he had come to rely on it.

"You look comfortable," Fontana interrupted. She hovered in the doorway. "Mind if I join you?"

"Not at all."

"Great. Here I come." She flew into his compartment, pausing to close the hatch behind her. Deft movements propelled her over to where he was floating. Executing a barrel roll to line up beside him, she peeked at the blueprints on the laptop's monitor. "The tech manuals? Don't you know that stuff by now?"

Kirk couldn't admit that he had a lot of catching up to do. "What can I say? It relaxes me."

He closed the lid on the computer, not averse to taking a break. His fingers and wrists were tired of pecking away at the keyboard. What was that peculiar-sounding ailment people suffered from in this era? Carpal-tunnel something?

"Really?" she said. "I thought spy novels were your vice of choice." She spoke with easy familiarity. "I figured you'd be reading some trashy new cloak-and-dagger thriller."

Good to know, Kirk thought, filing away that bit of personal trivia. That explained all those twenty-first-century espionage novels he had found loaded in the ship's entertainment files. Most of them were potboilers destined for obscurity, but he had recognized the titles of a few future classics. *The Chrysalis Experiment,* for instance, and *Assignment: Armageddon.* Those books, by "Lincoln Roberts," were still being read in his time.

"Just trying to expand my horizons, I guess."

"By reading tech manuals for pleasure?" Fontana

shook her head. "That doesn't sound like the Shaun Christopher I know."

He shrugged. "Maybe you don't know me as well as you thought."

"You know, I'm starting to think so."

He sensed a serious undercurrent in her remark. "Something on your mind, Alice?"

If she was having doubts about him, he needed to remedy that. If possible.

She rolled over onto her side, the better to examine him. Striking green eyes met his. "Have you given any thought," she said tentatively, "to what we talked about before? That time you were shaving?"

"About us, you mean?"

"Yes." She glanced back over her shoulder at the closed hatchway. "Marcus is up on the flight deck, reviewing the telemetry on that damn probe, and the brat is downstairs updating her stupid blog." She took hold of his jumpsuit to put herself closer to him. "We've got time for a heart-to-heart—and more, if you feel like it."

"I see," he hedged, uncertain how to proceed. He was not one to refuse the advances of an attractive woman, but this was another man's love life he was in the middle of. Fontana wanted Shaun, not James Kirk. He was reluctant to romance her under false pretenses, even for the sake of maintaining the timeline. And then, of course, there was Zoe. What if she was the one Shaun was supposed to be with?

"Is something the matter?" she asked.

"I don't know, Alice," he said, holding himself back. "Don't get me wrong. You're a remarkable woman. Any man would be lucky to be with you, but . . . maybe now is not the right time."

"Why? Because of the mission? NASA policy?" Her eyes narrowed. "No, that's not it, is it? There's something different about you, about us. There was always a spark between us, even after we called things off, but now . . . you've changed somehow." A note of suspicion crept into her voice. "Is it her? The stowaway? Is there something going on between you two?"

Not that I know of, Kirk thought. *Or at least, not yet.*

"This isn't about Zoe," he said. "Things are just . . . complicated right now."

"Complicated how?"

Before he could come up with a halfway plausible answer, a siren went off, startling them both. The ear-piercing wail echoed off the bulkheads.

"Oh my God!" she exclaimed. "That's the fire alarm!"

Their awkward personal issues were instantly put on hold. A fire on a spaceship could be deadly even in his own time, let alone on an isolated, fragile vessel like the *Lewis & Clark*. This far out from Earth, with no Starfleet to rescue them, evacuation was not an option. The escape pod was only intended for near-Earth disasters. Out here, there was no hope of recovery and nowhere to flee to. They could end up stuck on a burning ship.

I don't understand, Kirk thought. *This wasn't in the history tapes.*

Then again, neither was he.

"Move it!" he ordered as they both went into red alert mode. Pushing off from him, Fontana dived for the hatch. She placed her palm against it, testing the temperature, before cautiously sliding it open. An acrid smell invaded the compartment.

"Smoke," she reported.

Kirk smelled it, too. He lunged for the video-com. "Christopher to Command. What's happening?"

O'Herlihy's face appeared on the small screen. Thick gray smoke obscured his features. *"There's a fire in the mid-deck,"* he reported, coughing hoarsely. *"Downstairs!"*

Kirk recalled that O'Herlihy was working on the flight deck. Standard shipboard fire-prevention measures, drilled into Kirk back at the Academy, flashed through his brain. "Kill the ventilation system," he ordered, to slow the spread of the fire and smoke. Any flowing air currents would just speed up the danger. "And shut down all power to the mid-deck."

"I'm on it!" O'Herlihy rasped. *"Hurry!"*

"Hang on!" Kirk said. "We're on our way."

Smoke was the immediate threat, he realized, even before the flames. In this confined environment, suffocation was a very real danger unless they took precautions in time. After all, they couldn't exactly throw open a window.

"Respirators!" he called out to Fontana.

"Way ahead of you!" She unclasped a blue plastic case from a bulkhead and extracted a rubberized full-face breathing apparatus attached to a portable oxygen canister. He expected her to don it herself, but instead, she flew it across the room to him. "Catch!"

He snatched the mask out of the air. "What about you?"

"There's another one in my compartment." She flew out into the corridor. "Be right with you. Don't wait for me!"

There wasn't time to argue the point. He secured the mask to his face and made sure the seal was airtight. A toggle initiated the oxygen flow, and he breathed deeply of the uncontaminated air before exiting his quarters and heading for the hatch to the lower level. Smoke was already wafting up from below. He clicked on an attached searchlight to make his way.

He heard someone coughing downstairs. *Zoe!*

He dived headfirst through the hatch into the rec area and looked around hurriedly for the stowaway. The fans had gone silent, slowing the smoke's progress, but a sooty haze still made it hard to see.

"Zoe!" he called out, but the mask muffled his voice. "Where are you?"

At first, he couldn't find her, and he feared she was passed out or worse, but then she swam out of the smoke toward him. A wet rag was wrapped around the bottom half of her face, making her look like an old-time bandit. Sweat gleamed on her bare arms and legs, as though she had been working out on the treadmill. Her dark eyes were watering from the smoke. Despite the rag, he could hear her gasping for breath.

He fumbled with the straps on his mask, intending to share his oxygen with her, but Fontana beat him to the punch. Joining him in the smoke-filled compartment, she thrust a spare respirator at Zoe. Her own mask was already affixed to her face. He guessed that she had acquired the third unit from O'Herlihy's quarters.

Good thinking, Kirk thought.

Zoe pulled the mask over her head. Kirk checked quickly to make sure that it was working. She gave him an encouraging thumbs-up, then saluted Fontana, who more than deserved it. The fact that Fontana, of all people, had possibly saved Zoe's life was not lost on him. That was worth a commendation or two, as far as he was concerned.

Unfortunately, they still had the fire to deal with.

The respirators made verbal communication difficult, so they had to rely on hand signals. Kirk located a fire extinguisher and indicated that Fontana should grab one, too. Leading the way, he pushed off toward the command module. Zoe started to follow him, but Fontana held up her hand and pointed back at the hab emphatically. Her message was clear: *Stay here.*

She slammed the hatch shut, sealing Zoe in the hab,

and trailed Kirk into the murky vestibule leading to the command module. A blast of intense heat hit Kirk as they cautiously approached the open hatch at the opposite end of the tunnel. His eyes widened behind his mask.

The blaze was worse than he had feared.

Unrestrained by gravity, a bright blue fireball, at least a foot in diameter, spread out from the center of the mid-deck, scorching the surrounding minilabs and payload racks. The roaring inferno fed eagerly on the ship's air supply, throwing off fiery orange sparks and gouts of flame in all directions. Irreplaceable lab equipment crackled and burned. Chemical reagents in airtight containers exploded, blowing apart overheated cabinets. Rubber gloves bubbled and melted. A sealed containment box cracked, releasing toxic fumes. The bulkheads blackened alarmingly.

He briefly considered sealing off the module and venting its atmosphere to extinguish the fire, but the hatch door was already too hot to touch—and O'Herlihy was trapped one deck above. They could seal off the vestibule at the other end, try to contain the blaze to the command module, but what about O'Herlihy? Kirk wanted to call out to the man, find out if he was okay, but he couldn't remove his respirator mask. He could only hope that the endangered scientist was still alive and that they wouldn't have to sacrifice him for the good of the ship.

Here's hoping it doesn't come to that, Kirk thought.

He flew as close to the hatchway as he could, feeling the heat of the blaze through his mask and jumpsuit, and hefted the bright orange fire extinguisher into position. He wondered briefly what they used in the twenty-first century to fight fires. Carbon dioxide? Nitrogen? A more advanced compound? Whatever it was, he prayed it was effective.

Before he could aim the nozzle at the fire, however, Fontana tapped him on the shoulder to get his attention. She used her hands to pantomime a missile flying back the way they'd come.

Right, Kirk thought. In zero gravity, the spray from the fire extinguisher would act as a thruster, propelling him in the opposite direction. They needed to brace themselves securely first. But how?

An idea occurred to him. Putting his extinguisher aside, he wedged his feet beneath a guide rail, grabbed a nearby truss with one hand, and wrapped his other arm around Fontana's waist. Getting the idea, she braced herself against him and aimed her own extinguisher at the conflagration. She twisted the nozzle.

A spray of white fire-retardant foam shot from the nozzle, the unleashed pressure driving her backward into Kirk. Grunting, he absorbed the impact and held fast while she emptied the extinguisher into the heart of the fireball. Steam rose from the flames, adding to the smoky chaos. Burned foam splattered the walls, floor, and ceiling.

But the fire kept on burning. To Kirk's alarm, he

saw globules of molten metal boiling off the charred bulkheads. Sparks erupted from exploding terminals. His heart sank. There was no containment field outside the ship to protect them in the event of a hull breach. If the fire burned through the outer hull, they would vent their atmosphere whether they wanted to or not. Explosive decompression would blow them all out into the vacuum.

They needed to kill this fire!

Fontana's extinguisher sputtered. The spray slowed to a trickle, before dying out entirely. She shook it angrily, but it was no use; the entire contents of her extinguisher had barely made a dent in the inferno. Chucking the empty container aside, she claimed Kirk's extinguisher and resumed her efforts. A fresh supply of foam battled the blaze.

Keep it up, Kirk thought, holding on to her against an equal and opposite reaction to the spray. Peering over her shoulder, he watched anxiously to see if the second helping of foam was doing any good. For a second, he wondered what had started the fire, then pushed the question aside. They could worry about that later, if and when they saved the ship.

A hatch opened in the ceiling above the mid-deck. More foam sprayed down from the upper level, joining Fontana's efforts. Combined, the twin sprays attacked the blaze from different angles.

O'Herlihy, Kirk realized, relieved to discover that the other man had not suffocated yet. But the ceiling separating the flight deck from the fire was in trouble. Kirk watched in dismay as the flames ate away at the bulkheads. Molten steel sprayed from the ceiling, weakening it. A sudden gout of flame lunged at the open hatch, forcing O'Herlihy to slam it shut again. He was alive, but for how much longer?

Fontana let loose with the extinguisher. Kirk wasn't sure, but it looked as if she might finally be making progress. The flames and sparks retreated, compacting back into the central fireball, which began to dim in intensity, going from blue-hot to red to orange . . .

That's it, Kirk thought, feeling a surge of hope. *You've got it on the ropes. Don't stop.*

The extinguisher ran out of foam.

"Dammit!" he cursed inside his mask, even as Fontana hurled the empty canister away in anger. He shared her frustration. Just when it looked as if they were on the verge of extinguishing the blaze!

Was there time to go searching for another extinguisher? Kirk doubted it. He glanced back at the tunnel behind him. If they hurried, there might still be time to seal off the vestibule and the command module. Had the moment come to sacrifice the module and O'Herlihy?

Kirk had faced this decision before, during ion storms and radiation leaks back aboard the *Enterprise.* Sometimes a captain had to jettison a pod or seal off a deck to save his ship, even if unlucky crew members had to pay the price. But it never got any easier.

I'm sorry, Marcus, he thought. *But we're running out of options.*

He heard a metallic bump behind him. Glancing back over his shoulder, he saw a petite, shadowy figure rushing toward them through the smoke. Zoe flew awkwardly out of the haze, clumsily bearing a third fire extinguisher. The metal canister smacked noisily against the side of the tunnel. She thrust the extra extinguisher at them.

Kirk could have kissed her.

Fontana snatched the canister from Zoe. She opened the valve and delivered a foamy coup de grâce to the blaze. To Kirk's relief, the third extinguisher seemed to do the trick. Fontana kept on spraying until the foam completely smothered what was left of the fire and didn't stop until she exhausted the new canister's supply. By now, there was more foam than embers floating through the blackened mid-deck. Kirk let out a sigh of relief.

That had been a close one!

Zoe applauded their success, clapping her hands loudly. She started to take off her mask, but Kirk signaled her to wait. There was still too much free-floating smoke and ash; they needed to give the ship's air filters a chance to scrub the atmosphere thoroughly.

Letting go of Fontana, he squeezed past her to inspect the charred ruins. The mid-deck, which had primarily served as the ship's onboard laboratory, had been gutted by the fire. Loose debris and foam drifted amid the wreckage. Kirk doubted that they would be conducting any more experiments there.

Could have been worse, he thought. *We could have lost the hab or the flight deck. Or maybe even the engines.*

But one troubling question remained. What—or who—had started the fire?

"Take a deep breath," the doctor instructed.

The fans were churning noisily as O'Herlihy checked out Kirk and Zoe in the infirmary. Paper filter masks, clasped over their mouths and nostrils, had replaced the more cumbersome respirators. The air was getting cleaner by the hour, but they still needed to avoid inhaling any lingering smoke or soot. Kirk sat on the examination pad, while O'Herlihy applied a cold stethoscope to his bare chest. Kirk breathed evenly.

"Not bad," the doctor pronounced. "Your lungs sound clear enough. Looks like you got that respirator on in time." He put away his stethoscope. "But I'm going to want to check everyone's blood-oxygen levels regularly for the next forty-eight hours at least. Lord knows what sort of fumes and contaminants have gotten into the air."

They had all washed and changed into fresh clothing, rather than risk spreading more soot and ash through the ship's atmosphere. Sometime soon they would have to scrub down the mid-deck and the rest of the ship to contain the contamination. This was going to be a laborious and painstaking task, but there was no way around it. Left alone, the residue from the fire would make it into their air supply and their lungs.

"No problem, Doctor." Kirk pushed away from the pad. "I'm just glad you're still around to look after us. For a while there, I was afraid we had lost you."

"I was worried about that myself," O'Herlihy said. "Thank God for that fire alarm. I might not have even noticed the smoke otherwise. As it was, I barely had time to secure a respirator and close the hatch."

That wouldn't have been enough if they hadn't managed to put out the fire, Kirk knew. "So, you have no idea how it started?"

O'Herlihy shook his head. "I was engrossed in my work, completely oblivious, when the alarm went off. Next thing I knew, smoke was billowing into the flight deck."

"Weird," Zoe commented. "Who knew this ship was a fire trap?"

She floated nearby, sipping water through a tube. Kirk had insisted that the doctor examine her and Fontana first, since he had donned his respirator before them. Zoe was still coughing occasionally, and the doctor wanted to keep a closer eye on her, but apparently, there was no immediate cause for alarm. It seemed they had all managed to come through the crisis without any serious burns or injuries. Kirk figured they owed that to their prompt response to the fire and a hefty dose of luck.

"It's not supposed to be," he said. "Something here doesn't smell right, and I don't mean the smoke."

"You can say that again," Fontana said, rejoining them in the rec area. She had insisted on investigating the site of the fire the second the doctor had given her a clean bill of health. She carried a blackened steel cylinder that looked as if it had been baked inside and out. The cylinder was wrapped in a clear plastic bag to keep any charred residue out of the air. "Take a look at this."

O'Herlihy squinted at her burden. "Is that one of the spare oxygen generators?"

The device, which was roughly the size of a wastebasket, was intended to supplement the ship's life-support system in the event of an emergency or a temporary power failure. The solid-fuel canisters contained a chemical mixture that, once activated, could generate several hours' worth of oxygen. They were stored at key locations throughout the ship.

"You bet," she said. "I can't be sure, but pending a more thorough investigation, it looks like this was the initial source of the fire."

Kirk peered at the cylinder. Certainly, it was capable of generating enough oxygen to produce a fireball of that magnitude and keep it going indefinitely. But surely it wasn't supposed to ignite like that.

"A malfunction?" He searched his memory, vaguely remembering a similar incident from the early days of space travel. "Didn't something like that happen before? On a Russian space station?"

"*Mir*, 1997." She gave Shaun a puzzled look. "Come on, Shaun. You know that. Every astronaut does. Don't tell me you're fuzzy on the details!"

Well, it was *nearly three centuries ago,* Kirk thought, *and there's been a lot of space history since then—at least, for some of us.*

"The point is, there's a precedent."

Fontana shook her head. "That was more than twenty years ago and shoddy Soviet-era craftsmanship to boot. The ones we're using today have been redesigned with safety in mind. You'd have to make a real effort to ignite one that way. It wouldn't just happen by accident."

"What are you saying?" Kirk asked, frowning. "That somebody tampered with the canister?"

"That's exactly what I'm saying, and I think we all know who the obvious suspect is."

She glared at Zoe, who suddenly realized that she was on the hot seat. She lowered her straw. "Whoa there, Detective Fontana! Are you implying that I'm responsible?"

"I'm not implying anything. I'm accusing you flat-out. Somebody sabotaged this ship, nearly killing us all, and you're the only one who doesn't belong here!"

"But I was nearly killed, too!" Zoe protested. "I helped you put out the fire!"

"So? You wouldn't be the first terrorist to be willing to sacrifice themselves. Maybe you just chickened out at the last minute."

"That's crazy!" Zoe said. "I wouldn't do something like that. I'm no terrorist!"

"That's what they all say," Fontana scoffed. She swung the bag containing the cylinder around, as if she was thinking of throwing it at Zoe. "Who else could have done it?"

Kirk put himself between the two women. "Hold on. Let's not rush to judgment here." He turned toward Fontana. "Alice, are you certain it was sabotage? Is there a chance that the generator ignited spontaneously?"

"Well, I'm no arson investigator," she conceded reluctantly, "but those things are supposed to be foolproof. The odds that one would just go off like that must be a hundred to one. They've been carefully designed *not* to do that."

She had a point, Kirk realized, but he knew from experience that even the most reliable technology could malfunction sometimes. Like the transporters back on the *Enterprise,* for example. Those had actually split him in two once. And on another occasion, they had transported him to a mirror universe. A primitive oxygen generator igniting by accident seemed fairly plausible by comparison.

"What do you think, Marcus?" he asked.

"I hate to say it," the doctor answered, "but Alice may be right. Zoe's motives and background are iffy. We don't really know why she smuggled herself aboard." He spoke more in sorrow than in anger. "This whole business is suspicious."

"What?" Zoe sounded hurt and surprised. "*Et tu, Doc?*"

"I'm sorry, Zoe," he replied. "But you *are* a stowaway. And oxygen generators don't just ignite themselves."

"I never trusted you," Fontana snarled. "And it looks like I was right all along."

Zoe grabbed Kirk's shoulder and spun him around to face her. "Please, Skipper! Don't listen to them. You've known me for months now. You know I wouldn't do something like this. That's not me!"

His gut told him she was telling the truth, but that wasn't good enough, not when the safety of the ship was at stake. He couldn't take the chance that she was more dangerous than she seemed. Another "malfunction" like that could kill them all.

"I'm sorry," he told her. "But you're going back into the airlock, for the duration this time."

"But I'm innocent! You know I am!"

"Maybe so," he said grimly. "But that's for a full forensic examination to determine, maybe back on Earth. In the meantime, I can't have a suspected saboteur running loose on my ship." He took her by the arm. "Fontana, please help me escort the prisoner to the brig."

"With pleasure," she said.

Seventeen

"It's dead, Mr. Spock. As the proverbial doornail."

Montgomery Scott stepped away from the inert probe, which had been beamed directly to a force-shielded laboratory pod. In an emergency, the entire pod could be jettisoned into space to avoid harm to the rest of the ship. Antigrav lifts suspended the massive probe above the floor. A battery of specialized scanners, far more powerful and sophisticated than a standard tricorder, were aimed at the relic. Data from the scanners scrolled across a wall screen at the opposite end of the pod. Spock studied the data, which appeared to confirm Mr. Scott's colorful diagnosis.

"I have to agree with Mr. Scott," Qat Zaldana added. She faced the screen alongside the two men. "We've been studying the probe for hours now, and all indications are that it's completely inoperative. Its internal components are nothing but slag. Its memory banks are fused." She looked away from the screen to the blackened wreck itself. "Honestly, from the looks of things, it's a miracle that the probe made it to this system at all. It's been through a lot."

"Aye," Mr. Scott agreed. "There are radiation burns, microfractures in the hull, fused circuits, even traces of extreme phase changes on the quantum level." He whistled at the extent of the damage. "This thing was built to last, you can tell that even now, but it's taken a heap of punishment over who knows how long. We're talking a couple of level-twelve ion storms at the very least, disruptor fire, solar flares, maybe even a brush with a black star or two."

"I see."

Spock did not find the engineer's report encouraging. He had hoped that the combined efforts of Mr. Scott and Qat Zaldana would yield some insights into the probe's mission and origins, as well as some clue to its connection to the current crisis.

"Did you learn anything of use?" he inquired.

"Not really," Qat Zaldana confessed. "To be honest, even if its internal workings were still intact, I'm not sure I'd be able to make head or tail of it. I'm no engineer like Mr. Scott here, but even I can tell that we're dealing with technology that's way beyond anything the Federation or its peers have come up with yet." A rueful chuckle escaped her veil. "I feel like a medieval astrologer trying to make sense of a crashed Romulan bird-of-prey that was burned to a crisp on its way down."

Spock sympathized with the challenge. He was tempted to examine the probe himself but doubted that he would find anything that Qat Zaldana or Mr. Scott had missed. *Perhaps later,* he mused, *when the time comes to investigate the captain's fate.* At the moment, however, he had more pressing matters to attend to.

"We can take the bloody thing apart piece by piece," Mr. Scott volunteered, "but I canna guarantee it will do any good. Not in time to help those poor souls on Skagway, at any rate."

Spock nodded. "Very well. It appears that the probe will not provide an answer to our present dilemma. Let us put it aside for future study while we prepare the *Enterprise* to take on as many evacuees as possible. Mr. Scott, please see to it that all available cargo areas and recreational facilities are converted to temporary living quarters and that the ship's life-support capabilities are operating at peak efficiency. We have a long way to go and a good many refugees to accommodate."

The nearest starbase was more than three weeks away. Spock mentally calculated how many extra passengers the ship could support for that period of time, depending on various controllable factors. The numbers were not encouraging.

"What about the others?" Qat Zaldana asked. "The ones you can't evacuate?"

"The *Enterprise* will remain to protect the colony for as long as it endures," he promised her. "You, of course, are welcome to remain aboard until we reach a safer harbor."

"Thank you," she said somberly, "but I'll have to think about that. It's a hard decision, like being a passenger on the *Titanic* or the *Solar Queen*. Do you take a spot in the lifeboats or not? And if you do, how do you live with yourself afterward?"

"That is an emotional question. I cannot help you answer it," Spock said. "I can only say that it would be a great loss if your intellect and scientific expertise were not preserved."

"That's nice of you to say, Mr. Spock, but . . . let me think about it. I'll give you my answer when the time comes."

Spock respected her wishes. There was still time, although not as much as he would have preferred. They now had twenty hours before Skagway entered the inner rings; he hoped to have all of the evacuees aboard by then. He wondered briefly what he would do in her place. Would it be logical to sacrifice himself to save another?

Possibly, depending on the circumstances. He had faced that choice before, as when he and Kirk and McCoy had been subjected to the Vians' experiments in the Minervan system or when he had piloted a shuttle into the nucleus of a destructive space amoeba, but those had been matters of duty to the ship and his fellow officers. The needs of the many had outweighed the needs of the one. That did not necessarily apply in the case of Qat Zaldana and her fellow colonists.

He could only hope that she would choose to save herself.

Eighteen

"Okay. It's decided, then. We're going home."

Less than twenty-four hours after the fire, Kirk presided over a meeting on the flight deck. The mid-deck below had been meticulously scrubbed, but a smoky odor still wafted up from the scorched wreckage. Kirk and Fontana were strapped into the pilots' seats, while O'Herlihy drifted restlessly around the compartment. Zoe was locked up in the airlock at the other end of the ship. Kirk hoped she was comfortable. He still wasn't convinced that she was responsible for the fire.

"No surprise there," Fontana said. "We probably should have turned back days ago."

The nearly catastrophic fire had been the last straw as far as Houston was concerned. The decision had been made to cut the mission short, seven days early, and head back to Earth. Mission Control had already worked out a new flight plan, which had been uploaded to the ship's computers. Granted, Earth was still three months away, but Houston wanted the ship back as soon as possible, before anything else could go wrong.

From what Kirk gathered, NASA was still working overtime to keep all of the unexpected complications out of the press.

No wonder I've never heard of them, he thought. *It was all covered up.*

"The hell with that!" O'Herlihy swore. "It's not fair! We haven't finished our studies yet. What with all the commotion, we've barely even begun our surveys of Saturn's magnetosphere, not to mention Titan and Enceladus and the other moons." He turned toward the pilots, frustration written all over his face. "Are we sure we can't get NASA to reconsider? Even with the loss of all that equipment in the mid-deck, there is still plenty to be done out here. Just think of all we could accomplish if we complete our mission!"

Kirk sympathized with the scientist's disappointment. This had been a once-in-a-lifetime opportunity for him. "I know how you feel, Marcus, but we've taken an important first step here. Future missions will carry on in our footsteps, count on it."

He wished he could tell the other man that this was hardly the end of humanity's exploration of Saturn and its moons and that someday there would be thriving colonies out this way. Kirk had recently spent an enjoyable layover on Titan during his most recent visit to Earth. The outer solar system was home to millions of intelligent beings in his time, not all of them human. The historic voyage of the *Lewis & Clark* had been just the beginning.

Fontana stared at him. "You're taking this pretty philosophically," she said. "Frankly, I expected you to make more of a fuss, instead of waxing eloquent about the future like this." Her eyes narrowed. "It's not like you."

Kirk winced inwardly. Not for the first time, he wished that she hadn't known the real Shaun Christopher quite so intimately. It wasn't making his imposture any easier.

"Look, I'm not happy about this, either, but I can see Houston's point of view." He ticked off the reasons on his fingers. "The stowaway, the alien probe, the unexpected changes in Saturn's rings and weather patterns, the fire, the possibility of arson. I can't blame them for wanting to play it safe and cut their losses. If I was in charge, I'd probably feel the same way."

In truth, he had profoundly mixed feelings about NASA's decision. While this mission was definitely proving more perilous than anyone could have possibly anticipated, he was in no hurry to be reunited with Shaun's friends and family. Trying to fool just his fellow astronauts, and especially Fontana, had been tricky enough. How on Earth, literally, was he going to face Shaun's kids? Not to mention John Christopher.

What if Shaun's father recognizes me somehow?

"I suppose." Fontana sounded skeptical. "Well, if nothing else, I guess you'll be back in time for Rory's birthday."

He took her word for it. "Yes, that's a definite plus,"

he said, pretending to be excited by the prospect. Changing the subject, he tried to console O'Herlihy. "Look at it this way, Doctor. You're going to get to see your wife and daughter a week early."

"Yes, that's true enough," O'Herlihy said, rather less enthusiastically than one might expect. The man's muted reaction struck Kirk as out of character; he chalked it up to the scientist's understandable disappointment at not being allowed to complete his work. "It's just such a waste," O'Herlihy lamented. "Three months in transit, and all those years of planning and preparation, only to turn back early?" He slammed a fist into his palm. "What difference could a few more days make?"

Kirk couldn't remember ever seeing O'Herlihy so agitated. He wondered if the stress of this tumultuous voyage was finally getting to the man. Perhaps it was just as well that they were calling the mission short.

"I'm sorry, Doctor," he said firmly. "The decision is final."

He turned his chair toward the navigation controls in order to review their new flight plans. NASA had needed to make adjustments to allow for the changing positions of both the ship and Earth. The impulse engines could make up the difference once they were under way.

Fontana unstrapped herself from her seat and came up behind him. For a second, Kirk feared another romantic overture, but he realized that was unlikely

with O'Herlihy present. Still, it was also unlikely that
he could avoid being alone with her for the next three
months. He wondered how long he could resist her and
if he really wanted to.

At times like this, a warp drive could come in handy.

"What about you?" he asked her casually. "You
looking forward to seeing your dog again?" He was not
about to mistake her pet for a child again. "I imagine
Gus will give you quite the tail-wagging welcome when
you get back."

"Well done," she said acidly. "You got his name
right."

An edge to her voice tipped him off that something
was wrong, but he was still caught off-guard when she
spun his chair away from the controls and locked her
elbow around his neck, catching him in a choke hold.
Gasping, he grabbed her arm and tried to tug it away
from his throat. Despite months in zero gravity, her
grip was formidably strong. Had she been working
out that much, or had they both lost equal amounts of
muscle tone?

"Don't even think about touching those controls,
mister!" she growled. "I don't know who you are, but
you are *not* Shaun Geoffrey Christopher!"

"Alice!" O'Herlihy reacted in shock. "What are you
doing? Have you lost your mind?"

"This isn't Shaun!" she insisted. "I know it sounds
insane, but you've got to believe me!" Her legs floated
in the air as she anchored herself to Kirk's neck,

squeezing hard. "Rory's birthday is tomorrow. The *real* Shaun would know that!"

O'Herlihy hovered impotently, confused by Fontana's accusations. "Shaun?"

Kirk realized that his cover was blown, unless he could convince O'Herlihy that Fontana was mistaken. He stopped struggling, reasoning that the real Shaun would want to talk to his crew, not fight them.

"Listen to me," he wheezed, despite the pressure on his windpipe. "You've got this all wrong. I'm not an impostor!"

"Oh, yeah?" she taunted him. "Then tell me something only the real Shaun would know. Where was the first place we made love?"

Kirk had no idea. "Your place?"

"Nice try," she said bitterly. She didn't volunteer the correct answer, not that it mattered. Hurt and anger spilled from her voice. Obviously, she didn't care who knew about their history now. "That probe did something to his brain, Marcus. That's when this all started. I didn't want to believe it, but . . ." She tightened her painful hold on his throat. "Who are you, and what did you do to Shaun?"

He wished he could tell her. She deserved the truth, but there was too much at stake. He couldn't risk changing history by telling her the truth. Her broken heart was the price for preserving the future.

"My memory," he squeaked. "I lost my memory, that's all. I didn't want you to know—"

"Bullshit!" She yanked his head back. "You're not Shaun. You're someone else!"

"Stop it, Alice!" O'Herlihy flew toward them. "You're choking him!"

"Tough!" She loosened her grip slightly, just enough for Kirk to breathe. "Trust me, Marcus. We're not talking mere amnesia here. Get me some restraints."

O'Herlihy hesitated, clearly not sure what or whom to believe, despite Kirk's obvious lapses in memory. "Talk to me, Shaun. Tell me she's wrong."

"I'm sorry, Doctor," Kirk said, panting. "I should have told you the truth about the holes in my memory, but I was afraid you'd relieve me of command."

"Liar!" Fontana said. "Don't listen to him, Marcus. You must have noticed the change in him, too. You know Shaun. Is this him?"

"I don't know." The doctor wavered, trying to keep up. "What are you suggesting? Some manner of alien mind control?"

"You got a better explanation?" She appealed to the other man. "We can't trust him, Marcus. That probe did something to him. Even if you don't believe he's someone else, you have to realize he's not right in the head. He's been lying to us for days. Hell, for all we know, *he* started the fire!"

"Not Zoe?"

"If only!" Fontana said. "God, do I wish I could lay this all on her, but I can't!"

Kirk spied her reflection in the cockpit window.

Her eyes gleamed wetly. "No," he said hoarsely. "I was with you when the fire started, remember?"

"Big deal. You could have set a fuse or added some sort of slow-acting reactant to the chemical slurry." She choked back a sob. "The restraints, Marcus? Please!"

"All right." He surrendered. "Give me a minute."

On a vessel where loose objects and utensils tended to drift freely unless tied down, there was no shortage of bungee cords and Velcro straps on hand. Under Fontana's watchful gaze, the doctor bound Kirk's wrists and ankles together, then undid the straps binding him to the pilot's seat. Kirk did not put up a fight. This wasn't like being taken prisoner by the Klingons or the Romulans. Fontana wasn't wrong; he *was* an impostor who didn't belong there. She was just doing her duty. And even if he could overpower the two astronauts somehow, what then? He could hardly hijack a historic NASA space mission!

At the moment, all he could do was keep his mouth closed and hope for the best.

Where are you, Spock? I could use a hand here.

Fontana yanked him roughly away from the flight controls and propelled him across the flight deck like a weightless sack of potatoes. He slammed into a hard steel bulkhead at the rear of the compartment. Dazed, he winced as she tethered him tightly to a ladder leading down to the mid-deck.

"No need to be so rough," he said. "I'm not going anywhere."

"You bet you're not." She pushed back to inspect her work. "So, you ready to talk yet?"

"I'm not sure what else I can say. You seem to have made up your mind . . . unfortunately."

"Don't make this about me. You're the guilty party here."

Kirk tried his restraints. There was no give in them. Fontana had known what she was doing.

"I know you think you're doing the right thing," he said. "I respect that."

"Screw your respect!" She yanked John Christopher's dog tags from his neck, snapping the chain. "You don't deserve to wear these!" She clenched her fist around the tags. "God, when I think that I almost . . ." She couldn't bring herself to complete the sentence.

"I told you it was complicated," he said.

O'Herlihy cleared his throat. "What now?" he asked, sounding defeated. "What are we to do with him?"

"Throw him in the airlock with the other trespasser, what else?" She chuckled bitterly. "You'll like that, won't you? I've seen the way you look at her, ever since the probe. That was another giveaway, incidentally. Shaun wasn't interested in her that way, but you were. I could tell. And then, of course, things were different between us."

Hell hath no fury like an astronaut scorned, Kirk thought wryly. He should have known the messy love triangle would blow his cover. No doubt Spock would have something pithy to say about the folly of human emotions.

"I'm sorry," he said sincerely. "I didn't want you to get hurt."

"Well, it's too damn late for that, isn't it?"

She unhooked him from the ladder and shoved him toward the hatch. "Come on, Marcus. Help me get him to the brig. I want this bastard out of my sight!"

Kirk couldn't blame her one bit. The whole situation was spiraling out of control, not unlike Saturn's rings had been. Now he was looking at three months of captivity while he tried to figure out what to do next and worried about his real ship, somewhere far in the future.

If I never get stuck in the past again, it will be too soon!

Nineteen

"I want to say you look like your father," McCoy commented, "but I guess that's not really the case."

"Tell me about it," Shaun said. His fingers explored the unfamiliar contours of Captain Kirk's face. It was like a sore he couldn't stop picking at. He supposed he ought to be thrilled to have a newer, younger body, but he didn't feel that way. He wanted his old body back, and he wanted out of this so-called sickbay. He paced back and forth across the futuristic hospital room. It felt strange not to be floating. "I still can't believe you actually met my dad."

"Time travel." The doctor snorted. "Don't get me started."

Shaun wasn't sure how McCoy could be so blasé about it. Personally, he was still trying to get used to the idea that he was really hundreds of years in the future and in another man's body, no less. Not that his hosts had actually let him see much of that future. He had been confined to quarantine for what felt like days.

"How are you holding up?" the doctor asked. He seemed a decent sort, with a distinct hint of Georgia in his Southern drawl. Shaun found him easier to deal with than that alien iceman, Spock. If nothing else, McCoy had a much better bedside manner.

"Besides going stir-crazy?" Shaun gazed at the sliding door cutting him off from the rest of the ship. He had tried to open it, but apparently, it had been programmed not to release him. Ditto for the guards posted outside. "C'mon, Doc. You can't keep me cooped up here forever."

"I know," McCoy said. "But bear with us. Like I explained before, we need to limit your exposure to our time if we ever want to return you to your own place in history. We learned that lesson with your father."

"How's that going, anyway? Am I going home any-time soon?"

The doctor's pained expression warned Shaun not to expect good news. "To be honest, that's sort of on the back burner at the moment. I'm afraid we're in the middle of an urgent mission right now, and that's caused an unavoidable delay in dealing with your situation."

"What sort of mission?"

"You know I can't tell you that, for your own good, as well as history's."

"But it's serious, right? An emergency?"

He had not missed the yellow alert lights flashing inside sickbay or the obvious tension in McCoy and Nurse Chapel. Even Spock seemed slightly on edge in his own spooky Vulcan way. Shaun could tell something was up. The *Enterprise* felt like Area 51 right after the DY-100 was hijacked.

"Yes," McCoy admitted. "But as soon as this matter is settled, one way or another, you'll be our top priority." He tapped Shaun's chest. "Trust me, we want to get our captain back where he belongs."

Shaun believed him. "And you really think he's back in my time, in my body?"

"That's the theory, believe it or not. And if Spock thinks there's something to it, then I wouldn't want to bet against him." McCoy heaved a sigh. "He's annoying that way."

Not for the first time, Shaun tried to imagine this James T. Kirk character back aboard the *Lewis & Clark* with Fontana, O'Herlihy, and Zoe. Everybody seemed to think Kirk was a stand-up guy and a first-rate captain, but Shaun still didn't like the idea of somebody else taking over his mission and his body. Nobody would tell him what history recorded about the Saturn mission. Shaun hoped that wasn't a bad sign.

Take care of my ship, Kirk. Whoever you are.

He plopped down into a seat by his bed. He was still getting used to gravity again, but at least Kirk's body had not been debilitated by months of weightlessness. The *Enterprise*'s "artificial gravity" had just caught him by surprise before.

"What am I supposed to do in the meantime, Doc?"

He had always been an active guy. Just sitting around doing nothing was driving him nuts. His fingers drummed impatiently on the arm of the chair. His feet tapped against the floor.

"I'll see what I can do about the library viewer," McCoy said, calling his attention to a portable TV screen by the bed. The monitor was attached to a movable arm. "We can't give you full access to the ship's library, for obvious reasons, but we should be able to set up a filter program that will allow you to call up a wide variety of recreational reading and programs."

Shaun got the idea. "But nothing after 2020, right?"

"That's the idea," McCoy confirmed. "Of course, somebody else is going to have to program the filter. I'm just a simple country doctor, not a computer whiz."

Shaun wasn't sure he bought that. He guessed that everybody in this era knew more about computers than Bill Gates, Steve Jobs, and Sumi Lee put together.

"So, I'm stuck watching reruns for the duration?" Suspended animation on a sleeper ship sounded better. He shook his head. "Can't you even tell me if Buck Bokai beat DiMaggio's record?"

"'Fraid not," McCoy said. "I don't even know what that means." He shrugged. "Look at this as a chance to catch up with your reading."

"Now you sound like my ex-wife," Shaun said. Debbie had always urged him to read more. "You married, Doc?"

"Not anymore," McCoy said dourly.

Shaun recognized the tone. "Guess some things

never change, no matter what century it is. Sounds like we have that much in common."

His fingers beat out an impatient rhythm.

"You keep doing that," McCoy noted with a touch of professional interest. "A nervous tic?"

Shaun glanced down at his hand. He stopped tapping his fingers.

"Not that I'm aware of." He had barely noticed he was doing it. "And I'm pretty sure the space shrinks back at NASA would have called me on it before."

You didn't get placed in command of a seven-month mission to the other end of the solar system without a thorough psychiatric evaluation—or ten. Frankly, he didn't need to talk about his feelings and childhood issues ever again.

"So, this is something new?" McCoy asked.

Shaun felt as if he was back on the couch. What was it about doctors that made them think everybody was on the verge of going space-happy? Not that he wasn't entitled to a nervous breakdown right now, considering. He thought he was holding up pretty well given that he wasn't even himself anymore.

"I've just got this stubborn drumbeat stuck in my head," he tried to explain. "Like a catchy melody you can't shake, you know?"

At least the *Enterprise* didn't seem to be afflicted with Muzak. That was something, although he had to wonder what constituted easy listening in the twenty-third century. Lady Gaga was probably considered classical music these days.

"And how long has that been going on?" McCoy asked.

Shaun thought about it. His eyes widened. "Ever since that probe zapped me here," he realized. "Now that I think of it."

Glancing down, he saw that he had automatically starting drumming his fingers again. He fought to keep his feet from joining in.

"What the—?" He gazed anxiously at McCoy. "What does this mean, Doc?"

McCoy frowned. "The hell if I know."

An intercom whistled. *"Dr. McCoy,"* a female voice paged. *"Please report to the landing deck. The first wave of evacuees has arrived. Some of them require medical attention."*

"Evacuees?" Shaun echoed. That didn't sound good.

"Not your problem." McCoy pressed the speaker button on a wall-mounted intercom unit. "McCoy here. On my way." He headed for the exit, then paused to look back at Shaun. "You going to be okay here?"

"Sure," Shaun lied. Aside from being trapped in the future with an alien beat stuck in somebody else's head, he had nothing to complain about. "Go ahead. Do your job." He relocated to his bed and stretched out on it, staring at the ceiling. "I'm not going anywhere."

McCoy looked uncomfortable abandoning him. "I'll have Chapel look into that viewer," he promised.

The door slid open before him. Shaun caught a glimpse of a larger medical facility before the door *whoosh*ed shut again, closing him in. His spirits sank at the prospect of being cooped up with nothing but his thoughts for company. An overwhelming wave of homesickness, for his own time and place, washed over him. He wondered if he would ever see his friends and family again. In theory, his dad, his kids, and his crew had all been dead for centuries. He choked back a sob. A beautiful face surfaced from his memory.

Fontana, he thought. *Alice.*

He wished he could have said something to her before he disappeared.

Twenty

2020

"Feel like a bite?"

O'Herlihy ascended into the flight deck bearing a meal on a tray. Magnetic utensils clung to the reusable metal tray, which also held slots for various disposable foil and plastic containers. Fontana caught a whiff of rehydrated macaroni and cheese, along with freshly nuked apple cobbler. O'Herlihy had brought ketchup and Tabasco sauce, too. Life in space deadened the taste buds for some reason, so most astronauts tended to pile on the condiments and seasonings to compensate. The sticky food stayed in place in zero g.

"Not really," she said. Dejected and not particularly hungry, she sat in the cockpit while reviewing the preflight checklist for their trip home, which was now scheduled for 0700 tomorrow. She was not looking forward to being the sole pilot for the next three months, let alone explaining to Houston why that was the case. She was still trying to figure out how to break the news to Mission Control that she had confined the ship's commander to the airlock on suspicion of being possessed by an alien probe.

They're going to think I've gone crazy, not Shaun.

"Eat something anyway," the doctor urged her. He sat down beside her, occupying her usual seat at the helm. "You need to keep your strength up. You've had a rough day."

"That's putting it mildly." The aroma from the food did little to restore her appetite; her stomach felt tied up in knots. Second thoughts tormented her. She fiddled anxiously with Shaun's father's dog tags. "You don't think I'm crazy, do you? We had to lock him up, right?"

"Honestly, I don't know," he said wearily, sounding appropriately saturnine. "This entire trip has been one shock after another. I feel like I'm at the end of my rope."

Fontana knew the feeling. This wasn't the carefully planned mission she had signed on for.

"He didn't even know his own kid's birthday!" she blurted, unsure whom exactly she was trying to convince. "On top of everything else, like forgetting my dog and the fire on the *Mir* and what we meant to each other . . ."

It felt odd speaking openly of her history with Shaun, but frankly, that was the least of her worries. A little scandal and gossip was nothing compared with what had happened to Shaun, whatever that was. She just wanted the old Shaun back.

"I can't explain any of that," O'Herlihy admitted, "unless the jolt from the probe really did wipe his memory clean. Electroshock is well known to induce various degrees of memory loss."

"No, it's more than that," she insisted. "I know Shaun, better than anyone on this ship, and that's not him. I can feel it in my gut, even though I know that doesn't sound very scientific."

"I fear we left conventional science and logic behind a long time ago," he said. "Perhaps when Saturn's rings started unraveling and then snapped back into place." He pushed the tray at her. "Really, Alice. You need to eat."

"I'm not hungry." She appreciated his concern, but food was the last thing on her mind right now. If anything, she felt sick to her stomach. She waved the tray away. "Maybe later, okay?"

"At least have some hot tea," he pressed. "To soothe your nerves."

"Fat chance." She found his solicitous attitude both amusing and annoying. "Stop clucking at me, Doc. You're in danger of becoming a cliché."

"Just drink the damn tea," he said patiently. "Doctor's orders."

She knew a losing battle when she saw one. "Yes, Mother." She accepted the sealed, microwave-safe bottle, which was warm to the touch. Conventional teacups were useless in space; you couldn't pour without gravity. She sipped the hot beverage through a straw. "Happy now?"

"Yes, thank you." He hooked the tray to the control panel in front of him. "For later, if you feel like it."

"We'll see."

She finished off the spicy tea, not quite recognizing the flavor. It had a peculiar aftertaste that she chalked up to the effects of zero gravity on her taste buds. Despite the doc's prediction, the tea did little to ease her anguished spirit. She couldn't stop thinking about Shaun and what might have become of him.

"Do you think they'll be able to fix him?" she asked. "Back on Earth?"

"I wish I knew. If you want, I can examine him again, once we're under way. But I'm not exactly equipped to perform brain scans out here. That may have to wait until we're back home."

Three months from now . . .

"I understand," she said glumly.

Fontana knew she had to face the possibility that the real Shaun, the one she'd loved, was gone forever, replaced by whatever impostor was wearing his face and body. She recalled kissing him in the airlock right before he jetted out to try to capture the probe. That was probably the last time she had seen the real Shaun.

At least I got to kiss him good-bye.

It was all too much. An overwhelming sense of exhaustion caught up with her, and she swayed unsteadily in her seat. Despite the lack of gravity, her limbs felt as if they were growing heavier by the moment. Her arms drifted limply at her sides. Bottled-up emotions bubbled up inside her, spilling out into the cockpit.

"Oh, Marcus! I'm not sure I can handle this. What if he's really gone for good?"

"Don't worry," he said in a comforting tone. Capturing her hand, he patted it gently. "It's all right. It will all be over soon."

Huh? What did he mean by that?

"Maarcusss . . . ?" She slurred his name, suddenly finding it hard to speak. Her tongue felt as if it was wrapped in foil, like one of the snacks on the meal tray. The tea bottle slipped free of her fingers. She felt groggy and light-headed. A jolt of panic briefly dispelled the fog enveloping her mind. She watched the loose bottle drift away.

The tea, she realized in shock. *It was doped.*

O'Herlihy had drugged her.

She tried to ask him why, but all she could manage was a single mumbled syllable. "Whyyy . . ."

"I'm sorry, Alice. I truly am." His mournful face blurred before her eyes. He plucked the tainted bottle from the air and returned it to the tray. His deep, sepulchral voice seemed to be coming from light-years away. "I'm proud to have served beside you and Shaun. You have to believe me."

The flight deck seemed to be spinning around her. Creeping shadows, as black as space, encroached on her field of vision. Her eyelids drooped.

"It's better this way," he said. "You won't feel a thing."

The darkness swallowed her up.

Twenty-one

"Skagway approaching the inner rings, sir."

Chekov once again manned his post on the bridge. Unfortunately, the situation had only worsened since his earlier attempts to defend the colony. As the errant moon neared the fringe of the rings, it came under assault from multiple vectors. There was no clear line of demarcation between the gap and the inner rings, so Skagway was already crossing into the path of orbiting debris. The potential for collisions increased, even as the barrage from the outer rings accelerated. Ice and dilithium crystals of varying sizes battered the lunar colony and the surrounding terrain. On the viewer, geysers of pulverized rock and ice erupted from the moon whenever a sizable meteor struck home. The dome's fading shields flickered ominously.

"I can see that, Ensign," Spock replied from the captain's chair. He spoke a bit more sharply than he intended; he had not slept in days, and fatigue was taking its toll on his Vulcan reserve. He frowned at the screen. The crisis had escalated even faster than he had calculated. The evacuation was not yet complete. "Maintain defensive fire."

Targeted widespread phaser salvos broke apart the boulder-sized ice balls into smaller particles that continued to slam into the moon and the vulnerable colony. Despite the crew's best efforts, an ever-increasing number of meteors made it past the phasers to hit the moon. The dome shuddered visibly under the assault. Hairline cracks began to show on its surface. Spock assumed that repair crews were frantically attempting to shore up the failing dome from the inside.

Nor was Skagway alone under siege. Although the *Enterprise* was cruising above the rings, it was still being buffeted by random debris escaping their orbits. The bridge rocked beneath Spock. Repeated impacts tested their deflectors. A blow to the port side of the saucer jarred him, almost throwing him from his seat. Over by the turbolift entrance, a yeoman stumbled against a rail. Her data slate clattered onto the floor.

"Shields at seventy-two percent," Chekov reported.

That was less than ideal, Spock noted, but his primary concern remained the colony, which was in a far more precarious situation than the *Enterprise*. He calculated that the dome had at most ninety minutes before it was breached beyond repair. While there were limited emergency shelters beneath the moon's surface, he suspected that few colonists, if any, would still be alive by the time Skagway made it through the inner rings to spiral into the turbulent atmosphere and crushing pressure of Klondike VI. In any event, the moon itself would soon be lost in the gas giant's swirling depths.

"Evacuation status?" he asked.

"Still under way," Qat Zaldana reported from the science station. She had volunteered to act as their liaison with the colony during the evacuation efforts. "Four hundred seventy-eight colonists are aboard, but there are still thirty-two more en route and waiting down on Skagway." She looked away from her monitors. "We're going as fast as we can, but this is a huge job. And that storm out there isn't making it any easier."

Spock appreciated the challenges involved. Shuttles had been employed around the clock to ferry the evacuees from Skagway to the *Enterprise*, but each shuttle could carry only twenty passengers at most. Tearful farewells at the spaceport had slowed the process, too, or so he was informed. Under the circumstances, however, he could hardly begrudge the colonists their emotions. He could only imagine what it would be like to lose one's home and family to a cosmic disaster. Not even a Vulcan could be unmoved by such a catastrophe.

"If only we could just beam those people aboard," Qat Zaldana lamented. "We'd be done by now."

"That would require lowering the colony's shields, as well as our own," Spock reminded her, "which is hardly advisable under the circumstances. Even leaving the shuttlebay doors unshielded during landings and departures constitutes a significant risk."

"I know," she said. "It's just so frustrating. We can't even take everybody as it is."

Per the governor's orders, children and adolescents had been evacuated first, followed by rank-and-file miners, assayers, technicians, clerks, and others who were not required to keep the colony functioning. Governor Dawson, her staff, emergency crews, and other essential personnel had chosen to remain at their posts until the end.

Spock was impressed by their courage and dedication in the face of certain death. There were those on Vulcan who did not understand why he chose to serve aboard a starship crewed primarily by humans. Many of his fellow Vulcans, he knew, regarded humans as regrettably illogical and questioned his willingness to live among them. Moments like this reminded him that there was more to the human race than their often flagrant emotionality and made him quietly proud of his human half.

"Continue evacuation procedures," he instructed. "Save as many as we can."

"Aye, sir," Uhura said. "*Columbus* reports that it is taking off from Skagway now with a fresh load of evacuees. *Galileo* is preparing to head back to the colony."

"Thank you, Lieutenant," Spock replied. "Urge them to exercise all necessary caution."

With the barrage of high-velocity particles increasing in intensity, the shuttle flights were growing steadily riskier. Already, the shuttles had been forced to blast their way through the hailstorm with their shields on full.

Qat Zaldana turned the science station over to Lieutenant Kwan, who had been standing by to assist her. She crossed the shaking bridge to the command module, holding on to the safety rails to keep from losing her balance. Tremors rocked the floor beneath her feet.

"Mr. Spock," she said quietly. "The moment has come. With your permission, I would like to board the last shuttle down to Skagway. Somebody else can take my place aboard the *Enterprise*."

He nodded. "Are you quite certain of your decision?"

"Yes, Mr. Spock. This is something I must do." Her veil concealed whatever emotions she might be experiencing. Her voice was as calm and steady as his own. "Please do not attempt to dissuade me."

"I would not presume to do so. You are not a member of this crew under my command. I respect your right to choose your own fate."

"Thank you for understanding." She made her way toward the turbolift. "It has been a pleasure working with you. Please thank Captain Kirk for me. I hope he will be himself soon."

Her remark struck Spock as curiously apropos. He arched an eyebrow. Had that been merely a casual turn of phrase, or did she know more than she ought to about the captain's unusual condition?

"Mr. Spock!" Kwan called from the science station. "I'm detecting multiple launches from the colony!"

"What?" The announcement snared Qat Zaldana before she could exit the bridge. She lurched unsteadily back to the rail and stared up at the viewer. "That can't be happening. There's only one shuttle due back."

But *Columbus* was not the only vessel departing the moon in a hurry. More than a dozen other vessels, ranging from shuttles to two-person prospector ships, lifted off from the battered hangars and landing pads surrounding the colony. Scouts, tugs, and ambulance ships fled the colony. Many of the ships were clearly not intended for anything more than a short jaunt about the moon itself, while others had been designed merely for mining the nearby rings. None of them was capable of making it to the nearest starbase or habitable planet. They had no place to go—except to the *Enterprise*.

"There's too many of them!" Chekov exclaimed. He cut off his phaser blasts for fear of striking one of the refugee ships. "We've no place to board all those vessels!"

"Nor do we have the capacity to take on excess refugees," Spock noted. "This is not an orderly evacuation."

"No," Qat Zaldana agreed. "This is panic. Blind desperation."

"Mr. Spock!" Uhura said. "A priority transmission from the governor."

He had expected something of the sort. "Put her through. Visual at fifty percent."

"Aye, sir."

The image on the viewer was split down the middle. Governor Dawson appeared on the left side of the screen, while a view of the frantic exodus occupied the right. She looked distraught and disheveled, her silver hair hanging loose across her face. An untreated bruise on her cheek was evidence of a recent accident or struggle. The lights flickered in her office. Spock heard shouting, sirens, explosions, and phaser fire in the background.

"Enterprise!" she addressed them. "We've lost control down here. My people are panicking. They don't want to be left behind." A loud crash off-screen caused her to flinch and look to one side before resuming her alert. "A mob stormed the spaceport, trampled over my security people. We believe they're heading your way."

"We are aware of the situation," Spock reported tersely. "But surely you realize that we cannot accommodate all of these extra refugees. Our life-support systems have their limits."

"I told them that, Mr. Spock," she said. "All they know is that you're their only hope." She sagged in her seat, looking utterly defeated. "I'm so sorry. We tried to reason with them, but they wouldn't listen. They broke into the armory and pushed past our lines. Many of our security people refused to fire on their own friends and family. People are terrified. They don't want to die."

Spock was forced to reassess his view of humanity. Vulcans would not have succumbed to panic and hysteria like this. It was not logical.

Or was it? It occurred to him that even a remote chance of survival was mathematically superior to no chance at all. Even if only a handful of the rioters made it to safety, there was at least the possibility that you or your loved ones might be among them. Seen from that perspective, a desperate attempt to force one's way onto the *Enterprise* was a perfectly logical choice, if not a very commendable one.

None of which made this particular complication any less vexing.

"I understand, Governor. I am confident that you and your people did your best." He contemplated the chaotic exodus on the other half of the screen. "It appears that this is our problem now."

"Don't judge them too harshly," Dawson said, apologizing for her people. *"They're not Starfleet, only ordinary miners and their families. They just want to live."*

"That may not be possible," he said. "Spock out."

Dawson's image disappeared. A full view of the latest crisis filled the screen. A disorganized, ragtag flotilla braved the storm to close on the *Enterprise*. They buzzed around the much larger starship like a swarm of Lakodonian gnats. Scanning the chaos, Spock spotted *Columbus* trying to weave its way through the congestion to get back to the *Enterprise*. Random vessels crowded the shuttle, no doubt hoping to squeeze past it into the shuttlecraft bay. *Columbus* executed evasive maneuvers, trying to shake its unwanted escorts, but the other craft stuck to it as though caught in its wake. They bounced and scraped against one another as they jockeyed for position. An older-model ferry, which looked as though it had been salvaged from a junkyard, lost power and fell behind.

"Mr. Spock! We're receiving dozens of hails," Uhura reported. She feverishly worked the communications console, looking almost, but not quite, overwhelmed by the flood of transmissions. Anguish showed on her features. "They're pleading to be allowed to board the *Enterprise*. Begging for their lives!"

Spock did not envy Uhura. "Issue a general announcement on all frequencies," he instructed. "Tell them to turn back to Skagway."

She complied with his orders, but her board continued to light up with incoming transmissions. "I'm trying, Mr. Spock. They're not listening!"

He chided himself for not fully anticipating the colonists' reckless behavior. It was not as though there were not historical precedents. The unfortunate images on the screen reminded him of the interplanetary "boat people" of ancient Blinogu, who had fled the imminent destruction of their planet in a fleet of flimsy solar-sailing vessels. Their desperate voyage, alas, had not ended happily. The Bline were now extinct.

"*Columbus* is hailing us," Uhura announced. "They're requesting new instructions."

On the viewer, the shuttle could be seen trying to make it through the debris and the refugee ships to get to the *Enterprise*. The other vessels hemmed *Columbus* in, often blocking Spock's view of the shuttle. He recalled that it was currently carrying eighteen authorized evacuees, plus a Starfleet pilot and a security officer. The shuttle crews had been kept small to make room for the evacuees.

"We can't open the space doors to the bay," Chekov realized aloud. "It would be a free-for-all. We'd be overrun!"

Spock had to agree. The situation immediately outside the ship was already untenable. Without any manner of space traffic control in effect, the various craft zipped past one another in a random fashion. A speeding prospector ship cut off a minishuttle in its haste to get ahead of the other refugees, nearly causing a collision. Two jostling scout ships grazed each other. The smaller ship's starboard thruster went flying off, sending the scout spinning out of control. Sulu gasped as the disabled ship tumbled past the *Enterprise,* barely missing its saucer section. Undaunted, the other scout joined the mob crowding *Columbus.*

"Madness," Qat Zaldana whispered, so low that possibly only Spock's ears could hear. "Sheer madness."

Spock considered his options. If necessary, he could order the *Enterprise* to warp away from Klondike VI, but that would wreak havoc on the many small vessels surrounding the ship and would also mean abandoning *Columbus* and its passengers. He was not yet ready to employ such drastic measures.

"Keep hailing them," Spock instructed Uhura. "Remind them that they are endangering the children already aboard."

"It's no good," she said, shaking her head. "Nobody is listening. They're all shouting, screaming, begging over one another." Wincing at the tumult, she fiddled with her earpiece to reduce the volume. "They're demanding that we let them board. They say they're not going to let us leave without them." She grimaced. "It's getting pretty ugly, Mr. Spock, and heartbreaking at the same time."

He was inclined to take her word for it. "Please disregard them, Lieutenant. Maintain an open frequency to *Columbus* instead." He recalled that Lieutenant Schneider was piloting the shuttle; she was an able pilot who had logged many hours in flight drills. "Tell them to stand by and be prepared for an immediate landing or beam-out."

He considered the probability that they could lower the *Enterprise*'s shields long enough to beam the shuttle's crew and passengers aboard. Was it worth exposing the entire ship to danger to rescue one last party of refugees? He did not dare dispatch *Galileo* to Skagway for another run. That would be foolhardy in the extreme.

"My apologies," he said to Qat Zaldana. "It appears that we will not be able to return you to the colony as you requested. Circumstances have changed."

"I could pilot my own shuttle," she reminded him.

"But we cannot risk opening the space doors to let

you leave." Spock wondered if a human would see Qat Zaldana's inability to sacrifice herself as a "silver lining." Dr. McCoy might think so, as would Captain Kirk, were he not lost in time. "In any event, the fact that we can no longer dispatch *Galileo* to retrieve more evacuees means that your presence will not cost anyone else a place aboard the *Enterprise*. You might as well survive."

She tilted her head. "Was that a joke, Mr. Spock?"

"Merely an observation," he replied. "The matter is out of our hands."

"We'll see," she said cryptically.

Before he could inquire what she meant, a more urgent dilemma presented itself.

"Hold on, everyone," Sulu warned. "We've got some bumpy weather coming up."

A thick patch of ring matter pelted the *Enterprise* and the swarm of flyers surrounding it. Repeated impacts rattled the bridge, but Spock was more concerned with *Columbus* and the other smaller spacecraft. He watched tensely as craggy chunks of ice, some nearly as large as the shuttle, invaded the already-crowded space outside the *Enterprise*. Lieutenant Schneider had her work cut out for her if she was going to avoid being struck by one or more frozen particles.

"Mr. Chekov," Spock said. "Can you clear a path for *Columbus*?"

"Negative, Mr. Spock." His fingers hovered over the firing controls. "There are too many other vessels in the way! I can't target the debris!"

Without phaser cover, *Columbus* was on its own. The shuttle rolled out of the way of an oncoming iceball that flew past its upside-down landing gear to barrel into a compact prospector ship on the other side of the shuttle. The unlucky prospector was smashed to pieces in a soundless collision that killed at least two colonists. Flying wreckage added to the hazards threatening the flotilla. A hijacked lunar transport received a severe gash along its stern. Vapor jetted from the breach before someone inside sealed the wound. The transport lost speed and maneuverability, falling away from the rest of the pack. Spock wondered if it would attempt to return to Skagway.

Unlikely, he decided. Nothing waited for them on the moon but certain annihilation.

"This is just the warm-up act," Sulu warned. "Sensors indicate that the main event is coming up any minute now."

The refugees were not going to turn back, Spock realized. Circling the *Enterprise,* pleading for sanctuary, they could not possibly withstand the hazardous environment they had rashly thrown themselves into. So far, fatalities had been minimal, but that had been more happenstance than anything else. The vulnerable flyers were at the mercy of the storm.

Unless . . .

"Mr. Chekov, expand our shields outward by one hundred sixty percent."

Startled, Chekov looked back at him. A baffled expression indicated that he was confused by his orders. "Excuse me, sir. Did I hear you correctly? Extending the deflectors that far out will severely diminish their strength and integrity."

"That is correct, Ensign." Spock knew that the shields had been designed to conform to the profile of the ship, adding a layer of protection akin to a secondary hull. Ordinarily, their protection seldom extended more than fifty meters beyond the ship's exterior plating. But these were not ordinary circumstances. "You have your orders."

"Aye, sir." Chekov resigned himself to his task. "Extending shields."

Spock moved to notify Engineering of his plan, but Mr. Scott responded even more quickly to the drastic change in the shields. An agitated brogue erupted from the intercom. *"Mr. Spock, what sort of games are ye playing up there? I canna believe what my readouts are telling me."*

Spock took the engineer's reaction in stride. It was to be expected. "No games, Mr. Scott. It has become necessary to expand our shields to encompass the space surrounding the ship."

"But that's not what they were built to do!" the engineer sputtered. *"As Dr. McCoy might say, are you out of your Vulcan mind?"*

Possibly, Spock thought. "Emulating the good doctor is unworthy of you, Mr. Scott. Please see to it that sufficient power is diverted to the task and that the deflector grid remains operational."

"I'll do my best, Mr. Spock, but that's going to put a

considerable strain on our resources. I'm not sure how long we're going to be able to manage this daft stunt of yours . . . sir."

"Your caveats are noted, Mr. Scott. Spock out."

On-screen, the results of his tactic were already visible. A force-field bubble, roughly following the contours of the *Enterprise,* now extended for approximately four hundred meters around the ship in every direction. The bubble was invisible except where the ubiquitous debris struck it, which was almost everywhere. Brilliant flashes of Cherenkov energy lit up the screen, making Spock grateful for his protective inner eyelids.

"Dim luminosity," he instructed. "Thirty-point-two percent."

For the moment, the refugee ships were safe within the *Enterprise*'s shields, but Spock knew that this was only a temporary solution. He needed to take advantage of the opportunity while he could.

"Shield status?"

"Thirty percent and holding," Chekov reported. "For now."

That will have to be enough, Spock judged. He activated the intercom. "Transporter rooms. Lock onto shuttle crew and passengers."

With the shuttle no longer outside the *Enterprise*'s shields, it was now possible to beam its endangered human cargo aboard. Unfortunately, this entailed abandoning *Columbus* and the last several evacuees waiting back on Skagway, but that could not be helped. The evacuation was over now. All that remained was to stand guard over Skagway until it reached its inevitable end. Spock hoped that those left behind would make good use of what little time they had left.

"Transporter rooms reporting, sir." Uhura was visibly relieved by the news. "The shuttle crew and passengers have been beamed aboard."

On the viewer, *Columbus* veered away from the *Enterprise*. Spock assumed that Lieutenant Schneider had set an automatic course that would reduce the chance of any unwanted collisions. The tugs and scouts that had been shadowing the shuttle broke away from it to stay close to the starship instead. Spock watched as *Columbus* headed away from both Skagway and the *Enterprise* before slowing to a stop against the force-field barrier. In time, it, too, would be sucked in by the planet's fluctuating gravity. A minor loss, compared with the epic tragedy facing the lunar colony.

"Shall I keep the shields extended, sir?" Chekov asked. "Now that our people have been beamed aboard?"

An excellent question, Spock mused. He was reluctant to abandon the refugee flotilla to its fate but wondered how long the *Enterprise* could be expected to shelter the fragile craft beneath its metaphorical wings. "Shield status?"

"Twenty-eight percent," Chekov said dolefully. "Eighty-five percent of generator output diverted to deflectors. Other systems operating below capacity."

The shields were consuming an excessive share of the ship's energy and resources. Spock decided to issue one final warning to the hijacked vessels swarming the *Enterprise*.

"Lieutenant Uhura, inform the refugees that no further evacuees will be brought aboard the *Enterprise*. Alert them, as well, that we will be withdrawing the protection of our shields in exactly ten minutes. They are strongly advised to return to the safety of the colony."

"Such as it is," Qat Zaldana said sadly.

"Yes," he confirmed. "Such as it is."

He hoped none of the ships would attempt to ram its way through the *Enterprise*'s space doors into the landing deck. "Mr. Chekov, be on the alert for boarders. Fire on any vessel on an approach track for the shuttle-bay."

"Aye, sir."

Proximity alarms sounded on the bridge.

"Mr. Spock!" Sulu called out. "I'm tracking a huge iceball . . . heading straight for us!"

He relayed the threat's coordinates to the main viewer. An immense white object filled the screen, dwarfing the other missiles around it. At first, Spock thought that Sulu might have accidentally ordered full magnification, but a quick glance at the viewer settings, as displayed on his chair readouts, invalidated that theory.

"*Bozhe moi!*" Chekov blurted in his native tongue. "It's as big as a house!"

"Distance two hundred meters and closing," Sulu reported. "Azimuth twenty-one-point-six. Collision in one minute."

"One minute, forty-eight seconds," Spock corrected him. "Evasive action."

"But there are ships all around us!" Sulu protested.

"And precisely nine hundred thirteen individuals aboard the *Enterprise*," Spock stated. With their shields at less than thirty percent, they could not risk a collision of such magnitude. "Evasive maneuvers."

"Aye, sir!" Sulu fought his control panel. "The helm's not responding! It's sluggish!"

The extended shields, Spock realized. They were consuming too many generators and subroutines at the expense of other systems, helm control among them. "Mr. Scott," he ordered Engineering. "More power to the helm."

On the viewer, the ice ball came at them like a mountain. Spock realized that they could not evade it. Nor were the diminished shields enough to deflect it.

"All hands and passengers! Brace for impact!"

Twenty-two

2020

The airlock was damp and uncomfortable. Free moisture had condensed on the bulkheads. Empty spacesuits were stowed on the walls. Rolled-up sleeping bags had been jammed into one corner. The cramped compartment had never been intended to house one prisoner, let alone two. Kirk found himself pining for the relative luxury of Shaun's personal living quarters. It was hard to imagine spending the next three months there.

"So, Fontana really thinks you're an impostor?" Zoe asked. She seemed bemused to find him sharing her cell.

He shrugged. "A minor misunderstanding."

"Boy, I knew she was paranoid, but this takes the cake."

He felt obliged to defend Fontana, who was just trying to protect her ship from an apparent intruder. He would have acted the same way as he had whenever an alien intelligence had possessed a member of his crew. The safety of the ship and other crew members always came first.

"She seems to think that I've changed since my encounter with the probe."

"Well, duh," Zoe said, floating freely around the compartment. "You had a close encounter with a genuine alien artifact and nearly got fried in the process. An experience like that is bound to have an impact on somebody. How couldn't it?"

Kirk wished he had thought of that argument, not that it explained his memory lapses. "Did you notice a difference, too?"

"Absolutely. You seemed more . . . mysterious somehow, like you were hiding something important. It made you more interesting, to be honest, not to mention a good deal sexier." She winked at him. "You know me, I love a mystery."

So I gather. He remembered Zoe coming on to him shortly after he found himself aboard the *Lewis & Clark.* Had she picked up on the fact that he was guarding forbidden secrets? No doubt that would be catnip to an inquisitive journalist like her. Apparently, the real Shaun had not been nearly so tempting an enigma.

"I'm not sure Fontana feels the same way. I don't suppose you'd care to explain that to her?"

"Talk sense to that green-eyed monster?" Zoe snorted at the notion. "Like she would ever listen to me, especially now."

He had to agree. "Then it seems I'm here for the duration."

"Sucks for you," she said. "Not that I'm complaining, mind you. I appreciate the company . . . and how."

She pushed off from the ceiling, launching herself toward him.

Kirk made no effort to avoid her but nodded at the closed-circuit camera monitoring the interior of the airlock. "Don't forget. We have an audience."

"No problem." She peeled off her tank top and draped it over the lens of the camera. "Let them get their cheap thrills elsewhere." She held her arms out, inviting him in. "C'mon, Skipper. I don't know about you, but I could use a little human warmth right now."

Kirk gazed at her enticing face and figure. Fontana had been right about another thing: he did find Zoe extremely attractive. He still wasn't sure what Shaun would do right then, but maybe that didn't matter so much anymore. He was already under arrest on suspicion of being an alien body snatcher; perhaps he might as well take advantage of the situation and Zoe's generous charms.

"You know," he said, "they're going to notice that the video feed has been obstructed."

"Then let's not waste time."

They embraced in midair, clinging to each other to keep from rebounding apart. Her taut, compact body molded to his as their lips found each other's. Locked together, they tumbled about the airlock, occasionally bouncing off the walls and ceiling. They were going to have some interesting bruises afterward, but it seemed more than worth it. Their hands busily explored exciting new life-forms. Kirk wondered just how much time they had.

A sudden burst of acceleration threw them against the outer hatch. Kirk's back took the impact, and his body cushioned Zoe. Their lips came apart, and they stared at each other in surprise.

"Whoa! Did you feel that?" she asked. "I mean, I knew I was good, but—"

"We're breaking orbit," he said, concerned by the unexpected jolt. The ship wasn't scheduled to start its return voyage for another twelve hours or so. "This shouldn't be happening."

Zoe got the message and stopped fooling around. "Okay, that doesn't sound good."

Letting go of her, he flew across the compartment to the video-com. "Fontana! O'Herlihy! What's happening up there?"

O'Herlihy's face appeared on the screen. He looked sweaty and distraught, as if he was cracking under the pressure. His eyes were bloodshot. His hair needed combing. Kirk was reminded of Ben Finney—after his breakdown.

"I'm sorry, Shaun, if that's who you truly are. Alice can't speak to you right now. I've taken control of the ship . . . for what little time we have left."

Kirk realized at once that the scientist had gone rogue somehow. "Where is Fontana?" he demanded. "What have you done with her?"

"She's fine," the doctor said. "*I just gave her something to sleep, that's all. It was necessary. I couldn't have her interfering with . . . what has to happen now.*"

"What do you mean?" Kirk asked. "What are you up to?"

"*I suppose you deserve the truth, both of you.*" O'Herlihy looked positively consumed by guilt. "*The Lewis & Clark is not returning home. I've set a new course. I'm using up all of our thruster fuel to send us spiraling into the planet in a matter of hours. We should get going fast enough to pass through the rings a few more times before we finally crash into Saturn itself.*"

Kirk's blood went cold. O'Herlihy was talking about a suicide run. Even in his own time, no vessel could survive a plunge into the heart of a gas giant. The titanic pressures would eventually crush the ship like a paper plane in a hurricane. And the *Lewis & Clark* didn't even have a structural-integrity field.

"That's insane! You're going to kill us all."

"*You think I don't know that?*" Anguish contorted O'Herlihy's face. "*You don't understand. I don't have any choice!*"

"But why, Marcus? You can't condemn us to death without telling us why!"

"*It's my daughter!*" he said, sobbing. "*My precious Tera. They're going to kill her if I don't!*"

Kirk had seen pictures of Tera O'Herlihy. She was a

lovely young woman in her early twenties. Her father had always seemed very proud of her.

"Who is, Marcus? Who is threatening her?"

"HEL," he admitted. *"The Human Extinction League. She got mixed up with them in college, and now they're holding her hostage. They demanded that I sabotage the mission, create a disaster that would 'teach the world a lesson' about the folly of spreading humanity to the stars, or they would torture her to death."* He was shaking now, his voice hoarse with emotion. *"You have to understand. She's my only child, my baby. I couldn't let that happen to her!"*

Kirk got the idea. Looking back, he recalled how emotional the doctor had been at times, especially when the subject of his family had come up. Kirk had ascribed that to simple homesickness, but obviously, there had been a lot more going on beneath the man's cool, avuncular demeanor. Small wonder O'Herlihy had choked up on occasion; Kirk could only imagine the strain he had been under.

None of which made their current situation any less perilous.

"You started the fire," Kirk realized. "Not Zoe."

"Yes. I stalled as long as I could, wanting to get as much science accomplished as possible, but HEL was getting impatient. They were sending coded messages to me via my wife's e-mails, and they wanted results. I had to do something to keep them from hurting Tera." The revelations poured out of him, as though he felt a need

to confess. *"I thought that maybe if I died in the fire, that would be enough to satisfy them, but I see now that I was just fooling myself. They won't be happy unless this entire mission crashes and burns in a way that can't possibly be covered up. I have to destroy the ship. That's the only way to make sure that Tera is safe."*

Kirk tried to reason with him. "But you can't sacrifice four lives for one. There must be another way. Perhaps if we notify the authorities back on Earth?"

"No! I can't take that chance. I'm sorry, but this is my baby we're talking about." He wiped his eyes, trying to regain his composure. His voice had a resigned, fatalistic tone that worried Kirk more than any emotional outbursts. He had clearly made up his mind. *"We're astronauts,"* he rationalized. *"We always knew we might not come back."* He reached for the comm controls. *"Good-bye, Shaun, Zoe."*

"Wait!" Zoe cried out before he could cut off the transmission. "How much time do we have?"

"Approximately five hours," he said, *"depending on how long it takes the planet's internal pressure to crush us. If it's any consolation, we're taking the scenic route to gather as much scientific data as possible before the end, passing through the rings themselves. I intend to keep transmitting our findings back to Earth for as long as possible. No matter what happens to us, we won't have died in vain. We will have carried out our mission and increased humanity's knowledge of the universe. Not a bad legacy to leave behind."*

"A noble sentiment, Doctor," Kirk retorted, "but I would prefer to live, too."

"Ditto," Zoe chimed in. "What he said."

"I'm sorry," O'Herlihy said sadly. *"I'm afraid that's the only comfort I have to give. Please forgive me."*

He switched off the comm.

Twenty-three

A bowl of hot chicken soup and a cup of coffee appeared on a tray in the food slot. Shaun sampled the soup, which was just the way he liked it, not too salty. He had to admit that the food service aboard the *Enterprise* definitely beat the prepackaged NASA cuisine back on his old ship. So far, the starship's galley had been able to produce almost every form of comfort food he had asked for, from root beer floats to sushi. There even appeared to be some exotic alien dishes on the menu.

Okay, he conceded. *I could get used to this.*

He started to carry the tray over to a waiting desk, despite the turbulence shaking the ship. It felt as if the *Enterprise* was in the middle of an outer-space hurricane—or a battle? A red alert light flashed above the locked doorway, and Shaun wished he knew what was going on. He gathered from what he had overheard before that the ship had been taking on refugees. But refugees from what?

The unsteady floor made it hard to keep his balance. Hot soup sloshed over the lip of the bowl, scalding his fingers. "Crap!" Shaun swore.

Maybe I should have ordered pizza instead.

A warning siren blared, and he almost jumped out of his (Kirk's) skin. An urgent voice came over the intercom system.

"All hands and passengers! Brace for impact!"

Although well intentioned, the warning came too late. A deafening jolt flipped the ship over on its axis, too fast for its internal gyros or whatever to compensate. Shaun was thrown across the room into the ceiling. The food tray flew from his fingers. The cup, bowl, and cutlery clattered loudly. Soup and coffee splashed against the walls and ceiling.

"What the—?"

The ship completed a full rotation, righting itself. Shaun landed hard on the floor, only a yard away from his bed. Stunned, he scrambled to his feet and glanced around. Years of NASA training kicked in as he hurriedly attempted to assess the situation.

Whatever had just hit the *Enterprise* had done a real number on the ship. The overhead lights flickered and went out, momentarily stranding him in darkness, before the emergency lights came on. Klaxons blared outside sickbay. Sparks erupted from the diagnostic screen above the bed, forcing him to throw up his arm to protect his eyes. Charred fragments rained onto the bed. The acrid smell of smoke and burning circuitry contaminated the air. Even the artificial gravity wobbled, causing his stomach to turn over queasily. The possibility of a hull breach—every astronaut's worst nightmare—forced its way into his brain, but there was no evidence of explosive decompression. If a breach had occurred elsewhere on the ship, perhaps it had already been sealed off. He had to assume that the *Enterprise* had the capacity to isolate any compromised sections of the ship. It would be insane to build any sort of spacecraft that couldn't.

They surely have their safety procedures, backups, and fail-safes, he reminded himself. *I have to assume that they're prepared to handle any emergency.*

But that didn't make being in the dark any easier.

A wet noodle dropped onto his sleeve. He looked up to see spilled soup and coffee dripping from the ceiling. He stepped out of the way, only to see the drops stop falling. Glistening round globules began to float above his head. His stomach flipped over again. Loose pillows, silverware, notepads, noodles, and bite-sized morsels of chicken floated freely through the room. His feet lost their grip on the floor.

So much for the artificial gravity.

All of a sudden, he felt as if he was back on the *Lewis & Clark,* but that wasn't even the most interesting development. The sliding door began to malfunction, too, opening and closing at random. Peering through the gap, he caught periodic glimpses of the rest of sickbay.

And freedom.

His eyes narrowed. A sly smile came over his face. Sure, he remembered Dr. McCoy explaining that he couldn't see too much of the future, and for a moment, he even considered staying put for the sake of the "timeline."

Then he shook his head.

Screw that, he thought. He'd been locked up in solitary long enough, and he wasn't about to float around doing nothing while all hell was apparently breaking loose. He needed to find out what was going on. Besides, who said they were ever really going to put him back where he belonged? They sure hadn't seemed in any hurry to get him home. Maybe McCoy had been feeding him a line of bull this whole time.

There was only one way to find out.

He studied the door's spastic openings and closings until he thought he had the timing down. He couldn't delay too long; McCoy or Chapel or somebody might come checking on him at any moment, although he was hoping they had their hands full elsewhere. Shaun decided that he was ready. Bracing himself against the foot of the bed, he tensed his leg muscles, glad that Kirk had apparently gotten plenty of exercise. He counted down the seconds.

Three . . . two . . . one . . . liftoff!

He pushed off from the bed, launching himself at the stuttering doorway. Gliding through the air, he feared for a moment that he had timed it wrong, but then the door *whoosh*ed open before him, and he flew into the larger sickbay facility beyond, where he nearly collided with a burly security officer in a red uniform.

The man was floating unconscious just outside the door. Shaun guessed that he had been knocked out when the ship rolled over. A fresh bruise marred the man's forehead.

He moaned groggily. "Not the captain . . . don't tell . . ."

Shaun gathered that the guard had been let in on the big secret that Kirk wasn't actually Kirk these days. He wondered how many crew members knew the truth.

"Not the captain . . ."

"Nope," Shaun agreed. "Not by a long shot."

A glance around the sickbay confirmed that they had the place to themselves. Shaun guessed that McCoy and his staff were probably dealing with medical emergencies all over the ship, although it probably wouldn't pay to stick around. Checking on the guard, he determined that the man was just dazed and not seriously injured. Shaun figured he'd be okay where he was.

"Hang on," he told the guard. "The doctor will be with you shortly."

An array of beds, similar to the one he had just abandoned, faced what looked like the main exit. The doors opened at his approach, and he ventured cautiously into the corridor outside, where he encountered a scene of frenzied activity and chaos.

Warning lights flashed. Sirens blared. Men and women in bright, primary-colored uniforms scrambled to deal with the emergency, whatever it was. Tendrils of smoke wafted through the hallways. Vapors gushed from broken conduits. Damage-repair teams fought to bring sparking panels under control, although they were hampered by the lack of gravity, which they were obviously unaccustomed to. Frustrated crewmen bounced awkwardly off the walls and one another. A lost tool, whose function Shaun couldn't begin to guess at, drifted past his head. He couldn't help smirking at their clumsy efforts. These Starfleet folks might be more than two centuries ahead of him, but they had clearly been spoiled by their artificial gravity.

Let an old-school astronaut show you how it's done.

He effortlessly navigated the confusion, only to realize that he had no idea where he was going. Pausing to get his bearings, he had to duck a boot that came spinning toward his head. "Whoa!" he called out. "Easy there!"

The boot was attached to a leggy crew member in a short red dress, who was somersaulting through the air. He grabbed her ankle to halt her uncontrolled tumble. She anchored herself to the ceiling.

"Sorry, Captain." She was an attractive black woman who looked to be in her early twenties. A beehive hairdo seemed curiously retro. "Guess I need to brush up on my zero-g maneuvers."

Captain?

He was used to dealing with McCoy, and it took

him a second to remember that everyone saw him as Captain Kirk. Perhaps he could turn that to his advantage.

"No problem," he said confidently, in his best mission-commander voice. He pretended to grope for her name. "Miss . . ?"

"Voss." She didn't seem to find it odd that the captain couldn't immediately place her. A ship this size probably had a substantial crew. "Yeoman Celeste Voss."

"Right," he said, as though it had simply slipped his mind. Thinking ahead, he decided that he wanted to be at the center of the action. "Do you know where I can find Mr. Spock?"

"On the bridge, I assume." She looked him over uncertainly. "Are you all right, sir? I understood you were injured."

"Nothing to worry about," he assured her. "Please accompany me to the bridge, Yeoman." He gestured chivalrously. "After you."

She just looked more puzzled. "Er, the bridge is *that* way, sir."

"Of course it is." He smacked his forehead in mock dismay. "That rollover must have spun me around a bit. Maybe you'd better lead the way, just in case."

He spoke lightly, trying to palm it off as a joke. Did Kirk josh around with his crew like this? Shaun hoped so.

"Aye, sir," she said, a trifle uncomfortably. "This way."

Pushing off from the ceiling, she led him down the busy hallway to a bright red door that opened to reveal some sort of elevator compartment. They floated into the elevator, which impressed Shaun with its size and convenience. Back on the *Lewis & Clark,* they had gotten by with just ladders and hatches. Then again, there had been a lot less territory to traverse on his old ship. For all he knew, it was quite a hike from here to the bridge.

The door closed behind them. Voss looked expectantly at him, and Shaun wondered what he was supposed to do. After an awkward moment, she took hold of a handle jutting from a rail at waist level. It chirped at her touch.

"Bridge," she announced.

The elevator surged into motion. *Voice-operated,* he noted. *I'll have to remember that, assuming I stick around much longer.*

The trip was short and smooth. Within minutes, the elevator came to a stop, and the door *whoosh*ed open. "Here we are, sir," she said, unable to look him in the eye. Shaun hoped he wasn't hurting the captain's reputation among his crew too much.

Sorry about that, Kirk. Then again, who knows what you're doing on my ship right now?

Two hundred fifty years ago, that is.

Before he could exit the elevator, the gravity came back without warning. He dropped deftly onto his feet, avoiding a clumsy fall. Voss stumbled slightly but managed to land on her feet, too. He grabbed her arm to steady her.

"Thank you, sir."

"Anytime, Yeoman." He flashed what he hoped was a winning smile. "Time to put our best foot forward."

He strode onto the bridge.

Twenty-four

"So, is this it?" Zoe asked. "Are we screwed?"

"Not on your life," Kirk said. He had never believed in no-win scenarios, and he wasn't about to start now. "We still have five hours to take back the ship."

"Er, in case you haven't noticed, we're locked up in maximum security."

"Hardly." He glanced around the compartment. "This is an airlock, not a brig. It wasn't built to keep people in." He inspected the hatch leading back into the habitat module, while mentally reviewing the specs he had studied earlier. "In theory, there should be a manual override."

She shook her head. "You disabled it, remember?"

Not really, Kirk thought. He assumed that Shaun had done so when the stowaway was first discovered. It made sense. Shaun and Fontana would have made sure that Zoe couldn't open the airlock on her own. *I would have done the same thing.*

But he had more than two centuries of scientific expertise on these early astronauts. Perhaps there was some way to take advantage of that. His gaze fell on

Zoe's smart tablet, which she had been allowed to keep in her cell. "Give me that device of yours."

She batted the tablet over to him. "Why? What are you up to?"

"Wait and see."

A tool chest on one wall contained the equipment that the crew used on their extravehicular activities. Kirk used a zero-g screwdriver to pry loose the casing at the back of the tablet, exposing the crude silicon circuitry. Its wireless capacity had also been disabled, he noted, but he might be able to remedy that. The only question was whether he could do so in time with the primitive tools at his disposal, as well as making the necessary improvements to its programming.

Spock could do this blindfolded with chopsticks, he thought. *Too bad he's not here.*

Zoe watched over his shoulder as he tinkered with circuits. Needing additional components, he cannibalized the headphones in a spare "Snoopy cap." He was reluctant to pillage the EVA gear but didn't see any other option. Everything depended on giving Zoe's tablet a twenty-third-century upgrade.

"Wow!" she murmured. "Who knew you were MacGyver in disguise?"

He didn't get the reference but assumed that it was a compliment.

"Hand me those magnifying lenses," he requested.

"Yes, Doctor." She passed him the lenses like a nurse in sickbay. "What exactly are you doing?"

"Improvising."

Sweat beaded on his brow as he struggled with the archaic equipment. The lack of proper tools frustrated him. Time ticked by agonizingly, and he would have traded an entire ringful of dilithium crystals for one good laser solderer. His mind flashed back to that time in the Great Depression when Spock had managed to modify a tricorder using far more obsolete materials than these. He smiled tightly, encouraged by the memory. If Spock could put together a working mnemonic memory circuit out of nothing but "stone knives and bearskins," then he should be able to hot-wire a twenty-first-century computer tablet using NASA hardware.

Or so he kept telling himself.

"Almost there," he muttered.

A sudden impact shook the airlock. A metallic bang sounded as if it was coming from right outside the ship. The signal light above the inner hatchway went out.

Uh-oh, Kirk thought. *That could be trouble.*

"Yikes!" Zoe dropped a screwdriver, which drifted slowly toward the floor. "What was that?"

"The rings," Kirk guessed. It was the only plausible explanation for the impact. "The ship must be passing through the rings. An iceberg slammed into the hull."

Smaller impacts buffeted the hull, like hail pounding against a tin roof. For a moment, he thought he was back in the Klondike system, with its unstable rings, but Saturn's rings had their own share of hazards if you were suicidal enough to brave them, which O'Herlihy clearly was. Praying that none of the collisions would breach the hull, Kirk listened tensely for an alarm. When no siren sounded, he assumed that the ship's tough titanium skin had withstood the storm for now.

"Sounds like we're okay," he told Zoe. "That first bang must not have been big enough to sink us."

"You sure about that? 'Cause it sounded damn big to me."

"Yes," he had to agree. "It did."

The collision was an unwelcome reminder that they were running out of time. Even if they survived their periodic passages through the churning rings, Saturn's ferocious atmosphere still waited to crush the fragile spaceship to a pulp. Hurricane winds would whip the shattered fragments around the planet at speeds exceeding a thousand kilometers per hour. And then, of course, there was the danger of burning up in reentry.

Granted, history had recorded no such disaster, but perhaps he had changed history already just by being there. There were too many unknown variables. He couldn't count on the *Lewis & Clark* surviving as it had under Shaun Christopher's command.

"Start getting into one of those spacesuits," he ordered Zoe. "Just in case."

She hurried over to where the suits hung on the wall. "How come?"

If they lost their atmosphere, he wanted her prepared. A spacesuit would buy her precious time.

"Just do it," he said, "and hurry."

She didn't argue with him. "Hey, if you were into cosplay, you just needed to ask."

The barrage outside abated swiftly. Kirk recalled that the rings, although almost three hundred thousand kilometers across, were often less than a kilometer thick. They would have passed through the rings in no time. They were safe for the moment.

Until their polar orbit carried them through the rings again.

Biting his lip, he hastily finished his modifications to the tablet. Unable to replace the casing he had pried off before, he had to leave its inner workings exposed. He hoped the ship's sterile atmosphere would not contaminate its circuits too quickly.

"Done," he pronounced. "I think."

"Glad to hear it," Zoe said, climbing into a water-filled cooling garment. "Now, you want to tell me what you have in mind?"

He approached the locked inner hatch. "I believe the colloquial term is 'hocking.'"

"You mean 'hacking'?"

"Right," he confirmed, suitably corrected. "That."

He pointed the tablet at the sealed doorway. In theory, he should be able to "hack" into the ship's computerized locking system. The elementary programming had been child's play compared with, say, rewriting the parameters of the *Kobayashi Maru* simulation back at the Academy. Twenty-first-century firewalls were still a long way from foolproof.

"Wish me luck," he said. "Open sesame."

He keyed the override command.

Nothing happened. The hatchway remained sealed.

"Damn," he muttered. He tried another command, with equally disappointing results. The hatch refused to budge. The indicator light above the exit flashed neither red nor green.

"What's the matter?" Zoe asked. "Why isn't it working?"

"That collision," he realized, "back in the rings. The impact must have damaged the mechanism. I can't get it to respond."

"So, we're stuck in here after all? While the doc is playing kamikaze with the ship?"

"Maybe not." He turned away from the inner hatch toward the one leading to the open cargo bay outside. "There's still another way out."

She looked where he was looking. Her jaw dropped. "Seriously?"

"Wouldn't be a real NASA mission without a proper spacewalk," he said, "and I'm not sure we have any workable alternatives."

She stared at the outer hatch and gulped. "Beats sitting around waiting to crash into Saturn, I guess."

"My point exactly." He began removing the second spacesuit from its niche. "Help me get into this suit."

Under ordinary circumstances, donning the suits would take at least fifteen minutes. Adrenaline and necessity sped them through the elaborate process in ten. They rushed through the various checks and tests, cutting corners wherever possible. By the time they had put each other's helmet on and pressurized the bulky suits, there was barely enough room in the airlock for both of them. They tested their radio receivers.

"What's the plan?" Zoe asked. "Where are we going in these unflattering get-ups? Once we're out of this space-age dungeon, that is."

"You're not going anywhere. You're staying here."

"Hell, no!" she protested. "You can't just leave me here!"

"It's too dangerous," he insisted. "I've had spacewalk training. You haven't. And trust me, it's not like taking a stroll back on Earth. You're not equipped for this. I'm sorry."

She glanced down at the cumbersome suit, which was at least one size too big for her. Her head barely poked out of the metal ring at the top of the rigid torso assembly. The gold-tinted visor covered her face like a veil.

"Then why am I dressed like Barbarella *before* her striptease?"

"To survive when I depressurize the airlock," he explained. Even staying where she was, she was going to be exposed to the vacuum for a time. The life-support system on her back held at least eight hours of oxygen, which ought to be more than enough. "Don't worry. One way or another, this will be over before you run out of air."

"Got it," she said. "But what am I supposed to do while you're out traipsing through space?"

"Keep O'Herlihy distracted as long as possible." The scientist was bound to notice when the airlock was activated, if he wasn't too busy collecting data while simultaneously piloting the ship to its doom. He might even come to investigate. "You think you can do that?"

"You're kidding, right? I was born to distract people."

Kirk could believe it.

Almost ready to depart, he had a few last tasks to handle first. A command via the tablet started the depressurization mechanism, which, to his relief, was more functional than the inner hatchway. As the air was rapidly pumped from the chamber, he took a metal hammer and shattered the lens of the closed-circuit camera beneath Zoe's discarded top.

There, he thought. *If Marcus wants to find out what's happened here, he's going to have to check it out in person.*

That should give Kirk time to get where he needed to go.

As a final precaution, he tethered Zoe to the locked inner hatch to keep her from drifting out into the cargo bay with him. "Hold on to the door," he urged her, "and don't let go."

"Not going anywhere," she promised. "Don't be too long, though. Okay?"

"You won't even know I'm gone."

"Don't sell yourself short. I'm missing you already."

The green light over the outer hatch gave him the go-ahead. He secured the tablet to one of the clips on his suit, then tried to activate the second hatch. Despite the oxygen feeding into his helmet, he held his breath to see if the airlock would respond.

The metal slid out of the way, exposing the cavernous cargo bay beyond.

That's more like it, he thought. *Spock would be proud.*

He turned to wave farewell to Zoe. She blew him a kiss through her visor, then held on to the other hatch with both hands. They had agreed to maintain radio silence from now on, just in case O'Herlihy tried to listen in.

"See you soon," he whispered.

He floated out into the cargo bay, holding on to the handrails to control his progress. He had left the short-circuited jetpack behind. In all the tumult, they had never gotten around to repairing it; besides, its miniature jets could never have kept pace with the ship unless the pilot was deliberately trying to rendezvous with him. He was going to have to climb, not fly, to his destination.

The spacious bay reminded him of his first, disorienting introduction to the *Lewis & Clark,* right after he'd unexpectedly found himself in this century. It was hard to believe that less than five days had passed since then; he felt as if he had already spent weeks in Shaun Christopher's skin.

Here's hoping I don't end up dying in his place.

A ladder led out of the bay onto the hull. He climbed the ladder using carabiners of the sort used by mountain climbers to ascend rocky cliff faces. Kirk had always enjoyed climbing back on Earth; one of his long-term goals was to climb the towering peaks of Yosemite someday. Who knew? Maybe he would have time to accomplish that in this era, if any of them made it back to Earth.

Clambering onto the top of the ship, he paused to take his bearings. The *Lewis & Clark* was indeed cruising in a polar orbit, perpendicular to the rings. Its delicate solar panels had been retracted, no doubt to keep them from being shredded by the orbiting ring matter. Staring down the length of the ship, he spied the glittering tops of the rings spreading out from the equator, thousands of kilometers below. It was like gazing at the surface of a luminous river made of sparkling boulders and flakes of ice. The inner B Ring shone brighter than the planet itself, even as the rings appeared to be rushing up to meet the ship. Could he reach his destination before they passed through the rings again? Kirk wasn't sure.

I need to get a move on, he realized, *and pronto.*

He tore his gaze away from the dazzling spectacle to focus on the task at hand. The front half of the ship stretched before him, pointed straight down at the rings. His goal was to reach the command module—and, most importantly, the docking ring attached to the nose of the command module. If he could just get there in time, he might be able to get back onto the flight deck and regain control of the ship. O'Herlihy was bound to have other ideas, but Kirk would cross that bridge when he came to it, after he crossed the rest of the ship.

Spacewalk exercises had been mandatory back at the Academy, and Kirk had always excelled at them. He was a bit rusty, though. Command of the *Enterprise* seldom required him personally to stroll outside the ship. At best, he took part in an EVA once or twice a year, usually as part of an emergency drill. He hoped that those drills would pay off now.

Guide rails mounted on the exterior of the modules provided foot and hand holds for careful astronauts. Kirk hooked his carabiners to the rail for safety's sake, then pulled himself along hand after hand. He moved briskly, tempted to ditch the tethers to save time. They slid along the rail behind him, making no noise in the silence of space. His feet dangled behind him, avoiding contact with the hull. The last thing he wanted right now was for O'Herlihy to hear footsteps stomping outside the ship.

The captain wished he knew what the desperate scientist was doing right now. Feverishly transmitting priceless scientific data back to Earth in his last few hours or rushing to check on the airlock? It was possible that he'd assumed that both prisoners had been flushed into space, but what if he guessed that a captive or two were attempting an unauthorized spacewalk? He was a brilliant man; he might well have figured out what Kirk had in mind, which could severely complicate matters later on. Given a choice, Kirk wanted O'Herlihy to be otherwise occupied when he attempted to reboard the ship.

Keep him busy, Zoe. You can do it.

The hab loomed before him, wider and more heavily insulated than the other modules. Its sides jutted out between the cargo bay and the command module like a section of snake that was digesting a large, lumpy meal. He had to scale its stern to reach the top of the hab, which he hurried across to make up for lost time. Arriving at the end of the module, he descended onto the vestibule connecting the hab to command, the same vestibule where he and Fontana had battled the fire only yesterday. Had they survived the blaze only to be torn apart and crushed by Saturn's singularly violent atmosphere?

Not if he had anything to say about it.

He set out across the vestibule. *Almost there,* he thought. He looked ahead and saw the brilliant immensity of the rings towering over him like a tidal wave—or perhaps a colossal floating avalanche.

I was too slow, he realized. *Here they come again.*

He looked about for cover. A canopy-sized communications dish offered shelter, and he flew beneath it only a heartbeat before the ship entered the rings. The light from countless reflective particles, spread across more than a hundred thousand meters, blinded him, forcing him to shield his eyes. Minute pieces of dirty ice, most no larger than grains of sand, pelted the hull. More substantial chunks of ice mingled with the tiny particles. The myriad obstacles orbited Saturn like billions of miniature moons. A hailstone the size of a pebble smashed through the communications dish, barely missing Kirk's head. A second piece ricocheted off the hull, leaving a dent in the titanium shielding. He crouched low and kept his head down. The multiple layers of his spacesuit contained a lining of rubberized nylon to prevent damage from micrometeorite strikes, but he knew that if a fast enough or large enough piece struck his life-support system or helmet, he was as good as dead. A volley of lethal frozen bullets strafed the ship. He recalled that the temperature of the rings was minus one hundred ninety degrees Celsius. He could feel the cold even through his insulated suit.

Hang on, he thought. *It will all be over in a minute.*

Although they stretched above and below the ship for as far as the eye could see, the rings were only about twenty times deeper than the *Lewis & Clark* was long. The accelerating spaceship swiftly passed through the rings into the open space above Saturn's southern hemisphere. An immense aurora, produced by charged particles captured by the planet's powerful magnetic field, shimmered above the south pole. The ship wouldn't encounter the rings again, Kirk realized, until the ship passed over the pole and headed back up toward the equator on the opposite side of the planet. He decided that he wanted to be back inside before the next barrage.

That had been about as close to a firing squad as he cared to get.

Gliding out from beneath the punctured dish, he spotted numerous nicks and scratches on the hull, along with a few larger dents. A thorough inspection of the ship's exterior was clearly called for, provided they survived the present mutiny. Ignoring the damage for the time being, he pulled himself along the guide rail, which was now warped and crimped in spots. Pushing against the thick suit and gloves from the inside was strenuous work. By now, his arms ached, and he was breathing hard. He couldn't slow down, though. Not when time was running out.

He crossed from the vestibule onto the command module. Light shone from the windows, tempting him to scout out the situation before proceeding further. Moving stealthily, he peered through a porthole, which offered only a partial view of the flight deck. His eyes widened as he spotted Fontana bound to the same ladder she had tethered him to only hours ago. She appeared to be unconscious, but it was hard to tell. Hadn't O'Herlihy said something about giving her something to sleep? He guessed that hadn't been her idea.

Looking away from the drugged copilot, he searched for O'Herlihy at the helm and the computer terminals but failed to locate him. He hoped that meant that the saboteur was away from the command module at the moment. There was nothing downstairs, after all, but the blackened wreckage from the fire. Perhaps he was still investigating the disturbance at the airlock.

Good, Kirk thought. *This is going to be tricky enough.*

The docking ring was on the nose of the command module, attached to the mid-deck. Kirk prayed that the fire had not done serious damage to the airlock, or he could well find himself locked out in the cold. Descending past the cockpit windows, he got into position outside the docking hatch. Although procedure dictated that the hatch was to be opened only in conjunction with the onboard flight crew, the airlock had not been built to repel boarders. After all, space piracy was not really grounds for concern in this solar system yet. That was still generations away.

All the better for me, Kirk thought. He mentally patted himself on the back for memorizing the ship's specs when he'd had the chance. Zoe's tablet remained clipped to his wrist, having survived the bumpy passage through the rings. He clumsily stabbed the controls with his gloved fingers. *Barring any untimely malfunctions, this should work.*

He keyed in the final command.

The hatch slid open.

Let's hear it for twenty-third-century know-how, he thought. *I may have a future as a safecracker in this era.*

Moving quickly, he entered the airlock and closed the hatch behind him. One more hatch lay between him and the mid-deck. He just needed to repressurize the compartment first, or else the force of the ship's atmosphere rushing into the airlock would smash him into the outer hatch with bone-crushing force, if not blow out the hatch altogether. Unlike Spock, he could not instantly calculate exactly how many kilograms per square centimeter that would unleash, but he knew it was nothing to be taken lightly. Opening an unpressurized hatch would also set off alarms all over the ship, which he hoped to avoid if at all possible.

No need to alert O'Herlihy if he didn't have to.

Waiting impatiently for the airlock to fill up with air, he peered through the six-centimeter porthole into the torched mid-deck, on the lookout for O'Herlihy, but all he saw was scorched rubble and the new fire extinguishers they had placed in the module as a precaution. He wished he knew where the treacherous doctor was hiding. For all Kirk knew, O'Herlihy was lying in wait just out of view, waiting to ambush him.

He reached instinctively for a phaser, only to realize his mistake.

Wrong ship, wrong century.

He would have to take his chances the old-fashioned way.

Ready or not, Doctor, here I come.

Twenty-five

"Captain on the bridge!" Yeoman Voss announced.

All eyes turned toward Shaun Christopher, who needed a second to absorb the sight of the *Enterprise*'s impressively large and colorful control center. Mr. Spock was seated at the center of the circular bridge, facing a wall-sized monitor or window. His crew was arranged around the perimeter, except for two officers manning a large console directly in front of Spock. From its look and position, Shaun guessed that they were doing the actual piloting. Seatbelts and straps had held the crew in place during the short-lived lapse in gravity. A bewildering array of displays, monitors, and instrument panels was enough to induce sensory overload. Shaun focused his gaze on the main screen.

Dozens of smaller spacecraft, of varied design, zipped across the monitor. An icy moon, boasting a full-fledged lunar habitat, was dwarfed by a huge ringed planet looming in the background. Purple bands streaked the planet.

"Oh my God!" Shaun exclaimed. "Is that Saturn?"

There had been no spaceships or moon colonies in

the vicinity the last time he'd checked. Of course, that had been two hundred and fifty years ago . . .

"Klondike VI," Spock corrected him. Despite his stoic demeanor, it was clear that he was not pleased by Shaun's unexpected arrival on the bridge. "Captain, you should return to sickbay. You are not well."

Shaun didn't feel like playing along. "I'm not the captain, and I'm not crazy," he declared. "I'm Colonel Shaun Christopher, and you know it!"

A quick glance around the bridge gave him a good idea of who had been let in on the secret and who had not. Several crew members, including the helpful yeoman, were clearly startled and confused by his outrageous claim, but others merely looked worried. The veiled woman, whom he remembered from the transporter room, turned toward him. He noted that she wasn't wearing a Starfleet uniform like everyone else.

"Shaun Christopher?" she echoed, sounding intrigued. "Curiouser and curiouser."

Mr. Spock let out a barely perceptible sigh. "Attention, all hands," he addressed the bridge crew. "Please be aware that the individual before you is not actually the captain. There is no time to explain the situation fully, but I expect you all to disregard any orders except my own." He turned toward Shaun. "Colonel Christopher, you can clearly see that we are in the midst of a crisis. I must ask that you leave the bridge immediately."

"No way, Spock. I'm here in this time now, and I don't intend to sit on the sidelines." He shrugged Kirk's shoulders. "Who knows? Maybe that probe sent me here for a reason."

"Now, *there's* an interesting possibility," the veiled woman observed. "Mr. Spock, maybe we should find out what our unlikely guest has to offer. He may have insights into the probe—and our present situation— that we have missed."

"I have already interrogated the colonel," Spock stated curtly. "But you are free to take custody of him if you wish. At the moment, I have other matters to attend to."

Shaun got the distinct impression that he was being handed off to a babysitter, but he figured that beat being expelled forcibly from the bridge and possibly thrown into the brig. He joined the veiled woman at one of the auxiliary stations. "Shaun Christopher," he introduced himself. "At your service."

"Qat Zaldana," she identified herself. "And would that be *the* Colonel Shaun Geoffrey Christopher of space history fame?"

He nodded, both surprised and flattered that she recognized his name. "You've heard of me?"

"I'm quite familiar with your illustrious résumé, Colonel," she said, "although I admit I never expected to make your acquaintance, let alone under such bizarre circumstances."

She seemed to be taking those circumstances

remarkably well, especially considering that he looked like James T. Kirk at the moment. Did this sort of thing happen often in the future? He certainly hadn't gotten that impression from Dr. McCoy.

"This is a bit out of my comfort zone, too," he confessed. "NASA never trained me for anything like this."

On the screen, some of the smaller ships appeared to be retreating to a domed complex on the nearby moon. Chunks of flying space debris endangered the numerous vessels, although the *Enterprise* was clearly attempting to provide cover for them by blasting the larger missiles apart with powerful blue laser beams. The beams seemed to pack enough firepower to make the Pentagon drool with envy.

"Maintain defensive fire, Mr. Chekov," Spock instructed. "Target all hazards to ships or colony."

"Aye, aye, sir," a young ensign reported. His Russian accent reminded Shaun of the cosmonauts he had trained with at the Star City complex outside Moscow. "Shields restored to usual configuration. Deflectors at thirty-five percent and rising."

"That's more like it," said an Asian crewman sitting to the Russian's left. "Helm controls responding again."

"Excellent, Mr. Sulu," Spock said. "Take us further above the rings to reduce the chance of any future collisions."

"With pleasure," Sulu replied. "Altering trajectory

relative to the equator. Attempting to stay within firing range of Skagway."

The image on the wall screen shifted as the *Enterprise* ascended higher above the plane of the rings. The turbulence shaking the ship began to abate, even as Shaun tried to figure out exactly what was going on. He gathered that the moon colony was in jeopardy, and possibly the starship, too, but the details remained murky. Dr. McCoy hadn't exactly kept him informed about current events.

Shaun sat down next to Qat Zaldana. "Why don't you bring me up to speed?" he suggested.

"Since the twenty-first century?" she quipped. "That could take a while."

He nodded at the screen. "How about just what's happening out there?"

"That I can manage." She quickly explained that the planet's rings were coming apart and that the moon itself was spiraling into the inner rings toward the planet itself. To make matters worse, it seemed that more than a thousand people were still stranded on the moon, and even the *Enterprise,* as impressive as it was, wasn't big enough to carry them all to safety.

No wonder Spock looks so grim, Shaun thought. They were looking at a tragedy of catastrophic proportions, like Katrina or Mount Rainier. "And there's nothing you can do?"

She shook her head. "We suspect this disaster may have something to do with that alien probe and possibly an unusual hexagonal vortex down on the planet, but we haven't been able to put all of the pieces together, at least not in time to save the people left on Skagway."

"Hexagon?"

"That's right," she said. "There's a hexagonal storm at the planet's north pole, much like the one on Saturn, which started shrinking at about the same time the rings began to destabilize. We assume there's some kind of connection or causal link."

Talk about déjà vu, Shaun thought, if that was the right term for remembering something from your own past while occupying someone else's body in the future. "That sounds a lot like what we were observing back in my time, right before I ended up here. Saturn's rings were behaving strangely, the hexagon was shrinking, and so on. The scientists back in my time didn't know what to make of it." Shaun remembered how nonplussed O'Herlihy had been by his findings.

"How strange," Qat Zaldana said. "Mr. Spock, are you listening to this?"

"Indeed," Spock admitted. He spun his chair around to face them. "You have successfully captured my attention. Please continue your recollections, Colonel Christopher."

"Not much more to say," Shaun said. "We were studying the phenomenon from the *Lewis & Clark* when the probe distracted us." He chuckled at the memory. "Trust me, that voyage was full of surprises."

"None of that is in the historical record," Qat Zaldana said. "And I'm an astronomer. I would know."

"Must have been covered up," Shaun guessed. "I don't know how it is in your time, but back where— I mean, *when*—I come from, governments had plenty of secrets that they guarded zealously." His stint at Area 51 had taught him that and then some. "But it sounds to me like that big purple planet out there is going through the same thing Saturn did back in 2020."

"Except that Saturn and its rings and moons remain constant to this day," Spock said. "They are now much as you would have known them before your historic mission, which implies that the phenomenon you observed was reversed somehow."

That makes sense, Shaun thought. He tried to imagine what could have affected the rings way back when. "You think it was the probe?"

"Possibly," Qat Zaldana said. "What exactly do you remember, Colonel?"

He threw his mind back, trying to recapture every detail. In theory, centuries had passed since his dramatic run-in with the probe, but it had been only a couple of days for him.

"There were these pulses," he recalled. "Just before the probe zapped me here, it fired some sort of pulsed energy burst at the heart of the hexagon." He glanced up at the screen. "Kind of like those high-powered lasers of yours."

"Phasers," Spock corrected him. "Are you certain

the pulses were directed at the vortex on the planet's surface?"

"Absolutely." It was all coming back to him now. "I'll never forget it. I was floating in space, preparing to bring the probe aboard, when it suddenly fired off these incandescent bolts of bright blue energy, which triggered a reaction down on the planet."

Qat Zaldana leaned toward him. "What sort of reaction?"

"The whole hexagon lit up, glowing like a pinwheel, and a shock wave sent me tumbling away from the probe. Then the pulses just stopped, like I had just imagined them."

"And then what happened?" she asked.

"The hexagon," he recalled. "It almost looked as though it was going back to normal after the pulses. Its sides stopped contracting and started heading outward again at an incredible rate. It was probably a stupid thing to do, but I couldn't resist flying back to check out the probe again. I made the mistake of grabbing onto it and ended up here . . . in your captain's body." He still couldn't believe how insane that sounded. "I don't know what happened next."

"Saturn's rings and moons are still in place in our time," Spock stated. "And the hexagonal vortex at its northern pole can be seen to this day. I recall observing it during a scientific conference on Titan."

Shaun gathered that there were bases or colonies on Titan now.

"Then that's it," he said. "The probe must have fixed

Saturn back in my day. Maybe it can do the same now and save all those poor souls in that colony."

Spock did not seem hopeful. "Unfortunately, the probe is no longer functional. Whatever remarkable capabilities it may have possessed in your era have been lost to the ravages of time."

Oh, right, Shaun thought. He recalled banging into the future version of the probe back in the transporter room, right before Spock knocked him out with that neck pinch. That probe had looked like a wreck compared with the gleaming alien artifact he had encountered out by Saturn. Two centuries of change had clearly taken their toll on the probe, along with everything else he had ever known. The *Lewis & Clark* had probably rusted to pieces by now, if it wasn't gathering dust in a museum somewhere. *By all rights, I should be nothing but dust.*

"It's true," Qat Zaldana confirmed. "We've examined the probe thoroughly. It's dead as can be."

The news crushed Shaun's hopes. "Then we're screwed, and so are the poor bastards on that moon."

"Perhaps not," Spock said. "You say that the pulses resembled our phaser blasts?"

"I guess, maybe." Shaun threw up his hands. "I'm hardly an expert on 'phasers' or weird alien energy rays, for that matter."

"Understood," Spock said. He sounded reluctant to discard whatever theory he was formulating. "But what you observed *did* appear to be some manner of directed energy bursts?"

"I suppose." Shaun found Spock's interest encouraging. McCoy had said that the Vulcan usually knew what he was doing.

Qat Zaldana seemed hopeful, too. "What are you thinking, Mr. Spock?"

Spock left his chair to join them. "We have speculated that the hexagon is a manifestation of some unknown alien apparatus that serves to maintain the rings as we know them. Perhaps by making crucial adjustments to the planet's mass or gravity."

"Like the artificial gravity you generate on this ship?"

"Precisely," Spock said. "But on a much greater scale. And now that apparatus is failing, resulting in the catastrophic results we are now witnessing. What you observed in the past, however, suggests that the probe was once able to reset the mechanism somehow, via a pulsed signal."

Shaun saw where Spock was going with this. "You think the probe used those bursts to reboot the hexagon on Saturn, which straightened out the rings?"

"Essentially," Spock stated. "In which case, it is theoretically possible that we might be able to simulate the signal with our own phasers."

"I don't know," Qat Zaldana said. "That sounds like a long shot to me."

"Agreed," Spock said. "But it is the only option remaining to us, outside of abandoning Skagway to its doom." He looked at Shaun, seeing someone else. "And if there is one thing I have learned from serving under Captain Kirk for nearly five years, it is that long shots are often the difference between success and failure. I know that the captain would not hesitate to make one last effort to save the colony, no matter the odds against us."

Shaun grinned. "Sounds like a man after my own heart, Mr. Spock."

"You can feel his heart beating in your chest, Colonel. What does it tell you?"

"Go for it, Spock." Shaun chuckled. "Heck, it doesn't sound any crazier than everything else on this ship of yours." He tried not to look at the alien's pointed ears. "No offense."

"None taken." Spock pondered the problem before them; you could practically see his computer-like mind clicking away. "The challenge will be to replicate precisely the signal you observed more than two centuries ago. Do you recall the exact sequence of the energy pulses? It is no doubt essential that we transmit the signal correctly."

No doubt, Shaun thought uncertainly. "Maybe. I only saw the pulses for a couple of moments, in the middle of a complicated spacewalk, and as you know, a lot's happened to me since." He sank into his seat. "I'm not sure."

The responsibility weighed on him like gravity after a long space mission. His training had been intended to prepare him for almost every eventuality, but this was a new one. His fingers drummed on the flashing console in front of him. His feet tapped restlessly on the floor. *This would be easier,* he thought irritably, *if I didn't have this damn drumbeat stuck in my head.*

The same beat that he had been hearing ever since he touched the probe . . .

Shaun froze, then laughed out loud. "Of course! That's it. It has to be!"

Spock arched an eyebrow. "Is something amusing, Colonel?"

"Just let me at those phasers," Shaun said confidently. For the first time since he'd found himself in the future, he thought he knew exactly what he was supposed to do. "Trust me, Spock." He tapped his head. "I've got the correct sequence right here."

Spock took him at his word. "Mr. Sulu, set a course that brings us over the north pole of Klondike VI."

"But the colony . . ." the helmsman began.

"Will not long endure unless we pursue a different strategy."

"Aye, sir," Sulu acknowledged.

The *Enterprise* left its current orbit and climbed above the looming gas giant. As before, back at Saturn, Shaun was awestruck by the sheer size and majesty of the ringed planet. The *Enterprise* was like an aircraft carrier compared with the *Lewis & Clark,* but both ships were specks next to the gigantic celestial body before them.

"Please accompany me to navigation, Colonel."

Spock led Christopher over to the two-man station in front of the captain's chair, where they looked over the shoulder of the young Russian officer. Spock regarded Shaun curiously. "Do you believe you can describe the proper sequence to Ensign Chekov?"

"I'm no band conductor, Mr. Spock. I can feel the rhythm in my blood and bones, but I don't want to risk it getting garbled in transmission." He drummed his fingers against the back of Chekov's chair. "I think it might be better if I operated the controls myself."

"There is a certain logic to your request," Spock conceded. He tapped Chekov on the shoulder. "Mr. Chekov, please turn over the conn to Colonel Christopher."

Chekov gave Shaun a doubtful look that reminded Shaun of a particularly strict aeronautics instructor back at Star City. *Wonder if this Chekov is any relation. A distant descendant, perhaps?*

Sitting down at the conn, Shaun took a second to marvel at the fact that he was actually seated at the controls of a genuine faster-than-light starship centuries in the future. He felt as if he had suddenly gone from a Model T to a hover car out of an old science-fiction movie.

If only Mission Control could see me now.

"An honor to fly with you, Colonel," the helmsman said from the seat to the left. He gave Shaun a welcoming smile. "I've always been a big fan of you and your fellow astronauts."

"Thanks." Shaun was used to signing autographs and greeting space buffs. It was all part of the job. "Lieutenant Sulu, was it?"

"That's right." Sulu smoothly worked the helm controls. "Coming up on the north pole."

The hexagon, or what was left of it, appeared upon the viewer. Shaun was shocked at just how small and pallid it appeared, compared with the enigmatic landmark that *Voyager 1* had discovered back on Saturn in 1980. You could barely make it out against the churning purple clouds whipping around the pole. Shaun had to squint to see the honeycomb shape and its bizarrely artificial-looking angles.

"Jesus," he murmured. "What's happened to it?"

"That which the probe was intended to avert," Spock theorized. "And which we now hope to remedy . . . if it is not already too late."

Shaun searched his memory, trying to get every detail right. "The probe was pointed straight down at the hexagon."

"Mr. Sulu," Spock ordered. "Adjust our orientation appropriately."

"Aye, sir."

Shaun experienced a momentary tilting sensation as the *Enterprise* dipped forward so that it was pointed nose down at the anemic vortex below. He half expected to tumble forward over the console, but then the artificial gravity compensated for the ship's changed orientation, and he remained flat on his seat. The shriveled white hexagon was dead center on the screen.

Showtime, Shaun thought. *I'm on.*

He examined the instrument panel in front of him, feeling more than a little intimidated by the multiple lighted switches, buttons, and toggles. *Could be worse,* he thought. At least, they still used switches in the future and not some weird cybernetic interface or whatever.

"So, where are the firing controls?"

Leaning over Shaun's shoulder, Chekov pointed out a row of colored switches. "Just press that one . . . carefully!"

"What about targeting?" Shaun asked.

"I can handle that for you," Sulu volunteered. A pop-up viewer telescoped upward from his console. He peered into the binocular device and made some adjustments on his own instrument panel. "Done. Phasers are locked on target. All you need to do is pull the trigger, figuratively speaking."

Chekov sighed dolefully. "I just hope we don't trigger a self-destruct mechanism by mistake!"

You and me both, Shaun thought. He tried not to think about the hundreds of lives depending on him. *One good thing,* he consoled himself. *If I screw this up, nobody back home is going to hear about it for hundreds of years.*

He took a deep breath and listened to the persistent percussion in his head. If anything, it seemed to be growing even louder and more insistent every minute, as if it was demanding to be set free. He let the alien rhythm flow down to his fingers. He couldn't remember being this nervous since his junior-high piano recital, which had not gone terribly well. He swallowed hard.

"Okay. Here goes nothing."

The firing button was cool to the touch. He pressed it, paused, pressed it again.

There was no recoil, no explosion, but sapphire bolts pulsed across thousands of kilometers of space to strike the hexagon in what he prayed was the right sequence. Memories of the probe blasting down at Saturn flashed across his memory in sync with the rhythm driving his fingers. He kept pressing the button until the beat faded away.

At first, nothing happened. Shaun's heart sank. Had he gotten the signal wrong, or was their crazy theory mistaken? Maybe this was all a waste of time, and he had just been fooling himself to think that he actually knew what he was doing in this terrifying future world.

I don't belong here. This is all just some cruel cosmic joke.

"Look!" Qat Zaldana pointed at the screen. "Something's happening!"

A spark appeared at the center of the hexagon, then flared up until it shone as brightly as the sun. People on the bridge gasped and threw up their hands against the glare, until some sort of computerized filter program dimmed the image on the screen. For a moment or two, the light took the form of a gigantic glowing hexagon that matched the vortex's original dimensions. Gravitational ripples shook the *Enterprise,* pushing it farther away from the planet.

Sulu struggled to regain control of the ship. "Whoa!" he exclaimed. "It's like an antigrav wave, radiating out from the planet!"

"Do not fight it," Spock advised. "Let it carry us to a more distant orbit."

The shock waves seemed stronger than the one Shaun remembered. He wondered what the hell he had just done.

And then it was over. The light gradually subsided, and the actual vortex could be seen once more. Shaun wasn't sure, but he thought the hexagon looked larger and more energetic than before, more like the one back on Saturn. Its six sides spread outward, pushing through the surrounding cloud layers, while the vortex within the hexagon spun with renewed vigor. Blue spots, left behind by the glare, danced before his eyes. He wiped the tears away as he stared at the reborn hexagon.

Did I do that?

"Gravitational fluxes stabilizing," Qat Zaldana reported from her station. Despite her veil, she peered into a pop-up viewer of her own. "By the Faceless, I think we did it!"

"Fascinating," Spock declared.

Excited murmurs and chatter bounced off the

gleaming walls of the bridge. Shaun could practically feel the tension lifting. He half expected someone to break open a bottle of champagne or maybe some of that Saurian brandy McCoy had offered him once.

"Good job." Sulu congratulated him. He shook Shaun's hand. "Sure you never attended the Academy?"

Shaun glanced down at his golden tunic and insignia. "Well, I'm wearing the uniform, aren't I?"

Chekov grinned for the first time. "Captain Kirk would be proud."

The elevator doors slid open, and Dr. McCoy rushed onto the bridge. His uniform was rumpled, and his face was flushed. He looked as if he was having a bad day. His eyes widened at the sight of Shaun seated at the conn.

"There you are!" he said, aghast. "What the devil are you doing at the controls?"

"Possibly providing a solution to our dilemma," Spock informed the doctor. "And saving many hundreds of lives."

McCoy was speechless, but only for a moment. "Come again?"

"I don't believe it," Governor Dawson declared. *"It's a miracle."*

"Vulcans do not believe in miracles," Spock replied. "They are not logical."

Dawson gazed from the main viewer. *"Then what would you call what just happened, Mr. Spock? Our home has been saved. The rings are falling back into their usual orbits. Skagway is not going to spiral into the planet. Nobody else has to die.*"

"Merely the timely activation of an alien technology so advanced as to appear miraculous," he stated. "To be precise."

The governor didn't argue the point. *"Well, whatever you want to call it, we're grateful for everything you did for us."*

"We all are," Qat Zaldana added. She stood behind the governor, having returned to Skagway to assist in the rebuilding. *"And may I say it was a pleasure to work with your people."*

"We valued your assistance as well," Spock stated.

Christopher and his fellow astronauts were assembled on the bridge. Shaun occupied the captain's chair, feeling like an impostor, while Spock and McCoy flanked him. He was inclined to let them do most of the talking.

"It was a team effort," Christopher said. "I'm just glad we managed to be of service."

"We couldn't have done it without you, Captain," Qat Zaldana said. She sounded as if she was winking behind her veil. *"You definitely had the right stuff."*

He got the joke, even if the governor didn't. It had been decided that Dawson and the other colonists did not need to know about the captain's peculiar condition. They had their hands full rebuilding after the disaster and the riots. Shaun understood that the governor had issued a blanket amnesty to the refugees who had fled the moon in panic. That struck him as a shrewd and politically savvy move. The colonists needed to work together now, not waste time pointing fingers at one another. He suspected that most of the moon's inhabitants were just happy to be reunited with their loved ones.

"Do you require any further medical assistance?" McCoy asked.

"Thank you, Doctor, but the supplies you beamed down earlier should be enough. I think we've got things in hand now." She toyed with a shiny crystalline paperweight on her desk. *"In fact, my engineers tell me that we should be able to resume normal mining operations soon."*

"Starfleet will be pleased to hear it," Spock stated.

"Yes," Christopher agreed, wishing that he knew more about the colony and its significance. What the heck was "dilithium," anyway?

The governor smiled at Shaun. *"I'm glad to see that you're back on your feet as well, Captain. Hope you didn't miss too much of the excitement."*

"Oh, I think I got my share," Shaun assured her. "Don't worry about me. All in a day's work for a Starfleet captain."

Or so I assume, he thought.

Indistinct voices addressed the governor from off-screen. She sighed wearily.

"Well, as you can imagine, I have about a million

urgent matters demanding my attention." Stacks of reports were piled high on her desk. *"Thank you again for your assistance. Give my regards to your superiors back at Starfleet Command."* She stared glumly at her workload. *"Dawson out."*

The governor and Qat Zaldana disappeared from the viewer, replaced by a view of the massive repair efforts under way on Skagway. No runaway ring matter pummeled the icy lunar landscape. Shaun took a good, long look at the scene. Extraterrestrial colonies and mining operations were still the stuff of science fiction and NASA white papers back in his time. It did his heart good to know that despite wars and recessions and everything else, humanity had finally made it to the stars and seemed to be actually thriving. It made all his years at NASA and Area 51 worthwhile.

We did it, Alice. We really did it.

If this was the future, he could live with it.

Spock cleared his throat. "The chair, Colonel, if you don't mind."

"Oh, right." Christopher jumped up and turned the chair back over to Spock. "Guess I shouldn't get too comfortable in that seat."

Lieutenant Uhura, the communications officer, spoke up. "We've received word from Starfleet, Mr. Spock. We're cleared to leave Skagway."

"About time!" McCoy exclaimed. "*Now* can we go look for Jim?"

Twenty-six

2020

O'Herlihy flew through the ship, bouncing off the walls as he raced from the command module to check on the brig. His fist clenched a heavy steel wrench, the first weapon he had been able to lay his hands on. With luck, he wouldn't need to use it—he had never been a violent man until today—but he had no idea what to expect. How had the prisoners managed to depressurize the airlock and open the outer hatch? And why in heaven's name would they do such a thing?

This wasn't part of the plan, he thought. *It makes no sense!*

Ghastly images of Shaun and Zoe being flushed out into the vacuum tortured his fevered mind. Perspiration beaded on his face, and he wanted to scream in frustration. This was the last thing he needed right now. The ship was spiraling in toward Saturn; he needed to make the most of what little time he had left to transmit their final discoveries back to Earth. Indeed, he had been so caught up in this vital work that he almost overlooked the fact that the cargo-bay airlock had been activated. Nobody had responded when he had paged the brig via the comm, which only increased his anxiety. He had been tempted to ignore the situation, since they were all destined to perish anyway, but nagging questions and doubts had driven him to find out what had happened to Shaun and Zoe, even at the expense of losing precious minutes of scientific exploration. Something wasn't right. He could feel it in his bones.

If they've done something to endanger Tera . . .

Passing through the hab, he reached the airlock in a matter of minutes. The indicator light above the hatch was out, and he noticed that an adjacent bulkhead appeared slightly warped, possibly as a result of the ship's jarring collisions with ring matter. Had the impact somehow activated the airlock, killing the prisoners? That seemed unlikely, but part of him almost hoped that was the case. Shaun and Zoe would have died quickly, getting it over with.

An appalling possibility occurred to him. Could the prisoners have chosen to take their own lives, rather than prolong their final hours? Or had they accidentally killed themselves in some desperate, panicky attempt to escape? That didn't sound like Shaun, but then again, Shaun wasn't exactly himself anymore. Who knew what he was capable of now?

An empty blue jumpsuit was draped over the hatchway window like a curtain, blocking his view of the airlock's interior. Frantic for answers, he pounded on the hatch with the wrench.

"Hello? Is anybody in there?"

He had sealed and repressurized the airlock from command before heading there. He tried to open the hatch, but it refused to budge. The locking mechanism would not disengage. He banged on the hatch again.

"Are you still there? What have you done?"

A delicate hand drew back the curtain. Zoe's face, upside-down, smirked at him through the porthole. She appeared to be wearing a skintight elastic cooling suit.

"Hey there!" she shouted at him through the hatch. "What's up, Doc?"

He didn't know whether to be relieved or concerned that she was still alive.

At least she's still locked up, he thought. "I want answers! What happened here?"

"What's that again?" She cupped a hand over her ear in a transparent attempt to feign that she couldn't quite hear him. "Would you mind speaking louder?"

"What happened?" he hollered. "Is Shaun still with you?"

"Jeez, Doc! There's no need to shout."

For God's sake! He didn't have time to play games like this. Fuming, he activated the comm instead. "I know you opened the airlock to the outside!" he ranted. "What were you thinking?"

"Would you believe it was getting a bit stuffy in here?" She tugged at the collar of the cooling suit. "Not to mention chilly. You wouldn't believe how damp and clammy this place gets after a while. Not exactly the luxury suite, you know."

Her flippancy infuriated him. "Stop it! Can't you be serious for once in your life?" He tried to peer past her, but her inverted face filled the porthole, obstructing his view. "Where is Shaun? Let me talk to him!"

"Oh, it's 'Shaun' again, is it?" Her fingers formed air quotes. "I thought you and Fontana had decided that he was possessed by space ghosts or something. You forget about that part?"

"Shaun, the probe, amnesia . . . whatever!" He threw up his hands, unable to believe that she was actually wasting their last few hours like this. "Is he in there? Did he survive?"

"What do you care?" she shot back. "We're all supposed to die anyway, right, when we take our one-way plunge into Hurricane Saturn? What does it matter if 'Shaun' and I decided to air out this crummy cell first?" She wrinkled her nose in disgust. "Between you and me, it was starting to smell like a gym locker."

"Cut the comedy routine!" he demanded, as though dressing down a class clown back at the university. "How did you even get the hatch open? That should have been impossible!"

"You ever get tired of saying that, Doc?" she replied. "You'd think you would have figured out by now that *anything* is possible in this crazy universe. Just ask that weirdo hexagon down there."

"Just answer the question!"

"Say, how is my BFF Fontana doing? She still sleeping it off? Granted, there's a woman who really needed to unwind a bit, but slipping her a roofie seems a bit extreme."

She's stalling, he realized. *But why? What is she hiding?*

A worrisome possibility came together in his mind. His eyes narrowed suspiciously. There had been *two* spacesuits stored in the airlock, after all.

"Where is Shaun? Let me see him . . . if he's still there."

She shook her head upside-down. "The astronaut formerly known as Colonel Shaun Christopher is not available right now, but if you like, I can take a message."

I was right, he realized. *She's ducking my questions.*

His dire suspicions crystallized into certainty. Shaun wasn't in the brig with her. He had exited the airlock in the other suit. He was spacewalking, and there was only one place he could be going.

The command module.

"Blast you, Shaun," he murmured. "Why couldn't you just let me finish this?"

There was no time to lose. Like a swimmer reversing direction at the end of a lane, he somersaulted in the air and set off back the way he'd come.

"Wait! Where are you going?" Zoe hollered. "Come back!"

He ignored her. She didn't matter now. He needed

to get back to command—before Shaun ruined everything!

Kirk was anxious to get out of his spacesuit. Stuck in the docking ring, he waited impatiently for the airlock to finish repressurizing so he could enter the command module. He remained on the lookout for O'Herlihy, whose whereabouts remained unknown. Kirk suspected that the desperate scientist would not surrender without a fight.

What I wouldn't give for a phaser right now.

To his dismay, he spotted O'Herlihy in the vestibule on the other side of the module. Their eyes met across the charred remains of the mid-deck. O'Herlihy lunged from the vestibule, racing to seal the airlock before Kirk could emerge. Kirk's ears popped as he felt the air pressure rise within the compartment. A gauge reported that the pressure was almost normal.

Just another second . . .

The indicator turned green, and the hatch slid open. Kirk burst from the airlock to confront the other man. He unscrewed his helmet and tossed it aside.

"That's enough, Doctor. It's over."

"Don't try to stop me, Shaun . . . or whoever you are." O'Herlihy brandished a large metal wrench. "I won't let you!"

They circled each other warily, propelling themselves by handrails and gentle shoves. Kirk assessed his chances. He could handle himself in a fight, as everyone from Khan to Klingons had found out in his own time, but zero gravity complicated matters. It was going to be tricky to throw punches and kicks in this environment, and his zero-g combat training was years in the past and in a much younger body. He needed to think this one out instead of just wading in with his fists.

"Please, Shaun!" the doctor begged. "I don't want to fight you. Just let me save my daughter!"

"I'm sorry, Marcus. You know I can't let you do that."

O'Herlihy was fighting for his child's life, as he saw it, which made him a dangerous opponent, plus he had the advantage of a weapon. Weightless or not, that wrench could still do serious damage if it connected. Kirk started to regret taking off his space helmet.

He glanced around for something to even the odds. Zoe's slender tablet was still strapped to his wrist, but it wouldn't be much use in a fight. His gaze fell on a fire extinguisher taped to a melted lab counter. Outside of a phaser, the sturdy metal cylinder was just what he needed. Pushing off from a warped steel cabinet, he flew for the canister.

"Leave that alone!" O'Herlihy saw what Kirk was up to and frantically tried to stop him. He hurled the wrench at Kirk's head. The sturdy tool spun through the air between them. Kirk ducked and heard it clang against a bulkhead. Executing a barrel roll above the counter, he yanked the fire extinguisher free and rotated to face O'Herlihy, who was diving at him with a murderous expression on his face. Kirk fumbled with the trigger.

Foam sprayed from the nozzle. The blast struck O'Herlihy, driving him back, while simultaneously propelling Kirk in the opposite direction. Kirk grunted in pain as his back, already bruised from being tossed about the brig earlier, smacked into a wall. The padded spacesuit cushioned the blow to a degree, but it still smarted. He eased up on the fire extinguisher to keep from caroming around the deck.

"Stop it, Marcus! You don't want to do this!"

"It doesn't matter what I want!" O'Herlihy sputtered through a mouthful of foam. The frothy mixture coated his face and front, making him look like a survivor of a coolant explosion. He wiped it from his eyes. "I'll do whatever it takes to save my daughter!"

He grabbed the hatchway ladder to halt his flight. Choosing the better part of valor, he scrambled up through the open hatch, disappearing from sight.

Not so fast, Kirk thought. He couldn't give O'Herlihy the chance to lock him out of the flight deck above. Using the fire extinguisher as a makeshift thruster, he rocketed through the hatchway after his quarry. Drifting foam splattered against his face as he blasted up into the flight deck, past Fontana, who was still floating unconscious by the top of the ladder. Duct tape bound her wrists to an upper rung, while her legs floated free. She stirred restlessly.

But where was O'Herlihy? Kirk had lost sight of his

foe. Killing the fire extinguisher, he looked about for the other man. "Marcus?"

A metal meal tray smashed Kirk in the face, knocking him across the deck. The fire extinguisher slipped from his fingers. He tasted blood. Glistening crimson beads sprayed into the air, dispersing weightlessly through the atmosphere. He tumbled backward, dazed by the blow. The fire extinguisher banged into a bulkhead several meters away. Kirk felt as if he had just been slapped across the face by a Gorn. He spit out a tooth.

The ruckus roused Fontana, whose eyes fluttered open. A floating bead splattered against her cheek. She gazed about groggily. "Shaun?"

O'Herlihy tossed away the tray. Before Kirk could recover from the blow, he bounded over to the helm and hastily worked the controls. Not bothering to strap himself into the pilot's seat, he keyed new commands into the ship's computer.

"Wait!" Fontana said, coming to. "What are you doing? Get away from there!"

"You can't stop me!" His fingers jabbed at the instrument panel. "I have to save Tera!"

Even if it meant sending the *Lewis & Clark* on a suicide mission into the heart of a gas giant.

The thrusters ignited. A burst of acceleration tossed Kirk back against a bulkhead. Fontana was tossed about the ladder like a flag flapping in the wind. Saturn's turbulent atmosphere filled the windows of the cockpit, growing larger and clearer by the moment. Kirk could make out the planet's sulfurous yellow bands in alarming detail. Lightning flashed across storms the size of continents. The ship plowed through the inner rings.

"Shaun!" Fontana tugged at her bonds, fully awake now. "Stop him! He's changing our orbit, sending us into the planet!"

So much for the scenic route, Kirk thought. O'Herlihy had evidently given up on his plan to drag out the ship's final orbits long enough to make more observations of Saturn and its rings. Cutting to the chase, the crazed scientist and father was taking them on a downward trajectory straight into Saturn. The thrusters continued to fire, accelerating the ship. Kirk guessed that they had only minutes before the ship entered the atmosphere.

No, Kirk thought. *This has gone far enough.*

A crimson haze literally floated before his eyes. Shaking the cobwebs from his brain, he swept the drifting globules aside and tackled O'Herlihy at the helm. The doctor's face slammed into the instrument panel, and Kirk yanked the other man's hands away from the controls. Kicking against the console, he sent them both tumbling away from the helm.

"Let go of me!" O'Herlihy raged. "You're going to get Tera killed!"

Kirk disagreed. "Nobody's dying today, Marcus. Least of all us."

The two men grappled in midair, much as Kirk and Zoe had earlier, but much less enjoyably. O'Herlihy elbowed Kirk in the gut, but the captain's spacesuit shielded him from the blow; it was like wearing a heavily padded suit of body armor. Twisting around, O'Herlihy grabbed Kirk's throat and squeezed. His nails dug into Kirk's neck. Crimson bubbles percolated from his nose.

"Have you forgotten your oath, Doctor?" Kirk wheezed. He'd been choked once today already, and he'd had enough. "First, do no harm . . ."

He butted his head into O'Herlihy's bloody face. The scientist shrieked as his busted nose took another hit. More weightless red bubbles contaminated the air, joining drifting flecks of foam. Pushing down on O'Herlihy's shoulders, Kirk swung his legs up and kicked the other man squarely in the chest with his sturdy space boots. The force of the kick sent the scientist flying backward—toward Fontana.

She snagged him with her legs, wrapping them around his neck. "Hurry!" she shouted at Kirk. "Finish this!"

"Let go of me!" O'Herlihy struggled to extricate himself. "You don't understand what you're doing!"

Kirk bounced off a wall, launching himself at the trapped scientist like a missile. His right fist collided with the man's jaw. The thick white glove felt like a boxing glove, protecting his knuckles. O'Herlihy's head snapped backward, then swayed atop his neck. Frantic eyes rolled upward until only the blood-streaked whites were visible. He went limp.

Kirk had scored a knockout.

"Sorry about that, Doctor, but I left my phaser at home."

Fontana gave him a quizzical look. "Okay, consider me impressed, whoever you are." She let go of the unconscious scientist and nodded at her bound wrists. "I'd give you a round of applause, but I'm a little tied up."

"Let me do something about that."

The captain briefly wondered if it was a good idea to release her, since she was the one who had tossed him into the brig in the first place, after nearly choking the life out of him earlier, but he judged that circumstances had changed. After O'Herlihy's rampage, there was no longer any question who the real saboteur was, and Kirk guessed that he was going to need Fontana's help to undo what the doctor had done and save the ship.

He hastily tore away the tape. "Don't make me regret this."

"Not yet," she promised, massaging her wrists. "I think we've got bigger problems."

The thrusters flared at full power, recklessly burning through their fuel. No wonder the ship had been orbiting Saturn quickly enough to keep hitting the rings; never intending to make a return trip to Earth, O'Herlihy had felt free to expend all of their fuel on one final death spiral.

Fontana raced Kirk to the cockpit. She fired the braking thrusters.

"It's too late!" she shouted. "We worked up too much speed. We're caught in the gravity well." She strapped herself in. "Brace yourself! We're going in!"

Twenty-seven

2020

They entered Saturn.

Descending toward the planet, the *Lewis & Clark* skimmed the gas giant's upper atmosphere. Icy wisps of crystallized sulfur and ammonia blew past the cockpit windows as the ship bounced violently off the dense cloud banks below. Freezing winds buffeted the ship, fighting a losing battle against the heat of friction and causing the flight deck to spin on its axis like a carnival ride. Kirk strapped himself into the pilot's seat to keep from being tossed about the compartment. The hull began to creak alarmingly as the heat and pressure mounted outside. The temperature inside the cockpit climbed toward the hellish. Warning lights flashed all over the instrument panels. Alarms blared. The ship's outer plating had been built to withstand the unpredictable hazards of a six-month voyage far from home, but Kirk knew that the ship couldn't go much deeper into the atmosphere without burning up. It was a race to see what killed them first—the pressure, the storms, or the heat.

Kirk wanted to call down to Engineering, to tell

Scotty to divert all available power to the shields. Unfortunately, that wasn't an option.

"What about Querez?" Fontana shouted over the chaos. The bumpy ride rattled her voice, giving it more than a touch of vibrato. Sweat poured down her face. "Where is she?"

"The airlock. Safe, last time I saw her."

But for how much longer?

He let Fontana pilot the ship. She had more experience with this generation of vessel. He unhooked his clumsy gloves and tossed them aside. "Can you get us out of here?"

"I'm trying! But it's no use. I'm hitting the brakes for all they're worth, but the thrusters are running out of fuel. We can't achieve escape velocity!"

"There has to be some way to break free!" Kirk said. Saturn's tempestuous atmosphere descended for nearly a hundred thousand kilometers, but at this rate, the *Lewis & Clark* would burn up like a shooting star long before they reached the boiling seas of liquid hydrogen and helium far beneath the raging storms, let alone the planet's molten core. "We just need more power."

An idea hit him.

"The impulse engines! They're our only hope."

Fontana stared at him in shock. "From a cold start? There's no time!"

The impulse engines had been shut down since they had arrived at Saturn; the crew had been relying on controlled thruster burns to navigate around the planet. But it was possible that even the *Lewis & Clark*'s primitive impulse engines might have enough *oomph* to get them clear of the atmosphere again—if they could get them fired up in time.

"Trust me! It can be done." Kirk had seen Scotty work wonders with his engines in the past, usually in the nick of time. "You just need to kick-start the fusion reaction by superheating the deuterium, then keep a close eye on the plasma conduits."

"Or?" she asked.

"The ship blows up," he admitted. "But you have to believe me. I know this technology better than you do, and I know what it's capable of . . . with the right handling."

She hesitated, uncertain whether to trust him. "I don't even know who you are."

He didn't blame her for doubting him. He was asking a lot. "I know. But believe it or not, I've done this kind of thing before."

Lightning flashed far below them. Deafening thunderclaps shook the flight deck. Banshee winds wailed over the agonized groaning of the hull. The ship was tossed about like a dinghy on an angry sea. The overhead lights flickered ominously. Sparks erupted from one of the auxiliary computer terminals. Sweat soaked through Kirk's clothes; it was already hotter than Vulcan's Forge and getting worse by the second. He feared for Zoe, who was still trapped down in the airlock, with no clue of what was happening. He feared for them all.

"Oh, what the hell," Fontana blurted. "It's not like I've got any better ideas. Get to it, stranger."

"Thanks!"

Kirk rapidly called up the impulse controls and started streamlining the start-up procedure. The computer flashed a stream of alerts, warning him that he was exceeding established safety parameters. He ignored the cautions and overrode the computer's increasingly strident attempts to block him. He remembered reviewing the engine specs back in Shaun's quarters; what he was attempting was risky, to be sure, but it was doable if you didn't push these crude engines too hard. There was no way he could achieve the sort of thrust that more advanced impulse engines were capable of, but he wasn't trying to approach light speed, just to get them out of this oversized pressure cooker before they went too deep. *Good thing Saturn's gravity isn't proportionate to its size,* he thought, *or we wouldn't stand a chance.*

"Almost set." He let Fontana keep control of the helm, while he monitored the fusion reactor, the accelerator/generator, the drive coils, and the vectored plasma exhaust vents. All indicators were in the red zone, and the computer thought he was a maniac, but that couldn't be helped. He was asking the *Lewis & Clark* to do something no Earth-based ship had done before. He could only hope that she was up to it. "On my count, three . . . two . . . one . . ."

Blastoff.

The impulse engines awoke with a roar. A burst of acceleration drove Kirk back into his seat. A bone-jarring vibration rattled the flight deck. Kirk anxiously watched the gauges. If the overtaxed engines were going to explode, it was going to be now. Fontana wrestled with the nav controls. The ship's nose lifted upward.

"Yes!" she exulted. "We have liftoff!"

The deadly heat began to abate as the *Lewis & Clark* climbed toward safety. Wind, thunder, and lightning, coming from Saturn's furious depths, chased them out of the planet's atmosphere. Fontana let out a whoop as sulfurous vapors gave way to the frigid black emptiness of space and the dazzling brilliance of the rings.

"Oh my God!" she exclaimed. "We did it!"

Kirk wiped the sweat from his brow. "Tell you the truth, I wasn't sure that would work."

"Now you tell me." She eased back on the throttle, guiding the ship into a stable polar orbit that slipped through the gaps in the rings. The violent rattling subsided. For the first time in too long, the mission was back on track.

They were safe.

I'll have to tell Scotty about this someday, he thought. *If I ever get back to my own time.*

She turned toward him, a thoughtful look on her face. Shrewd green eyes examined him. "I still don't know who you are, mister, but I'm glad you're here."

"Thanks. That means a lot."

She eyed him pensively. "Can you please tell me one thing? Where is the real Shaun?"

"I wish I knew," Kirk said.

Before he could even try to explain, he remembered something else they needed to deal with first.

O'Herlihy.

He spun his chair around to check on the unconscious scientist, only to find the man missing. "Damn!" Kirk swore. "He's gone."

Fontana knew at once who he meant. After all, there was only one other man aboard the ship. An obscenity escaped her lips. "That bastard. He must have slipped away while we were saving the ship." She clenched her fists. "God, he had me fooled this whole time. I still don't get it. Why is he doing this?"

Kirk gathered that she hadn't heard about O'Herlihy's daughter. "I'll explain later. We have to find him!"

Unstrapping himself, Kirk lurched from his seat and headed for the hatch. With any luck, O'Herlihy hadn't gotten far. Maybe they could still catch him before he did any more damage. "Stay here!" he instructed Fontana, leaving her at the helm. "I'm going after him."

He dove headfirst into the mid-deck below. Fire-retardant foam still drifted about the compartment. He put a hand over his mouth and nose to keep from inhaling it. The fans and filters labored noisily to scrub the atmosphere, even as Kirk searched for the fugitive doctor. His eyes scanned the deck.

A warning light flashed above the airlock. An alarm sounded.

Kirk rushed to the entrance to the docking ring. Peering through the porthole in the hatch, he spied O'Herlihy inside the airlock, struggling with the outer hatch. According to the indicators, the compartment was still pressurized. He was not wearing a spacesuit.

"Marcus!" Kirk yelled at him through the door. "What do you think you're doing?"

O'Herlihy turned to face him. His face was haggard and bloody. His nose looked broken. He spoke like a man who had lost all hope.

"Don't blame yourself, Shaun. It's not your fault. I'm the one who failed Tera, not you."

Kirk realized that O'Herlihy intended to flush himself out the airlock.

"Don't do it. We'll find a way to save your daughter!"

"It's too late," the doctor said. "We're too far away to do anything. I'll never see her again, at least not in this life." He smiled ruefully. "Look at it this way. I'm going to be the first man on Saturn. If I'm lucky, people will remember that part . . . and not everything else."

An alarm squealed in protest as O'Herlihy fumbled with the hatch's manual override. The ship didn't want to open the hatch before the airlock was depressurized, but the suicidal scientist was determined to open it anyway. Kirk didn't underestimate the man's abilities. O'Herlihy knew this ship as well as anyone.

"Wait!" Kirk pleaded. "Give me a chance to fix things."

He remembered Zoe's upgraded tablet, which was still clipped to his suit. He took hold of it and hacked into the airlock's locking mechanism again. O'Herlihy cursed as the outer hatch refused to budge. The inner hatch slid open.

"Sorry, Doctor," Kirk said. "I told you before, nobody is dying today."

"I guess we've got a lot to talk about," Kirk said.

Kirk, Fontana, and Zoe had convened on the flight deck. Prying Zoe out of the broken airlock had been a challenge, but, working together, he and Fontana had managed to get the damaged hatch to open. O'Herlihy was under a suicide watch in the infirmary, strapped down to the examination pad and monitored 24/7 by a closed-circuit camera. At the moment, the suicidal scientist was sleeping restlessly, having been sedated by Fontana in an instance of poetic justice.

"And plenty of time to do so," she said. "Even with the impulse engines up and running, we've got a long trip back to Earth. Maneuvering is going to be tricky, now that we've used up most of our thruster fuel, but Mission Control is already working on a new flight plan to get us close enough to Earth. I'm going to cross my fingers and assume that everything will work out. I mean, we've beaten the odds so far."

"That's the spirit, Alice." Zoe had traded her elastic cooling suit for a spare T-shirt and shorts. "Speaking of rescues, what about the doc's daughter? What's going to happen to her?"

Kirk was worried about that, too. "We've notified the authorities back on Earth. Last I heard, they were planning a rescue attempt, but it's going to be a gamble. Apparently, HEL is holed up in a heavily fortified compound on an island in the Pacific Northwest. The odds are against anybody getting to Tera before her captors can execute her."

"You're not kidding," Zoe said. "I've been to that compound, to interview HEL's leaders." She shuddered at the memory. "It's a disaster waiting to happen."

If only he could do something to rescue Tera himself, but Earth was still three months away. Kirk could only hope that the special forces of this era were up to the task and that an innocent young woman wouldn't end up as collateral damage.

An electronic chime came from the main communications panel.

"Hark!" Zoe said. "We've got mail."

Fontana flew over to investigate. "Looks like we're receiving a transmission."

"From Earth?"

Kirk frowned, fearing bad news regarding O'Herlihy's daughter. No matter what the man had done, Kirk didn't want to have to tell him that Tera had been killed in a raid on HEL. He couldn't imagine what it would be like to lose one's only child.

Maybe it's just our new flight plan, he hoped.

"No." Fontana looked up from the terminal with a stunned expression on her face. She gazed at the empty reaches of space beyond Saturn's rings. "Unless this equipment is malfunctioning, the signal is coming from . . . out there."

Kirk felt a surge of excitement. He had almost given up waiting for a moment like this.

Could it be?

"What does it say?" he asked urgently. "Is there a message for us?"

"I'm not sure," Fontana said. Her smooth brow furrowed in confusion. "Let me put it on the speakers."

An unmistakable mellifluous voice emerged from the comm system.

"Hailing Captain Kirk," Uhura said. *"If you can read me, please respond."*

Twenty-eight

2020

Gravity hit Kirk like a ton of thermoconcrete. He staggered on the transporter platform, and McCoy rushed forward to prop him up. "Easy, Jim. Give yourself time to adjust."

"Thanks, Bones." He let the doctor help him off the platform. His bones and muscles, debilitated by weeks of zero gravity, felt like overcooked pasta. "Guess I've got some physical therapy in my future . . . if I don't get my own body back."

"Count on it," McCoy said. "And don't expect me to go easy on you."

Kirk chuckled. It was good to be home.

"Welcome back, Captain." Spock greeted Kirk. "I apologize for the delay, but as you know, we had other matters to attend to, and time travel is hardly an exact science."

"Understood, Mr. Spock." Kirk stood as straight as he could manage; it wouldn't do for the captain to appear too weak, even before friends. "I remember how tricky that slingshot maneuver can be. I'm just glad you made it to the right year."

Close to five days had passed for him since he had first arrived in this era; he wondered how much time had passed for the *Enterprise*. The Klondike system was months from Saturn, so clearly, he had missed a good deal of time. "The situation on Skagway?"

"Resolved, Captain, successfully."

"Good to hear it. I knew I could count on you, Mr. Spock. I look forward to getting a full report, after we take care of a few other pressing matters."

The *Enterprise* was keeping a low profile in this century, using Saturn's moons and the ship's own deflectors to reduce its chances of being detected by Earth. Kirk took a moment to appreciate the comforting familiarity of the transporter room. His welcoming party included Spock, McCoy, Scotty, and one other familiar face: his own.

Even though he had been expecting it, it still came as a jolt to see what appeared to be James T. Kirk standing beside Spock and Scotty. He had to remind himself that, this time around, he wasn't faced with an android double, a duplicitous shape-changer, or his own evil half. This was his actual body, which currently housed another man's mind.

"Colonel Shaun Geoffrey Christopher, I presume?"

"Pleased to finally meet you, Captain Kirk." The stranger with his face stepped forward and offered Kirk his hand. "I must say, you're a sight for sore eyes."

"The feeling is mutual." Kirk shook his own hand. "Sorry if I've been a bit rough on your body." He rubbed his sore jaw; cuts and bruises on his face served as painful reminders of his battle with O'Herlihy. "I'm afraid you're missing a tooth."

Shaun looked Kirk over. "Has there been trouble on my ship? Is everyone all right?"

"They're fine, more or less," Kirk said. "It's been an . . . eventful mission, but the situation was under control when I left. I can give you all of the details later."

"What about Alice?" he asked. "I mean, Fontana."

Kirk caught the urgency in his voice. It seemed that Fontana's deep affection for her copilot had not been one-sided. He decided not to mention his brief encounter with Zoe.

"Anxious to see you again," he assured Shaun. In fact, Fontana had wanted to beam over with him, until he'd pointed out that this would entail leaving Zoe in charge of the *Lewis & Clark*. Fontana had quickly relented, which was just as well; the fewer twenty-first-century astronauts to visit the *Enterprise,* the better. "I believe she's missed you."

"No more than I've missed her," Shaun said with obvious emotion. Kirk recalled that the displaced astronaut had not seen his own crew for months, by his reckoning. "Funny how getting zapped hundreds of years into a strange future and nearly dying on the other side of the galaxy makes you realize just what— and who—is really important to you. Alice and I have our own future to get on with."

Kirk believed him. He made a mental note to look both astronauts up when he got a chance. He was curious to find out what the future held for them, assuming that he and Shaun could straighten out their current situation.

"You'll see her soon," he promised, before glancing down at his borrowed body. "But first, there's the little matter of putting both of our minds back where they belong."

"Well, don't look at me," McCoy said. "I'm out of the brain-transplant business." He looked pointedly at Spock. "Once was enough."

Kirk wasn't particularly keen on swapping brains, either. He preferred to keep their gray matter in place, if possible.

"What about that infernal contraption that daft lassie used to switch places with the captain a few years ago?" Scotty asked, referring to Janice Lester and her foiled attempt to steal Kirk's body. "Camus II is a fair ways from here, but those alien machines should be just sitting there in this century, waiting for us."

"Not an option." Kirk had already considered that. "The effect wasn't permanent, remember? Our minds began to shift back of their own accord, and Janice theorized that the only way to make the switch stick was to kill me while my mind was still in her body." He looked at Shaun Christopher. "Obviously, that's not an option."

"Good to know," Shaun said. "What else can we try?"

Kirk turned to his first officer. "Spock?"

"I can attempt to facilitate some manner of psychic reintegration, Captain, but there are no guarantees. This would go beyond a simple mind-meld, not that there is ever anything simple about the joining of two or more minds." His somber tone conveyed the gravity of the challenge. "However, the only alternative is to condemn you and Colonel Christopher to reside in each other's body for the rest of your natural lives."

"Forget it," Shaun said. "I want my old body back, no matter the risk. No offense, Captain."

"None taken," Kirk said. "I feel the same."

"Hold on a minute!" McCoy blurted, clearly unconvinced. "Let's not rush into anything. Do you really think you can do this, Spock? Transfer minds from one body to another?"

"Ordinarily not, Doctor," Spock admitted. "You are quite correct that such a feat is most likely beyond my abilities or those of any other Vulcan. But I am relying on the fact that these two minds will want to return to their proper locations, just as the captain's and Dr. Lester's minds did on that previous occasion. In theory, I will simply be the conduit by which their respective psyches are able to restore their natural states."

"Like water flowing back to the sea," Kirk said, grasping the concept.

"Or a displaced electron returning to its previous

quantum state," Spock said. "Extraordinary energy was no doubt required to trade your minds, but it is possible that less effort will be required to put them back where they belong. Think of your brains as planets, exerting a gravitational pull on your thoughts."

"I don't know," McCoy grumbled. "It still sounds like a hell of a gamble to me. At least you're both still sound in body and mind. What if this stunt does more harm than good? You could end up brain-damaged or insane . . . or worse."

Kirk shrugged. "That's a risk I'm willing to take, Bones."

"Hell, yes," Shaun agreed. "Let's do this."

"Think back," Spock said. "Recall the precise moment you encountered the probe, the last moment your minds were where they belonged."

He stood between the men, who reclined on adjacent beds in sickbay. His fingers were splayed across their brows. Diagnostic monitors reported on their vital signs, with particular attention paid to their brain waves. Dr. McCoy and Nurse Chapel looked on anxiously. Spock closed his eyelids, both sets, to block out the distractions of the physical world. He cleared his mind, making it an empty conduit.

"Relive that moment," he urged the patients. "Reclaim it."

He reached out through his fingertips for the other

men's thoughts. Neural connections formed, linking them. Three minds became one.

"Reclaim yourselves . . . through me . . ."

Thoughts and sensations flowed into him from both sides, converging on his brain. Waves of clashing memories collided inside him.

Floating above Saturn, jetting toward the gleaming alien probe. Beaming the decrepit wreck aboard the Enterprise. *Staring in shock and wonder as the probe fires brilliant pulses of light at the hexagon far below. Marveling at the oddly familiar hieroglyphics etched on the charred bronze casing. Fontana, pleading for him to get away from the probe. Miramanee surfacing from his past. Curiosity overcoming caution. Poignant memories drawing him nearer.*

Reaching out to touch the probe . . .

Contact.

A blinding flash of light exploded in Spock's mind. "The rings!" he shouted, without knowing why. "The endless rings!"

He collapsed between the beds.

"Spock!" McCoy shouted.

Dazed, Shaun sat up in the bed. It took him a second to orient himself; for a moment, he wasn't sure who or where he was. *Right,* he remembered. *The* Enterprise. *Sickbay.* His hands explored his face, rediscovering crags and wrinkles he hadn't felt in months. Glancing down at himself, he saw that he was wearing a blue

NASA jumpsuit again, not a gold-and-black Starfleet uniform. His limbs felt weak and rubbery, as if they weren't used to gravity anymore. His heart leaped in excitement.

"Is this for real? Did it work?"

To his right, Captain Kirk looked back at him. He looked equally thrilled to be back in his own body. "So it appears, Colonel. We're us again."

But what about Spock? The Vulcan was sprawled on the floor between them, looking distinctly out of it. McCoy crouched over the fallen officer, scanning Spock with one of his futuristic medical gizmos. Spock groaned weakly. He clutched his head.

"How is he, Bones?" Kirk demanded, sounding every bit the captain of a starship, despite the profoundly unsettling experience they had just shared. "Will he be all right?"

"I think so," McCoy said cautiously. "His vital signs are normal, by his half-human standards, and he seems to be coming to. I think he's just in shock." He called out to Chapel. "A stabilizer, stat!"

"That will not be necessary, Doctor." Spock's eyes flicked open. He sat up with as much stoic dignity as he could muster. His face was pale, but the green was already coming back to it. "The experience was . . . unique, I admit, but Vulcans are not easily shocked."

"In a pig's eye," McCoy muttered. "You're not going anywhere until I give you a thorough checkup." He swept his gaze over the three patients. "And that goes for all of you."

"Whatever you say, Doc." Shaun lay back down, succumbing to gravity. "But don't think you can keep me here forever." The trip from Klondike VI to Saturn had been a long one, even by twenty-third-century standards. "I have a ship—and a mission—to get back to."

"You needn't worry about that," the doctor said. "I doubt we're sticking around." He turned toward Kirk, the real Kirk. "You probably ought to know, Jim, that Starfleet hasn't actually sanctioned this little jaunt into yesterday. We figured it might be easier to find you first and ask for permission later."

"Probably a good call," Kirk said. "You know how the brass is frowning on time travel these days. They don't want to risk changing history, not after some of the close calls we've had in the last few years. We'll probably have some explaining to do to that new temporal investigation agency when we get back. They seem to think we've been abusing the privilege lately."

"Imagine that," McCoy said wryly. "So, when are we heading home?"

"Soon," Kirk said. "But I have a few promises to keep first."

"Where is he? What's taking so long?"

Fontana was climbing the walls, waiting for she

didn't know what. Hours had passed since Shaun—or was it "Captain Kirk"?—had vanished from the cockpit in a sparkling column of light. Supposedly, there was another spacecraft nearby, just out of sight, but for all she knew, Shaun's body had just disintegrated right before her eyes.

"He should have been back by now, shouldn't he? If he was coming back?"

"Relax," Zoe said, floating cross-legged above the flight deck. "It will be okay. He seemed to know what he was doing."

Fontana couldn't believe how calmly the other woman was taking this. "Don't you get it? We don't even know who this 'Kirk' is, where he came from, what he was doing here, and, oh, yeah, what the hell happened to the real Shaun?" She stared anxiously out the cockpit windows, looking for answers somewhere beyond Saturn's glittering rings. "This whole thing is insane!"

"I know," Zoe sympathized. "But look, just a few hours ago, we were all booked for a kamikaze cruise to oblivion, but hey, we're still here. The way I see it, everything from now on is gravy."

"Maybe." Fontana almost envied Zoe's pathologically breezy attitude. "But what are we supposed to do in the meantime?"

"Make out?"

Fontana's jaw dropped. She bumped into a bulkhead.

"Geez, Fontana! It was a joke." Zoe rolled her eyes. "To lighten the mood, you know? No offense, but you're not my type."

"I'm crushed," Fontana said, recovering. "Truly."

She wondered if Zoe was actually more freaked out than she was letting on. Hadn't she said something once about cracking jokes whenever she was scared? In that case, it could be Open Mike Night on the *Lewis & Clark.*

Get back here, Shaun, she thought. *Soon.*

As if in answer to her prayers, an unearthly hum suddenly filled the flight deck. A coruscating pillar of sparks, about the size and width of an adult human being, manifested in the middle of the compartment, only a few yards away from the two women, then coalesced into a figure of flesh and blood. A familiar face looked around in wonder, as though amazed to find himself back on the ship.

"Shaun?" Fontana asked. "I mean, Kirk?"

"Right the first time." His face lit up at the sight of her. "It's really me, Alice. I'm back."

He rushed forward to embrace her. One kiss, and all of her doubts evaporated. She didn't need to quiz or interrogate him. She could tell at once that this was no impostor. This was the real Shaun, come home to her at last. Her heart gave her all the proof she needed.

"Whoa there," Zoe interrupted. "Get a room."

Fontana shot her a warning glance. "If you *ever*

mention one word of this on your stupid blog, I will make you wish you had been flushed out of that airlock."

"Got it," Zoe said, gulping. "My lips are sealed. As you were."

Pausing for breath, Fontana gazed into Shaun's warm blue eyes. Questions swirled inside her. "Where have you been all this time?"

His eyes devoured her, as though he hadn't seen her in weeks.

"That will have to be our little secret," he said. "I made a promise to some new friends to keep quiet about certain things, for all our sakes. But don't worry. I promise to give you the full story soon." He hugged her tightly. "It's taken me a long time to get back to you—months, in fact—but now we have all the time in the world."

"Months?" she echoed. "But it's been a week at most since that probe zapped you."

"For you, maybe, but for me . . . I've had a lot of time to think about us."

She took his word for it. Right now, it was enough that they were together again.

"What about me?" Zoe asked. "Don't I get a scoop?"

"Hang on," Shaun said, smirking. "You're in for a surprise."

The eerie hum returned. A shower of sparks enveloped Zoe, then whisked her away, leaving the two astronauts alone on the flight deck.

Fontana gaped in shock. "What the—? Where did she go?"

"Remember those new friends I mentioned?" Shaun seemed not at all taken aback by Zoe's abrupt disappearance. "Well, they need her help with something important."

Twenty-nine

2020

The walled compound, tucked away on a remote island in Puget Sound, had once belonged to an obscure doomsday cult that had gradually drifted apart after the world stubbornly refused to end when the Mayan calendar expired in 2012. Abandoned for years, the grounds and buildings had since been claimed by the Human Extinction League, whose members were not inclined to wait expectantly for mankind's demise. They aspired to hurry it along.

Tera O'Herlihy had been HEL's unwilling guest for months now. She couldn't remember the last time she'd seen the sun, the stars, or anyone who didn't want the human race to go the way of the dinosaurs. Since spring break, she'd been confined to an underground bunker beneath the compound's faux–Mayan temple. Concrete walls defined her world. Posters of past environmental disasters—Chernobyl, Bhopal, the Gulf spill, global warming—adorned the walls to remind her constantly of humanity's crimes against the Earth. A half-finished mural depicted a deserted Manhattan devoid of people and being reclaimed by wilderness.

Tera figured the artist had stolen the idea from that old Will Smith movie, not that it really mattered to her. A furnace chugged noisily in the boiler room down the hall. An armed guard was posted at the door. Tera knew better than to try to make a break for it.

Where could she go?

The compound was surrounded on all sides by barbed wire, sentries, motion detectors, and mine fields. Jase and the others had made it very clear to her that there was no way out. She was stuck here, held hostage by people she had once thought were her friends.

They're never going to let me go, she knew deep down inside. *No matter what they make Dad do.*

She perched on the edge of the rickety cot that had been her bed for months, picking at yet another plate of homegrown veggies from the compound's gardens. Worn yellow sweats hung loosely on her; she figured she'd lost at least ten pounds in captivity. She watched nervously as HEL's self-described visionary leader paced back and forth across the bunker, working himself up into another rant. She flinched in anticipation.

This was never good.

"Daddy dearest better come through soon," Jase snarled at her. "Or I'm reducing the human population by one stupid college girl." He helped himself to another beer from a small portable fridge and slammed the door shut. "Not a bad place to start, actually."

Although he called himself Jase Zero, she knew that his real name was Calvin Nickels. A rumpled army-surplus jacket was draped over his tall, lanky frame. He had a shaved skull, too much nervous energy, and an intense gaze that, tragically, she had failed to spot the madness in until it was too late. A faded T-shirt bore a graphic of Leonardo's "Vitruvian Man" with a blood-red slash across it. His jeans needed washing. A nine-inch combat knife was tucked into his belt.

Tera kept her mouth shut. It wasn't safe to talk to him when he got like this.

"Take it easy, baby." Simone, his girlfriend and bodyguard, stood by the door. A tall blond woman who looked like a biker chick, she was rumored to have done time in prison. Her black leather jacket had Shepard Fairey's iconic portrait of Khan painted on the back, and a Glock was holstered at her hip. She preferred guns to knives. "Give it time. That ivory-tower space nut's not going to let anything happen to his darling little girl. He'll play ball."

"You sure about that?" Jase said sourly. "What if—hang on! Maybe this is it!"

A plasma-screen television, tuned to a cable news network, was mounted on the wall opposite the mural. Jase froze in place as a computer animation of Saturn appeared on the screen. He snatched the remote and upped the volume.

". . . NASA reports that the *Lewis & Clark*'s historic visit to Saturn, now in its sixth day, continues to be an unqualified success. Scientists and space buffs around the world are marveling at the astounding new data and discoveries that the heroic crew is sending back to Earth on a daily basis. A spokesperson for the joint international effort, Dr. Emilia Sakamoto, has issued a statement declaring that 'the Saturn mission marks the next generation in space exploration, opening up a new frontier for all of humanity . . .'"

"Screw that! The universe is better off without us!" Jase hurled the remote at the screen, then whirled around to shout at Tera. "What the hell is keeping that idiot father of yours? He'd better not think he can dick us around much longer." He drew his knife and waved it in her face. "Doesn't he care what we can do to you?"

Cringing, she backed up against the wall behind her cot. The only good thing about Jase's manic episodes was that they regularly reminded her just how crazy he was, making Stockholm syndrome highly unlikely. But she knew that one of these days, he was going to go too far.

Maybe today?

"You think they're lying?" Simone speculated. "Maybe he already did it, and they're just covering it up. You know you can't trust the media. They're just mouthpieces for the pro-human agenda." Her face curdled in disgust. "They've got a vested interest in keeping their loyal audiences breeding like vermin."

Because of its reproductive associations, HEL

members abstained from sex. It didn't improve their moods.

"Give me a break!" Jase barked at her, turning away from Tera for a moment. "How do you cover up the destruction of an entire freakin' spaceship? We didn't ask him to scratch the paint job. We demanded a *disaster*, bigger than both shuttle explosions put together, something that will finally drive a stake through their obscene 'space program' once and for all and stop us from spreading the blight of humanity to unsuspecting worlds!"

"I know that," Simone said. "But does Dr. Daddy?"

"He had better!" he railed at Tera, spittle spraying from his lips. "What's wrong with him? Doesn't he love you at all?"

"Leave me alone!" she pleaded, even though she knew it wouldn't do any good. But she had to speak up, just to keep from getting sucked into their insanity. "You're fanatics, all of you. You're what's wrong with humanity, not my father!"

Tera couldn't believe how stupid she'd been to get mixed up with these lunatics in the first place. She had never really bought into their whole "voluntary extinction" agenda, which had always struck her as extreme, but she'd been impressed by their passion and commitment and had found their ideas exotically different from the pro-space, pro-science rhetoric she'd been hearing from her parents and their colleagues all her life. College was supposed to be all about exploring different philosophies and viewpoints, right? And the folks at HEL had been so friendly and enthusiastic at first, eager to share their beliefs with her. It had been easy to start hanging out with them, staying up all night to debate the pros and cons of human progress and expansion, sharing pizzas and beers.

Plus, to be honest, some of the guys had been kind of cute.

And look where that got me, she thought bitterly. *Now Dad's being forced to do something terrible, and it's all my fault.*

"Shut your mouth, college girl!" Simone fondled the handgun on her hip. "Okay, then," she asked Jase, "how long do we wait before we start taking Little Miss Hostage apart?"

"I don't know," he admitted, pacing once more. He gulped down the last of his beer and hurled the can into a corner. "Maybe—wait a second. Do you hear that?"

He ran over and switched off the TV. A peculiar high-pitched hum was coming from the corridor outside, maybe from down by the boiler room. A sparkling golden glow cast its light through the doorway.

"Crap! What's that?" He nodded urgently at Simone. "Check that out!"

"I'm on it." She drew her Glock and cocked it. "Stay here. I'll be right back."

Gun in hand, she slipped out into the hall.

"Damn, damn, damn." Jase went into full paranoid mode. Snatching a walkie-talkie off the top of a filing cabinet, he barked into the receiver. "Zero to Security! We may have company! Any bogies on the perimeter?"

The compound occupied a hilltop overlooking the shore. The surrounding terrain had been cleared for miles around. It would be almost impossible to approach the base undetected, never mind all the mines and motion detectors and guards.

"*Negative, Zero,*" a sentry reported. "*All clear.*"

"Well, keep looking!" Jase watched the door, holding his knife out in front of him. His face was flushed and sweaty. Wild eyes scanned for intruders. "Simone? Talk to me, Simone!"

A weird zapping noise came from the hall. A body thudded heavily to the floor.

"Simone?"

The guard did not respond.

"I knew it!" Jase growled. "Your father sold us out!" He yanked Tera roughly to her feet and placed his knife against her throat. His other arm circled her waist from behind as he turned her into a human shield. Months of deprivation and abuse had left her too weak to resist. "I've got the girl!" he shouted. "Show yourself, or I'll cut her throat!"

Tera felt the blade against her jugular. It nicked her skin, drawing blood. She whimpered, not certain what was happening. Was someone really trying to rescue her?

"Last chance!" Jase hollered. "I'm not bluffing here. Human life means less than dirt to me. It's what we're out to eradicate!"

"All right," a male voice responded from just outside the door. "Don't do anything hasty. I'm coming in."

Holding his hands up where Jase could see them, a stranger entered the bunker. He was a fit, good-looking white guy, in nondescript civilian attire, with sandy brown hair and the cool, confident manner of a professional soldier or cop. He reminded Tera of some of the astronauts and pilots her father had trained with, but as far as she knew, she had never seen him before. He held up two small electronic devices, about the size of compact phones. She didn't recognize the brand.

"Where's your weapon?" Jase demanded. "Get rid of it!"

The stranger dropped a small metallic gadget onto the floor. "The other one is just my communicator," he explained, his eyes meeting hers. "Good to see you, Ms. O'Herlihy. I was hoping to find you here."

"Who are you?" Jase interrogated him. "FBI? CIA? Special Forces?"

"My name is Kirk," he said, speaking to Tera instead. "I'm a friend of your father."

"Of course you are!" Jase tightened his grip around her waist, keeping her between him and the intruder. "You hear that, Tera? Your loving dad called in the troops, even after we warned him what would become of you if he did. Guess he cares more about his precious Saturn mission than his own daughter's life. How sick is that? What more proof can there be that the human species doesn't deserve to survive?" He spit at the floor. "The sooner we're gone, the sooner the Earth can start recovering from the damage we've inflicted on her."

"You've got the wrong idea," Kirk said. "Humanity is growing up and learning from its mistakes. It won't be easy, but we can discover effective ways to live in harmony with the Earth and, eventually, a multitude of other worlds, too. You just need to have faith in our potential as a species and give the future a chance."

"Bullshit!" Jase snarled. "We've had enough chances. We're a mistake, an evolutionary accident that should have died out ages ago, before we screwed up the entire planet. We're mutants. We're not entitled to a future!" He pricked Tera's neck with the knife. "Now, shut up and call off your people!"

"All right. You're in charge." Kirk held out his communicator. "Just let me tell my forces to stand down. No tricks, I promise."

"I have a better idea," Jase said, apparently in no hurry to become a martyr. Loosening his grip on Tera's waist but keeping the knife pressed to her throat, he turned his palm upward. "Toss that thing over to me."

"Okay. Here goes." Kirk lobbed it to Jase. "Just flip it open. They're expecting my signal."

Jase fumbled with the device, which chirped as he opened it. "No tricks," he reminded Kirk. He held the communicator up to his lips. "Hello? Is anybody there? Can you hear me?"

"*Aye,*" a voice answered with a pronounced Scottish brogue. "*And who might ye be?*"

"This is Jase Zero, commander of the Human Extinction League. We have hostages, who will be sacrificed if our demands are not met."

"*Is that so? And do I understand that ye are the gentleman who is holding that poor lassie against her will?*"

"That's right. And you'd better pay attention if you don't want to listen to her scream. Do you get me?"

"*Aye, I'm reading you, mister. That's all I need to know.*"

A sudden green glow lit up the bunker, stunning Tera from head to toe. She heard Jase's knife clatter to the floor. Her brain went blank.

And that was all she remembered.

Thirty

Kirk awoke in sickbay with a headache.

"Ugh," he groaned. "Remind me not to do that again."

McCoy applied a hypospray to his throat. "Here. This should help."

A hiss released the analgesic into his bloodstream. The pounding in his head dulled to a mild throb.

"Any better?" McCoy asked.

"Yes, thanks." Kirk sat up and looked around. Spock stood at the foot of the bed, waiting patiently for the captain to recover. Kirk was eager to receive his report. "Tera?"

"Safe," Spock stated. "The wide-dispersal burst from the ship's phasers stunned everyone within a one-kilometer radius. The landing party encountered no resistance and was able to recover the young woman without difficulty. She has been returned to her family with no memory of anything after the phaser rendered all of you unconscious. The authorities, alerted by an anonymous source, have made a successful raid on the compound. All terrorists present at the site have been taken into custody."

"Good," Kirk said, relieved to hear that the rescue mission had gone off more or less as planned. Given a choice, he would have preferred not to get stunned along with HEL, but a lingering headache was a small price to pay for Tera's safety. He wondered if word of her deliverance had reached the *Lewis & Clark* yet. In theory, the spaceship would already be creeping back toward Earth now. O'Herlihy still had several months to go before he could be reunited with his daughter, but at least both of them had survived their ordeal. "Well done, Mr. Spock. My compliments to your landing party . . . and Mr. Scott, of course."

"Thank you, Captain," Spock replied. "I must say, the human capacity for irrationality never ceases to perplex me. For sentient beings to advocate the extinction of their own species, even after a long history of environmental blunders, defies logic."

"You'll get no argument from me on that score." Kirk shook his head at the self-loathing nihilism that had spewed from the kidnapper's lips. "I'm just thankful that Zoe was able to give us the precise coordinates of HEL's headquarters and a rough map of its layout. That made rescuing Tera much less of a gamble."

"But are we sure we did the right thing?" McCoy said. "Don't get me wrong. I'm glad we saved the girl and all, but aren't we tampering with history?"

"Perhaps not, Doctor," Spock said. "I have been making a deeper study of the historical records of this decade, and it seems that the Human Extinction

League was indeed shut down by the authorities in the fall of 2020 and ultimately failed to inflict any significant harm on humanity. They are, in fact, nothing but an inconsequential footnote from this day forward. Furthermore, it seems that one Tera Franklin, née O'Herlihy, is destined to lead one of the early *Ares* missions to Mars in 2033. Carrying on in her father's footsteps, as it were."

Shades of Shaun Christopher, Kirk thought. "What about O'Herlihy himself?"

"Officially, he 'retires' from the space program shortly after his return from Saturn. His ground-breaking studies of Saturn and its moons, however, will help pave the way for future exploration of the outer Sol system, as well as the eventual colonization of Titan in the twenty-second century."

Kirk was gratified to hear it. "So, there's nothing about mutiny and sabotage in the tapes?"

"Not officially. Evidence suggests that the government will go to great lengths to cover up much of what truly occurred on the mission, including the encounter with the alien probe and the radical fluctuations in Saturn's rings and atmosphere."

"That seems a tad excessive," McCoy said. "I can see whitewashing O'Herlihy's misdeeds out of the history books, but why suppress major scientific discoveries?"

"Consider the times," Kirk said. "The economy is in trouble, World War III is on the horizon. I can see how the powers that be might fear that news of an unknown alien artifact tampering with our solar system might alarm an already jittery world. Or perhaps the Western powers simply don't want to share their secrets with the Eastern Coalition. We can't underestimate how paranoid people in this era are, sometimes with reason."

"It is a pity," Spock observed, "that the secrecy of the times will cause so much fascinating information to be lost to history."

"Until now." Kirk imagined that the ship's historian would want to debrief him thoroughly at some point. What was her name again? "I have to ask, Spock. What becomes of Shaun and Fontana? Do they end up together?"

Spock sighed, as though such unscientific matters were beneath him, but he had clearly anticipated the question. "History records that they will marry in 2021, almost immediately upon their return to Earth. They will have two children, one of whom, there is reason to believe, will be conceived during their long voyage back from Saturn. James Kirk Christopher-Fontana, to be precise."

"You see, Bones?" Kirk grinned at the doctor. "It seems everything's turned out just the way it's supposed to."

"Except for one persistent loose end waiting outside in the hall," McCoy said. "She's been asking to see you."

Zoe. Kirk had almost forgotten about her.

"What about her, Spock? What does history tell us about Zoe Querez?"

"Curiously little, Captain. In fact, there are no references to her after this date and scant few before then." Spock sounded mildly vexed that she had eluded his research. "Of course, records from this era are notoriously incomplete. Much of the data was lost during the ensuing world war."

"True enough." Kirk hoped that Zoe's future anonymity didn't mean that she would be thrown into some secret government prison after her antics in space. She deserved better, even if she did know more than she should. "All right, Bones. Send her in."

McCoy paged security. Moments later, Zoe was escorted into sickbay. He saw, with some amusement, that she had borrowed a red yeoman's uniform from somewhere. She twirled, showing off her legs.

"You like? If I had to wear those same old clothes one more day . . ."

"It suits you," Kirk said. "I mean it."

She squinted at his unfamiliar features. "Is that really you in there, Skipper? I admit, I'm still getting used to your brand-new face."

"Depends on which Skipper you mean. I'm the other Shaun you knew, the one after the probe. The more 'interesting' one, remember?" He smiled at the memory of their zero-g grappling in the airlock. "I hope the new face doesn't put you off too much."

"Nah." She winked at him. "It suits you."

He swung his legs over the edge of the bed and got to his feet. It felt good to have a young, capable body again, well adapted to artificial gravity. McCoy and Spock backed away to give them some privacy. "I appreciate your help with the rescue mission."

"No problem. I hear you folks pulled the doc's kid out of the fire?"

"She's fine, thanks in part to the intel you provided."

"Good," Zoe said. "I liked Marcus, even if he did try to kill us all." She glanced around the sickbay, taking in this peek at the future of medicine. "So, what now, Skipper? You beaming me back to the *Lewis & Clark*?"

"I'm afraid our transporters aren't quite that powerful. We're still orbiting Earth, using our deflectors to avoid detection, which raises an interesting possibility. If you'd like, we can drop you off anywhere on the planet. There's no need for you to spend the next three months in transit back from Saturn, especially since you weren't supposed to be on that flight in the first place. Plus, it might make it easier for you to evade the authorities if you aren't on the *Lewis & Clark* when it gets back to Earth in January."

She shook her head. "Thanks for the offer, Captain, and I'm sure Fontana and the real Shaun will appreciate the alone time, but it's not necessary." She stepped away from the bed. "You see, Earth isn't really my home."

She shimmered before him like a mirage. Kirk's eyes bulged, and Spock and McCoy rushed to rejoin them, as a familiar golden veil formed over her features. The red yeoman's uniform vanished, replaced by twenty-third-century business attire. Kirk immediately recognized the petite figure standing before them.

"Qat Zaldana?"

"Hello again, gentlemen. It's good to see you once more—in this persona, that is."

"Wait a second," McCoy blurted. "Am I getting this right? Zoe Querez and Qat Zaldana are one and the same?"

"So it appears, Doctor," Spock said, "albeit separated by more than two centuries."

She shrugged. "Time doesn't mean a whole lot to beings like me. We're not constrained by the fourth dimension the same way you are."

"But which one is the real you," Kirk asked, "and which is the disguise?"

"Both. Neither. That question kind of misses the point, Captain. You can call me Qat or Zoe, whatever feels natural."

Kirk felt as if he was talking to an unusually glib Organian or a Metron. Clearly, this entity was far more than she had appeared to be—in either of her guises. No wonder she had been able to stow away aboard the *Lewis & Clark* so easily. She could probably go anywhere she wished.

"I don't understand," he said. "What have you been doing among us? Why did you conceal your true nature?"

"To avoid spoiling the game, of course. It's been a nail-biter, but you came through with flying colors . . . in both centuries."

"A game?" Anger flared inside him. "Is that all this was to you? Some kind of sport, an entertainment? We almost died out by Saturn. People *did* die at Klondike VI!"

"That wasn't my doing. I was just playing along, watching as events unfolded according to the choices made by you and your fellow creatures." Her veil shimmered and evaporated, exposing Zoe's face underneath. "It was the doc who went off his rocker, remember, and the colonists on Skagway who panicked and rioted."

"But if you'd been honest with us," Kirk insisted, "revealed your true nature, couldn't you have fixed things yourself, before things reached a crisis? You obviously have knowledge and abilities beyond our own. Why didn't you use them to help us instead of watching us run around like rats in a maze?"

"More like adorable puppies learning a new trick," she teased him. "Seriously, it wasn't my place. Your plane of existence—your challenges, your victories. Think about it. Would you really want higher-level busybodies like me meddling in your affairs all the time?" She turned back into Qat again. "And honestly, material beings and worlds all seem fairly ephemeral from our perspective. Whether the rings collapse now or billions of your years from now doesn't really matter to us; they're still gone in a blink." Zoe emerged from beneath the shimmering veil. "The fun was in seeing how you all coped with that twisty little temporal puzzle at the center of your respective missions."

Fun? He was starting to wonder if she was less like an Organian and more like a Trelane. Come to think of it, Zoe's mischievous, frequently immature attitude bore a slight resemblance to a certain self-styled Squire of Gothos. He wondered if he should call for security— and if that would make any difference.

Probably not.

McCoy scratched his head. "Help me out here. The probe. The problem with the rings. Was that your creation?"

"Nope. I'm not what you call a Preserver. I'm something else altogether." She split down the middle, looking like Zoe on the left and Qat Zaldana on the right. "That whole business with the probe and the planets was simply an intriguing situation playing out in your cute little reality, one that I couldn't resist sitting in on. I just nudged things along a bit, made sure you both ran into the probe at the right times and places, transcendentally speaking. And you know what? It paid off. You got the clues you needed to figure everything out. Bravo!"

"What about the body swapping?" Kirk asked. "The mind transfer over time and space?"

"Okay," she confessed, "I may have had a little to do with that. Or a lot."

She knew who I was the whole time, he realized. *Even in the brig.*

He didn't know what to think about that.

"You said we came through with flying colors. What does that mean?"

"It means you're quite the interesting physical species. Just wait until I tell the others about you. You definitely warrant further study."

"In the future," Spock asked, "or in the past?"

Zoe/Qat shrugged. "Is there a difference?"

She blew Kirk a kiss, then vanished in a flash of blinding white light.

"Well, I'll be." McCoy rubbed his eyes. "I'm not sure I'm ever going to get used to that sort of thing. You think we'll run into her or her people again?"

"Who knows, Bones? It's a big universe out there, full of unexpected wonders and paradoxes." Kirk chuckled wryly. "You know, I was starting to forget that, but not anymore."

Spock arched an eyebrow. "Would you care to elaborate, Captain?"

"It's funny," Kirk said. He gazed at the empty space that their enigmatic visitor had exited only moments before. "Not too long ago, just before we shipped out for Skagway, I was afraid that I was starting to take what we do for granted, that after nearly five years on this mission, exploring the galaxy was becoming routine."

"But now?" McCoy asked.

"Now I've had a chance to remember just how exciting, and perilous, space travel can be." Kirk thought back to his days aboard the *Lewis & Clark*. "Maybe I needed to go back two centuries, experience primitive space travel in all its danger and novelty, to remind myself just what an astounding adventure we're on out here. And I can't wait to get back to our own time, where there are still strange new worlds and civilizations waiting to be discovered."

He strode out of the sickbay into the corridor outside. The never-ending bustle of life on a starship set his heart pounding. He marched briskly toward the turbolift. His bridge was waiting for him, and his future. Spock and McCoy hurried after him.

"Step lively, gentlemen," he called out. "Time's a-wasting."

"Why?" McCoy asked. "Where are we going?"

"Home."

Bibliography

Besides the usual *Star Trek* reference sources, I relied heavily on several books to help me capture the feel of a "realistic" twenty-first-century space mission to Saturn. Needless to say, any liberties I took were entirely my own idea and should not be blamed on the fine authors of the books below.

Asimov, Isaac. *Saturn: The Ringed Beauty*. Milwaukee, Wisc.: Gareth Stevens, 1989.

Becklake, Susan. *Space: Stars, Planets, and Spacecraft*. New York: DK, 1988, 1998.

Birch, Robin. *Saturn*. Broomall, Pa.: Chelsea House, 2004.

Graham, Ian. *E.guides: Space Travel*. New York: DK, 2004.

Linenger, Jerry M. *Off the Planet: Surviving Five Perilous Months Aboard the Space Station* Mir. New York: McGraw-Hill, 2000.

Miller, Ron. *Worlds Beyond: Saturn*. Brookfield, Conn.: Twenty-First Century Books, 2003.

Murray, Peter. *Saturn*. Chicago: Child's World, 1994.

Ride, Sally, with Susan Okie. *To Space & Back*. New York: Beech Tree, 1986.

Acknowledgments

Colonel Shaun Geoffrey Christopher appeared briefly in my *Eugenics Wars* novels a decade ago. I always meant to tell the rest of his story someday, but I never realized that it would take me ten years to get around to it!

That this book has finally blasted off into print is thanks to the invaluable folks at Mission Control, including my editors, Margaret Clark and Ed Schlesinger, and my agent, Russ Galen. I also want to thank my fellow *Trek* experts, such as Christopher Bennett, David George, Dave Mack, John Ordover, Marco Palmieri, Paul Simpson, and the gang at trekbbs .com, for letting me pick their brains and bounce ideas off them, even if some of those ideas took some wild ricochets. And I thank Paul Abell, a genuine rocket scientist, for generously offering to answer any questions I had about real-life space exploration. I probably should have taken more advantage of him! Thanks also to the Oxford Public Library, for letting me raid its shelves for books on Saturn and space travel and for letting me (and my dog) take advantage of their air-conditioning during a truly ferocious heat wave.

Finally, and as always, I could not have completed this mission without my invaluable copilot, Karen Palinko, and our four furry stowaways, Churchill, Henry, Sophie, and Lyla.

About the Author

Greg Cox is the *New York Times* bestselling author of numerous *Star Trek* novels and short stories, including *The Q Continuum*, *The Eugenics Wars*, *To Reign in Hell*, *The Black Shore*, and *Assignment: Eternity*. He has also written the official movie novelizations of *Daredevil*, *Ghost Rider*, *Death Defying Acts*, and the first three *Underworld* films, as well as novelizations of four DC Comics miniseries. In addition, he has written books and stories based on such popular series as *Alias*, *Batman*, *Buffy the Vampire Slayer*, *CSI: Crime Scene Investigation*, *Fantastic Four*, *Farscape*, *The 4400*, *The Green Hornet*, *Iron Man*, *The Phantom*, *Roswell*, *Spider-Man*, *Warehouse 13*, *Xena: Warrior Princess*, *X-Men*, and *Zorro*. He has received two Scribe Awards from the International Association of Media Tie-In Writers. He lives in Oxford, Pennsylvania.

His official Web site is www.gregcox-author.com.